Curses & Kitsune

A Paranormal Yakuza Duet Book 2

CJ Ravenna

Print ISBN: 979-8-9878197-7-7

First edition 2024

Editing by AlternativEdits

Proofreading by Lori Parks

Cover design by Natasha Snow

character when he was a minor that occurred off-page before the story

There is some other man drama. One of the main characters is forced to make a deal with a villain that he'll be "his" if the villain will aid them. However, the deal never actually happens, and the main character and the villain do not get together at any point in the story

Major story spoiler in

3...

2...

1...

You have been warned:

Temporary main character death (they are resurrected and both MCs are alive and well at the end. This is a romance after all, and the story has a HEA but the going gets rough around 70%! My books will always have HEAs but I like to make them hard-won. Please prioritize your mental health!)

The Namikawa-Kai:

Raiden Noboru: leader of the Namikawa-kai, also known as the Wolf of Asakusa. Jinta's mate. Pronounced Rye-dehn Noh-boh-roo.

Ren Makoto: Raiden's childhood friend, and second-in-command. Pronounced Rehn Mah-ko-to.

Goto Ishida: brother of Tadaomi Ishida. Pronounced Go-toe Ee-shee-da.

The Takada-kai:

Saito Takada: leader of the Takada-kai, and Raiden's abusive ex. Pronounced Sah-ee-to.

Hirano Kasamatsu: Saito Takada's second-in-command. Pronounced Khee-rah-no.

The Onodera Family:

Jinta Onodera: a reporter for the Jiji Shimbun. Mate to Raiden. Possessed by a kitsune spirit. Pronounced Jeen-ta O-no-deh-ra.

Katsuki Onodera: Jinta's big brother, who always stole

the spotlight. Heir to the family hospitality business. Pronounced Kahts-kee.

Fumiko Onodera: Jinta and Katsuki's mother. Pronounced Foo-me-ko.

Isshin Onodera: Jinta and Katsuki's father. Pronounced Ee-shin.

The Noboru Family:

Shoko Miyamoto: Raiden's mother. Pronounced Shoh-koh

Kenta Noboru: Raiden's father. Pronounced Kehn-tah.

Hideyoshi: Raiden's grandfather. Deceased. Pronounced Khee-Deh-Yo-Shee.

The Blades of the Onryō:

Akira: leader of the hunters. Pronounced Ah-kee-ra.

The Kitsune:

Tamano-no-Mai: an ancient and powerful kitsune possessing Jinta. Pronounced Ta-ma-no-no-My

CHAPTER 1

Jinta

I wake in the night feeling like something's wrong. I try to move, but I can't. There's something pinning me down. My chest feels painfully tight, and I can't get in a full breath. There's a noxious churning in my stomach, like the sashimi I had for dinner is coming back up to kick me. Groaning, I turn over, and my nails catch in the sheets and shred them.

Shit. Not my nails. *Claws.*

A low growl fills the room, and I realize *I'm* making that horrible, inhuman sound. My skin itches like I've got hives as fur grows over my body. There's a restless itch at the base of my spine, and when I scratch, I recoil with a shocked gasp. There's a tail growing there. No. Not just one. Several. *Nine.*

Double shit.

I lurch out of bed and throw open the door. "Raiden?" I cut my lip on my sharp canine teeth. "Ow, fuck!" I wipe away blood. "Raiden?"

Down the hall, the office door flies open and Raiden hurtles out into the hallway. His scent slams into me, making me woozy. He's never smelled like this. Raiden smells like himself, but amplified. My mouth waters with the sudden urge to bite, to *claim.*

What the hell is with me?

I must look as bestial as I feel. Raiden's eyes go wide. "Shit. It's happening. Come on, let's get you outside."

Once we're outside, the scents of the night come at me in a rush. A bird calls out within the trees, and something scurries around in the bushes. The sweet aroma of flowers, growing grass, and the musky tang of animals compels me to investigate every little scent trail.

"Can't think. What is... it's all so..."

"I know." Raiden tugs at my shirt. "Come on. Undress so you don't tear your clothes."

I can't even manage that as my knees shake, and I drop to all fours. I drive my claws into the ground and tighten my jaw, trying to push back the change coming over me. "W-will it hurt?"

Raiden's beside me, his hand gripping mine. "Only if you fight it. Let go."

I'm scared, but I trust Raiden. He says to let go, so I'll do it.

Closing my eyes, I force myself to relax. Fur sprouts and my body shrinks toward the ground. It happens faster than I can say. There's no time to notice the changes or to take anything in. One second I'm on my knees, and the next, I'm buried beneath a pile of clothes.

I reach out to push them away, and there's a white paw where my hand should be, the fur is streaked with a dusting of bright red. Not like blood, just a red pigmentation. I try to disentangle myself from my clothes. A frustrated sound escapes me as I stumble around, trying to paw the shirt off my head.

"Whoa! Easy, Sunshine. I got you." Raiden laughs deep and low, then reaches out. The world around me comes into view. Raiden kneels over me, grinning. "Wow. You're so fluffy! Here. Take a look." He holds out his phone and switches to selfie mode.

The white fluffy face of a fox appears on the screen. That's... me. Stunned, I turn in a circle, and all nine of my tails flutter around me.

"You're cute in this form." Raiden rests his hand between my ears, and his soft, warm touch makes me emit some embarrassingly high-pitched trilling sound. Foxes sound weird as hell. To my mortification, I roll over for a damn belly rub. Oh, no. He's never going to let me live this down.

"Friendly little bastard, ain't ya?" Raiden scratches my belly, then up my chest. When his hand is in reach, I bite him. "Ow! Shit. You little—" He stands, wrestling with his clothes. "Wait till I catch you."

I yip my delight, bursting with the energy to run and hunt with my mate.

Once Raiden is nude, he drops to all fours. Before his hands touch the ground, they've turned to paws, and his beautiful, enormous black wolf leaps toward me. I duck beneath his pounce and race off toward the trees.

With a playful bark, Raiden gives chase. I lose track of when it happens, but at some point, we stop chasing each other and instead run beside each other toward a single goal. Joy surges through me as I run side by side with the man I love. We're free. Nothing can touch us.

The winds change, blowing his scent toward me. My mate smells like sweet, citrusy yuzu. It's one of my favorite smells in the world. He smells so sweet, my mouth waters. A second heart races in my ears, and it's Raiden's. His heart pumps hard and fast as we run. For some reason, my eyes latch onto his neck. What would his blood taste like? Would it be coppery? Or would it taste as sweet as yuzus?

A flash of crimson blooms in the woods, as bright as a droplet of blood. A woman's pale face materializes from the trees. No matter how far or fast I run, she seems to follow me, as if I'm only running in place. Tamano-no-Mae's red lips curl.

"Go on"—her voice as clear as if she's speaking directly into my ears—"take a bite. See for yourself how sweet your precious mate's blood tastes. Drink him dry!" Her teeth flash, razor sharp.

A red haze falls over my vision as a sudden rush of rage possesses me. There's something else buried beneath all that fury, something sour and bitter, but there's no time to examine it. All thought flees my head except *bite, tear, kill!*

I pounce, claws slamming into Raiden's side. He's blown off his feet with a yelp, tumbling over in the grass.

"Sunshine? What the hell? That hurt!"

A growl rumbles up from my chest. Blue flaming orbs roar to life as I advance on him.

Raiden's ears flatten, brown eyes going wide. *"Jinta? Hey. What are you doing? This isn't funny!"*

No! What am I doing? How can I stop this? I'm not in control of any of my actions!

Tamano walks from the woods. "See how easy it is for me to take control, human? You're nothing like Namikawa. He was strong enough to control me. You think just because you're the host that you own me? It is I who owns you. Remember that, won't you, dear?" The wind blows, turning her to mist.

The rage boiling like lava in my blood simmers and dies. With a crackle, the foxfire disappears. A wave of nausea breaks over me, and I return to my human form. Oh my god. What just happened? I almost killed Raiden. *I wanted to kill him!* Cold sweat drenches my body. The breath tears from me in ragged pants.

"Jinta! Hey, are you okay?" Raiden leans over me, hands gripping hard onto my shoulders. I try to smile, but it breaks on my face as my eyes sting and blur.

I launch myself at him, arms flying around his shoulders as I nuzzle into his neck. Clutching him to me, I suck in a lungful of his citrusy scent. Thank god. I press my lips into his cheek, then against the shell of his ear. "I'm sorry. I'm so sorry." My voice shakes as I kiss the words into his skin.

Slowly, Raiden's strong arms wind around me and squeeze tight. "Good. You're back."

"Y-yeah," I say, exhaling shakily. I stroke his soft hair, curling my fingers.

"What happened?" Raiden's breath warms the crook of my neck, lips brushing over my skin.

My heart rate slows down, so I loosen my hold on him and slump back against a tree. Words don't come right away. My throat tightens as I swallow. "T-Tamano controlled me. Just to prove she could. Because I'm not strong like Namikawa was."

Lips thinning, Raiden gives his head a firm shake. "That was your *first* shift. Every shifter has to learn control at first. It's a skill."

But is it one that I can master? If I can't learn to control the kitsune, then this could happen again. Cold sweat trickles down my forehead. "She told me to hurt you, and I... I couldn't resist." Guilt gnaws at me, and I can't make myself look at him.

To my surprise, Raiden lets out an amused huff. "Damn. This bitch really has it out for me, huh? Sheesh. You sure I haven't done something to piss you off?"

The fact that he can laugh this off makes me feel a little better, and charms a chuckle out of me. Somehow, my boyfriend can still cheer me up even when I'm feeling low. "Well, you did overcook the pork last night. Oh, and your snoring is pretty atrocious. Then there's the fact that you haven't put out in twenty-four hours."

Reaching out, Raiden flicks my nipple. "Right. We all know you need your fix."

"You know I need my insides rearranged at least once a day, or I get grumpy."

He arches a brow. "Once?"

Okay, maybe more like twice at the minimum. My cock stirs at the idea of being beneath him. He was gone all day yesterday. "How was work yesterday?"

Work being his new duties as the boss of the Namikawa-kai.

"Don't wanna talk about it." Sighing heavily, Raiden flops down beside me. Leaning over, he presses warm kisses to my bare chest, lips tickling their way up my neck, then claims my mouth with his.

"Haven't brushed my teeth," I say between the soft

smack of our lips.

"You taste fucking incredible," Raiden assures me, voice low.

I could kiss him for hours, but my curiosity is stronger than my desire, for now. "Hey. Come on. Don't keep me in the dark." I push at his chest. "Has there been any sighting of the hunters? What was their name again?"

Rolling his eyes, Raiden glowers at me. "No. And they're the Blades of the Onryō."

I touch his arm where, not too long ago, a silver bullet laced with aconite had almost stolen him from me. During Raiden's initiation ceremony a week ago, their leader Akira had walked right in and said hello to me.

"And? What about the Takada-kai?"

Last time we'd seen him, he promised war against our pack.

"Nothing. Done?" Raiden leans back in.

I turn my face away. "How can things be so quiet? What are they planning?"

Jaw tight, Raiden shrugs. "No idea."

My stomach swoops with uncertainty. Between the hunters, the Takada-kai, and the kitsune curse, there's so much stacked against us. "We need to lift the curse soon. The last thing I want is to add to our pack's problems."

"Hey." Raiden tips my chin up so I meet his gaze. "You're not adding to anything. Namikawa controlled the kitsune just fine. This curse could be just the edge we need."

Yeah, but Namikawa had been the kitsune's host for one-hundred years. He'd had time. Time we don't have with Takada-kai and Blades sulking around in the shadows.

If I can't control the kitsune, then I'll just be a danger to everyone I care about. Suddenly, I want to run far away so I can't hurt him like I just tried to do. "I... need to take a shower." I make myself stand up and leave the pleasant heat of his body.

Raiden's eyes linger on my back, like he's trying to stare through me. "I'll get started on breakfast."

Once we're back at the house, we part ways—Raiden to the kitchen, and I head upstairs to the bathroom. Hot jets of water pelt down on my skin. The heat of the stream helps soothe the tension still clinging to me. The glass fogs up as I lather myself and rinse until I'm clean.

Leaning my forehead against the wall, I squeeze my eyes shut. I can do this, right? I just have to control it. There has to be a way. A hand slams against the glass. My heart leaps into my throat. Choking back a scream, I stumble into the wall. The pale hand slides down the shower door, revealing long, sharp claws that screech over the glass.

"As if you can control me." The mocking voice of Tamano-no-Mae makes me jump. "That fine mate of yours will realize how worthless you are... after I've slaughtered his whole pack and drained their souls from their bodies."

"You... you won't do that." My voice comes out small and pitiful in my panic.

Cold breath hits my neck. I whirl around, but there's nobody there. "Oh, but I can and I will. Namikawa had the means to give me what I wanted. Chaos. Death. Destruction. But you? You and your pack are far too soft. Boring. I'll break free and sow chaos all throughout Tokyo."

"We won't let you," I snap.

Two hands pound the glass, propelling my heart into my throat. Through the fog in the glass, two eyes as black as the void lock on mine. "You think that mate of yours cares for you? Wait until I've slaughtered his pack one by one. He'll be forced to make a choice... you, or his pack. And who do you think he'll choose?"

"No, he won't!" I cover my ears, trying to shut her out. But what if she's right? Raiden is the boss of the Namikawa-kai. If I endanger the pack, he's going to have to choose. Would he really throw me aside? My heart says no. We're mates. We haven't claimed each other, but our bond is strong.

The part of me who's been rejected before starts setting off sirens in my head. I'm struggling to convince myself of the truth, and to move on from the betrayal that cut me deep when my boyfriend cheated on me.

Maybe I never will, and I'll always be haunted by uncertainty and inadequacy.

The room spins as I suddenly go light-headed. My stomach lurches, sour bile coating the back of my throat. Fatigue makes my knees shake, and I grab onto the railing inside the shower so I don't fall. *What's going on? Why do I feel so weak?*

Tamano laughs lowly. "Perfect, dear. Your doubts only make me grow stronger!"

She's feeding off me like a damn parasite! "Raiden won't push me away." My voice gets drowned out by the rush of water. With my stomach twisting with dread, I lean on the wall and blow out a breath through my tightening lungs.

"He wouldn't," I whisper, and this time, it's only for me.

Chapter 2

Raiden

Freddie Mercury sings *I Want To Break Free* as I toss scallions into the scrambled eggs and whisk them. Jinta is taking longer than usual in the shower. He's usually in and out in under fifteen minutes. I add a splash of soy sauce, roll the eggs, then divide the omelet onto two plates. It smells fragrant, and the texture is good. I glance at the altar where my grandfather's photo sits. I think he'd be proud.

My grandfather taught me to cook back when he was still a chef. Before my parents abandoned me, I'd spent weekends with him at his restaurant, watching him cook. Things had been hard then, but cooking with my grandfather had been my escape. He always wanted me to leave the yakuza. Easier said than done when I'd owed Namikawa a life debt for my father's betrayal.

I wonder what he'd think if he could see me now. I've gone from Namikawa's lap dog to leader of the Namikawa-kai. Namikawa's nothing but ashes, but I'm still not free. For so long, I'd resigned myself to my fate. I'd live and die a yakuza thug, stuck in a life I never wanted since I was eight years old. Then again, I never thought I'd care about someone enough to be making them breakfast *and* living with them. Not until Jinta burst into my life.

The bedroom door closes, and Jinta's cherry blossom scent caresses my nose. Slender arms wind around my waist, and Jinta presses his body against mine. His soft, warm hands stroke up and down my chest, and when his gentle mouth brushes over the nape of my neck, a shiver nips my spine.

Turning around, my heart does acrobatics in my chest at the sight of his sweet face, framed by glossy, damp hair. His plush, pink lips look soft from the shower. "Try it." Grabbing chopsticks, I lift the egg to Jinta's lips. Dark eyes on mine, Jinta wraps his lips around the chopsticks. My cock gives a heavy throb when Jinta pulls off, chewing. When he moans his approval, a rush of primal satisfaction makes my stomach swoop.

With Jinta's seal of approval, we sit at the island counter and dig in. Every so often, I steal glances at him while he eats. It looks like he's feeling better. Relief warms my chest.

Or is it heartburn? Hell if I know. I'm seriously not used to feeling so... soft for another person. Somehow, Jinta's happiness has become intrinsic to my own.

I want to give Jinta Onodera the world because he deserves it, but all I have to offer are bloody pieces of it. My gaze drops to the tattoos that run down my arms, marking me for life. Can someone as pure as Jinta be a part of my world? Or will he leave when he realizes I can't offer him a damn thing?

My parents left when I was a kid, and that was hard enough. But losing Jinta? I'm not sure I'd come back from that. Jinta came along and brightened my world with his sunlight. Without him, I'll be lost in the dark.

"Got any super important yakuza boss tasks today?" Jinta asks.

"I need to hold a meeting, make sure everyone remembers their duties and keeps their eyes open for Takada-kai or hunters." It's still surreal that I've found myself in a position of authority after having no control over any aspect of my existence. "Everyone's depending on me to succeed Namikawa and get us out of the mess he left us in." I don't know if I can be what they need, what Jinta needs. How the hell can I balance both?

Jinta offers a smile. "Do your best."

It's hard not to want to give him the whole damn world when he smiles. "I'll try."

Jinta eats the last bite of egg. "Just think about when this is all over. It can be just us. You can leave the yakuza. We can go far away from here."

I lift up my arm and show him my tattoos. "What am I supposed to do? I'll never be able to get a normal job with these. I'm marked for life."

Frowning, Jinta runs his fingers up and down my forearm. "Become a tattoo artist."

I snort, and Jinta cracks a grin. "Don't think my customers would appreciate stick figure tattoos."

"You'll think of something. Come on, there really aren't any, I don't know, witches or something who can remove tattoos?" Lacing our fingers together, Jinta leans in and presses his lips to mine. "This isn't forever. Once the Taka-da-kai are gone and the hunters take a hike, things will calm down. It'll just be us."

He always speaks with such surety that I can't help wanting to believe him.

Even if I'm terrified, I'm incapable of giving him the life he deserves.

Closing my eyes tight, I focus on the softness of his lips and his sweet cherry blossom scent—until Jinta yanks his mouth away and stumbles off the seat. One hand over his mouth, he books it toward the bathroom.

Alarmed, I jump out of my seat and follow him. "Jinta! Hey!"

Throwing himself through the door, Jinta collapses on his knees and clutches the toilet seat as his body heaves.

My knees hit the tile, and I touch his lurching shoulders, wincing in sympathy as his body purges itself of everything he just ate. Fuck. My poor sunshine.

Finally, the nausea subsides. Jinta spits into the toilet a few times, then sits back. His sweat-slick skin has taken on a greenish tinge. I stroke the damp hair from his forehead and kiss his temple. "Okay?"

Jinta nods, clutching his stomach.

Seeing him so ill hurts like a knife in my heart. "Stay put." I run to the kitchen and grab a bottle of water. When I get back, I sit on the floor beside Jinta and hand him the water. Jinta flushes his mouth with the water a few times before he takes a big sip. Closing his eyes, he leans his head back against the wall.

"Are you okay?" I run my hand up his thigh.

"Feeling a little better." Jinta's voice is hoarse.

When I rest my hand on his forehead, his temperature feels normal. "You don't have a fever, but still, you should call out of work today."

Jinta shakes his head.

"Jinta," I growl. "Call out. You're sick. You should stay home and rest."

A muscle feathers in Jinta's clenched jaw. He pushes himself up and splashes water on his face over the sink. "I need to work! I've got to have some control over my own life, okay?" Toweling his face off, he stomps from the bathroom.

Damn it. I hate the thought of him going to work sick. What if he gets worse? I bolt after him and find him in the foyer, pulling on his shoes and a light jacket. "Why? What's so urgent that you can't skip a day?"

Jinta yanks on his shoes, cheeks flushed with anger, but I can't tell if it's at me or himself. "It's bad enough I can't control the kitsune. I'm a burden already, I can't be a financial burden to you, too."

How could he think he's a burden? I walk around him so I'm blocking the door, arms crossed tight over my chest. "Have I told you you're a burden?"

"No, but—"

"In case you haven't noticed, I'm more than capable of supporting the both of us. Namikawa trained me for years to take over his investing business."

"I know that!" Jinta snaps.

An exasperated sigh puffs out of me. "Then what—"

"If I can't contribute, then what good am I?" Jinta's sudden shout fills the foyer. "I already disappointed my family. I can't disappoint you, too!"

Jinta thinks he's... disappointing me? If he really feels that way, then I'm a lousy mate for not doing everything I can to assure him he could never disappoint me. "Jinta—"

Shaking his head, Jinta shoves past me and out the front door. In the sudden quiet, my sigh seems loud and defeated. What can I say to chase away all the doubts that plague that beautiful head of his? I'm the worst boyfriend and mate. He'd be better off with anyone but me—except I'd kill whoever took him away from me.

"Damn it." I close the door behind me and follow Jinta to the car. The guards patrolling the front yard bow to me as I pass through the bamboo garden and out the front gate. One of the guards sits at the wheel of my *Mercedes*. In the back seat, Jinta sits with his arms folded and his head hung low.

The gull-wing doors close behind me as I drop into a seat beside Jinta, who takes a sudden interest in the sleepy scenery beyond the windows. I bite my lip so I don't say something stupid. Words have never been my strong suit. Instead, I reach out and brush my pinky over his knuckles. Jinta's fist loosens, shoulders dropping down from where they'd hunched toward his ears. When he takes my hand and holds on tight, the ball of tension in my chest unwinds thread by thread until a contented sigh leaves my lips.

Before I can lean over and kiss his cheek, my phone rings. Fishing it out of my pocket, I answer. "Hey. I'm on my way into the city."

"Good." Ren's voice is thick with fury so cold, it's a wonder I don't feel her frosty breath on my ear. "We need to talk."

I squeeze Jinta's hand. "What happened?"

"We've been betrayed."

The doors crash open as I storm into my office, making the photos of all the Namikawa-kai bosses above my desk rattle in their frames. Ren paces up and down by the window so furiously, I'm expecting the rug to catch fire beneath her boots.

"I just called him," she says. "He'll be here any moment."

"Good." My stomach burns with anger. "And you're sure?"

"I'm positive!" Ren sweeps loose strands of hair back into her ponytail. "That bastard! When I get my hands on him—"

"I know." As much as I share her anger, I'm unsure how to handle the situation. If Namikawa were still alive, would this have happened? Betrayals were rare under Namikawa's leadership, but he was a firm believer in the crime fitting punishment. For repeat disobedience, he would take a finger. For more severe offenses, the punishment was a swift death.

Namikawa was respected. I am, too, but not nearly as much as he was.

Will my pack forgive me for what I have to do?

The door bangs open. Goto Ishida rushes into the room, hair askew, forehead damp with sweat. Before I can speak, Ishida drops to his knees and bows, forehead to the carpeted floor. "Please, boss, forgive my brother for his foolishness! Punish me instead, I beg you!"

I bunch my lips to keep the weak impulse to reassure him locked inside. No matter how much I wish things could be different, I can't afford to look weak by forgiving his brother for what he's done. Now, more than ever, the Namikawa-kai must present a strong and unified front, or our enemies will prey on us like sheep for the slaughter.

"Your brother committed a serious offense. He has to be punished for it."

With a ragged gasp, Ishida looks up at me. "I'll... I'll keep a close eye on him. This won't happen again, I swear!"

"Enough," I growl. "I've made my decision."

I hate that this will be the first big choice I have to make, but I should have expected this. I'm not an enforcer anymore. I'm the boss, and I have to act like it.

"Please, I—"

The doors open. Tadaomi Ishida steps into the office, hands in fists at his sides, shoulders tense. His eyes narrow as he sweeps his gaze from his brother to me. "Get up, brother. You're making a fool of yourself." His voice is heavy with resignation. Face wet with tears, Ishida scrambles to stand. When Tadaomi meets my gaze, he holds his head higher. "Well? Let's get this over with."

Straight to business, then. Tadaomi always did have some honor. Wordlessly, I motion for him to follow me up to the roof. The wind whistles as we step out under the overcast skies. It's not especially cold, but I still shiver as Tadaomi faces me. I can't say I ever knew him very well, but I considered him my brother, the same as anyone else in the pack. I've killed my enemies without batting an eye, but I've never had to kill one of my own blood brothers before.

This... won't be easy.

Tadaomi folds his hands at his waist and says, "So, you saw me. I guess I wasn't as careful as I thought."

Ren looks ready to start breathing fire. "Why would you go to a meeting with the Takada-kai? Explain yourself!"

Tadaomi laughs, shaking his head. "I pledged my loyalty to Namikawa. Not Noboru."

I should have expected not everyone would be thrilled with the abrupt change in leadership. But for Tadaomi to go so far as to meet with our enemy? It's unforgivable. "What did you tell him?"

Tadaomi jerks his shoulders. "Nothing he could use against you. I only said that I wished to join his pack in the fight to come."

Ren growls. "Why would you do that?"

"Because Noboru has turned this pack into a laughing-stock!" Tadaomi erupts. "Not only is your mate a human, he's a damn kitsune! How are we supposed to trust it won't kill us all?"

The calm I've been holding on to burns to ash as fury

blazes inside me. "Leave Jinta out of this."

Tadaomi ignores the warning in my voice. "Humans have no place among us! They are the enemy. He was a damn reporter, spying on us. He could spill all our secrets to the press, if he doesn't kill us first! He goes, or I do!"

My wolf snarls within, and my fangs sharpen. "Jinta is not a threat, and I'm going to work with him to help control the kitsune curse."

"As if I'm supposed to trust a thing you say! You'll be the death of this pack, Noboru! So make your choice. The human, or your pack."

My claws come out. There's no choice to make. I will always choose Jinta. Anyone who doesn't want to accept his permanent place at my side will have to take it up with me.

"Tadaomi, please!" Goto says, trying to get to his brother, but Ren cuts him off.

Tadaomi stares me down, claws sharp at his sides. He's made up his mind, and so have I.

Without breaking our stare, I roll up my sleeves, popping my neck from side to side. "Challenge me, then."

Teeth bared in a snarl, Tadaomi charges, and I meet him halfway. With a swipe of my claws, blood spatters the roof. Tadaomi stumbles, clutching at his throat as blood pours down the front of his shirt. I lower my hand, trying to ignore the way it shakes. Tadaomi drops to his knees and keels onto his side. Choked gurgles escape him as he twitches on the ground.

"Brother!" Goto shoves past me and gathers his sibling into his arms. "Please!"

Tadaomi's eyes glaze over, lips parting on a final bloody gasp.

Goto's lips wobble, and tears spill down his cheeks. When he glares up at me, rage burns in his eyes. "You... you killed him. Your own blood brother!"

I wipe my bloody claws on my trousers. "And the same will happen to anyone else who questions my leadership. Remember that, Ishida." Turning my back on the brothers, I walk past Ren. Something shifts inside me. My shaking hand balls into a fist, heart pounding to break free from my chest. I killed one of my own. Surely that should weigh on my soul, but it doesn't.

Instead, for the first time in my life, I feel... powerful.

CHAPTER 3

Jinta

The police press conference room is packed with reporters, but I manage to grab a seat up front before the conference starts. I'd been on my way to the office when my editor called, insisting I attend the conference.

The chief of the Tokyo Metropolitan Police Department walks onto the stage, sorting the papers on his podium. A lull falls over the room. I open my notebook and click the tip of my pen.

The police chief clears his throat. "Last night at nine-thirty, a vigilante group clashed with members of the Horikoshi-gumi in Chiyoda. The fight resulted in the deaths of Ken Kobayashi, Jintaro Ito, Akiro Suzuki, and Kyo Tanaka, several top members of the Horikoshi-gumi who we believe were in town on business. However, one gangster, Kenta Noboru, was identified at the scene, and he managed to escape."

My pen slips on the paper.

Noboru is a common last name, but still.

I raise my hand. "Excuse me, but are his whereabouts known?"

"Not at this time. All we know is that he managed to escape back to Osaka. We have asked local police to be on high alert for him."

"Why are you so certain a vigilante group was responsible?" a reporter asks.

"They wore wolfskin cloaks and reportedly shouted anti-yakuza sentiments before engaging the Horikoshi-gumi in a gunfight. Additionally, they wore a crest on their lapel that isn't associated with any of the yakuza groups in the city."

After a few more questions from the reporters, the conference concludes. While other reporters make for the doors, I remain sitting as my vision glazes over and my mind spins. The description the chief gave perfectly matches the Blades of the Onryō. The Blades must have had inside knowledge the yakuza group would be in town. Could someone within the gumi have tipped them off?

I ride the subway back to the office. While the train rolls along, I whip out my phone and type Noboru's name into the search engine. His face pops up. Noboru was featured in an article a few years back when he was imprisoned for five years for possession of illegal drugs. There's something undeniably familiar about his face. It's as if I'm looking at an older version of Raiden. Both have brown eyes, but Noboru's eyes are cold as dirt, whereas Raiden's are a warm whiskey-brown

Could Kenta Noboru be Raiden's father? I would have to ask Raiden himself. Somehow, Raiden's father cured himself of the kitsune curse and managed to run away from the Namikawa-kai. If we can find out how, I could be one step closer to being rid of Tamano-no-Mai before I harm anyone.

The train stops in the middle of the tunnel. People groan and sigh. The conductor apologizes over the PSA system, assuring us we'll be moving momentarily. I sigh and close my eyes. It's hot in here. Sweat rolls down my chest, and my mind wanders. The air conditioning isn't working in this car. Ugh, I feel gross, especially crushed between all these people.

An odd pumping fills my ears. It's rhythmic. Soothing. Almost like a heartbeat. Where's it coming from? I peer around the car, but I don't see anything to explain the source of the sound. More beats fill the train car, some pumping fast, others slow.

Am I... am I hearing the *heartbeats* of the other passengers? That's creepy. Since I became a kitsune, my hearing has become a lot more sensitive. Ren assured me once that I'd learn to filter out unimportant sounds and even control what specific sounds I take in.

Tension makes my teeth ache as the heartbeats get louder. It's maddening. I fumble in my pockets for my noise-canceling earbuds, cursing as I drop one into the sea of shoes.

"I've got it," a pretty young woman says, and she bends down and picks my fallen earbud up. With a smile, she offers it to me.

"Thank... you..." The words trail off as my eyes latch onto the pulse fluttering in her throat, moving in perfect sync to one of the heartbeats I'm hearing. Saliva floods my mouth, and suddenly, I'm *starving*. The pain in my stomach is enough to double me over.

"Are you okay?" the woman asks.

She smells so good.

My fangs cut into my lip, and strings of drool dangle from my mouth.

Can you hear it, human? Her plump little heart pumping lifeblood through her young, supple body?

Oh, god. It's Tamano.

It would be so easy. They're all trapped in here like hens in the chicken coop.

My nails lengthen to claws. *No. No, no!* Horror turns

the sweat to ice on my body. I drive my claws into my side, hissing when they puncture through my clothes and drive into my flesh.

I'm hungry, human. So hungry. I know you are, too. What are you waiting for? Take a bite. Drink her dry. You'll feel so much better once you've bathed in all of their blood, gorged yourself until you bloat.

I clam my eyes shut. Hunger pains cramp my stomach. My knees quake, and I collapse onto the floor. Passengers cry out in alarm and concern. I curl in on myself, desperately trying to make myself small and unthreatening.

God. I'm so hungry, and the smell of their sweaty flesh and the roar of their meaty hearts is going to drive me crazy.

What would it hurt?

"Just a bite, just a tiny sip of blood. Okay? That's all, that would be enough, wouldn't it?" I whisper.

Exactly, the kitsune purrs, *just a taste. You'll feel so much better, human. Stronger. You'll even be able to help your mate.*

Is that true? Hope blooms within me, but it's spattered with the blood of innocent men, women, and children.

I peer up at the woman holding out her hand to me, and whatever she sees in my face makes her complexion blanch.

Just take off her finger. Just one. You'll love it. They're small, but crunchy. It will give you strength.

My tongue moistens my lower lip. One bite and I could be stronger. I'd never burden my pack again. I... I...

"Jinta? Ren, he's waking up!"

The citrusy aroma of yuzu caresses my nose.

Raiden... he's here. Thank god. But where am I?

My throat is painfully dry. Sweat coats my skin and makes the sheets stick to me. Wherever I am, it's both too hot and freezing cold all at once. As I ease open one eye crusted with gunk, Raiden comes into focus above me. A relieved smile softens his tense jaw, and the furrow in his brow disappears.

"Hey, Sunshine."

"Where...?" What's wrong with me? I'm too tired to even lift my hand to touch him.

"You're in a hospital."

Alarm flares in me. "A... hospital? Why?"

How did I get here? I was on the train, and then my mind is just blank.

"You were on the train when you passed out. A passenger called for help." Raiden runs a cool, damp cloth over my overheated forehead. A sigh of relief escapes me. The cool cloth feels so good. Raiden's brow pinches, lips drawing into a thin line. "Told you to stay home. Why didn't you just listen to me?"

I hate that I made him worry. "Sorry, baby." I try to reach

out, but my arm is too heavy. Sighing like I'm the most exhausting person, Raiden threads our fingers together.

"Just promise me you'll take it easy."

But I need to be useful. If I'm not, what good am I? He'll leave me. Just like my ex-boyfriend. Just like my parents. Tears sting my eyes. I caused him so much trouble today, made him worry about me. *Fuck*. I'm such a burden.

"Hey. It's okay." His soft lips caress my forehead. "Just rest. If you're better in the morning, the doc will let you go home."

Closing my eyes, I try to savor his gentle kisses and soft reassurances, but guilt and shame burn me up on the inside. The doctor comes in to check up on me, providing some distraction. She insists I stay overnight so they can monitor me but believes I'll be well enough to leave in the morning.

"You have a fever," she tells me. "But you have no other symptoms of a flu or a cold. It seems to me like a reaction to intense stress. Try and take it easy."

Intense stress, huh? Yeah, being possessed by a blood-thirsty kitsune who demands I chew off people's freaking fingers will do that to a guy.

"Visiting hours are almost over—"

"I'm staying," Raiden says, glaring at her like he's daring her to try and stop him. She doesn't.

Ren leaves us alone for the night, and even though there's a sofa, Raiden pulls up a chair beside my bed. He'll wake up sore. When he hands me a plastic cup of water, I say, "You should sleep on the sofa."

"Just drink." Raiden takes the cup from me and holds it to my lips.

I'm capable of at least drinking on my own, but I have to admit, I like it when Raiden fusses over me. When I was sick as a kid, my father always acted like I was doing it on purpose and reprimanded my mother for trying to coddle me. So having him here looking after me... it heals some part of me that was hurt when I was a kid. The lump in my throat makes it difficult to swallow the water.

"You okay?" Raiden asks.

The edges of my lips rise despite the emotion clogging my throat. "Yeah. Just happy you're here."

A pleased sound rumbles up from Raiden's chest. Leaning over, he touches his mouth to mine. "Nowhere else I'd rather be."

I'm sure that's not true, but it's nice to hear it. My eyes grow heavy as he kisses me slow and sweet until my limbs are soft and relaxed. He switches off the light and holds my hand in the dark. In the morning, I'll tell him about the weird stuff that happened on the train. Right now, I just want to sleep and hope I'll feel better in the morning.

"Thank you," I whisper, and his fingers tighten around mine.

"Told you I'd always take care of you, didn't I?"

My heart flutters as I close my eyes and slip into sleep.

A fire burns within the pit of my stomach. Sweat soaks through the hospital gown and dampens the sheets. Hunger, like nothing I've ever felt, eats away at me. Got to eat something. No. Not just anything. A sweet aroma tugs at my nose, making saliva flood my mouth.

Raiden snores in the chair beside my bed. Over his shoulder, Tamano materializes by the door. "On your feet, human. We feed. Now."

My legs jerk, kicking off the blankets, but I'm not moving them. I can't speak, can't fight back. My instincts snarl, *feed, must feed,* and all I can do is shove open the door and follow that sweet, delicious scent. The hall is empty, and the silence makes the slap of my bare feet seem especially loud and grating.

Fear clutches my heart. She's going to make me feed on someone. We're in a hospital, so there are so many vulnerable people around. I'm a prisoner in my own body. There's no way to stop her. Except...

"Raiden, I need you. Wake up!" I call out to him through our bond.

Behind a door at the end of the hall, a heart thumps slow and feebly. My claws scrape against metal as I turn the knob. The room within is dark, but my eyes adjust in seconds. A woman lies in bed, her thinning hair clinging to her scalp, frail hands limp upon the sheets. An oxygen mask keeps her alive. She's old, sick, and weak.

"The perfect prey," I whisper in a voice that's both mine and Tamano's. "Go on, human. Break her wrinkled flesh. Drink her dry."

It's like I'm a prisoner, watching through the cell doors that are my eyes. I scream inside for her to stop this, beg her not to harm this poor old woman who's surely someone's beloved relative. Against my will, my feet take one step and then another. The old woman sleeps below me, unaware these moments might be her last alive.

Her pulse flutters in her neck, as sweet as the wings of a captured butterfly. My fangs sharpen to points, and a snarl chokes me. Her sacrifice will make me strong. I'll protect my pack, my mate, and he'll never throw me aside!

"Raiden. Help me. Please." There's no response.

I can't watch. I don't want to see.

But, god, I'm so hungry, and the pump of the blood through her veins *sings* to me.

"Prey," I snarl, and I bare my fangs and lunge.

CHAPTER 4

Raiden

Jinta's voice jolts me awake, but I only caught the end of whatever he said.

The bed is empty. Jinta's gone. My wolf rumbles in my chest. Something's wrong. Lurching from my seat, I knock on the bathroom door. I try the knob when no one answers, and he's not there either.

"Raiden. Help me. Please." Jinta's desperate cry blares through the bond.

Wherever he is, he's terrified. *If anyone's hurt him, I'll rip them to pieces!*

"Hang on, I'm coming!" I throw open the door. Jinta's scent spirals through the halls, and I jog to pursue it. His scent disappears into a patient's room. I hurl myself into

the room.

A woman screams and thrashes in the bed, arms raised and shaking as she attempts to push a man off her. No. Not just any man. *Jinta!* I barely recognize him as he bares his fangs and snarls, eyes blazing red.

"Hey!" I throw myself at him, clawing at his robe and hurling him backwards. With a snarl, Jinta kicks and claws like a wild cat being held by the damn scruff. His claws fly across my skin, tearing my clothes and drawing blood. "Jinta, enough!" The kitsune must have her claws in him. "Jinta, stop!" With my rabid mate locked in my arms, I wrestle him out into the hallway, and I slam him against the wall.

Jinta lunges before I can stop him. His jaws lock around my arm and chomp down. A roar of agony tears from me as his sharp fangs shred flesh and crunch down to the bone. As much as it hurts, I make myself go still to conserve my energy. If I struggle, he'll strip the flesh off my arm. My eyes sting as Jinta snarls around my arm, the vibrations of it rumbling in his chest.

Then, he sucks hard. My breath hitches as Jinta starts to... drink from me. Like a damn vampire. What the hell? I didn't know kitsune did that. Jinta's snarling dies to what almost sounds like purring as he drinks and drinks. His eyes close, and he moans contentedly as he feeds on me.

His bite feels like a fire burning under my skin, making my molars crack as I gnash my teeth to keep from screaming. His sickness yesterday makes sense now. He can't tolerate human food anymore. Tamano demanded a sacrifice to appease her rage. She has a taste for human blood and now, so does Jinta.

Fuck. This is going to wreck him when he realizes what he did. I can't tell him, for his own sake.

Finally, Jinta releases my arm, and I gasp my relief and cradle my arm to my chest. Jinta wipes his mouth, smearing blood over his fist. He bares sharp fangs at me. "You taste so good. I can see why he likes you so much."

Anger makes my fingers curl. "You can't have him, fox."

Jinta laughs, the sound sharp and cruel, so unlike Jinta's melodic voice. "Oh, but I already do. He's awfully easy to control. Weak and unsure of himself. Nothing like Namikawa. Soon, I will bend him to my will. And there's nothing you can do to stop it!"

"Like hell I'll let you take him from me!"

Jinta stumbles. His eyes flicker from red to brown and then to white as they roll back into his head.

"Shit!" I lunge to catch him as he faints. The fever that was consuming him is gone, leaving his skin cool. That fever... could it have been a symptom of the kitsune's bloodlust? *Damn it*. I wish I knew more about this curse. Namikawa kept this side of himself totally secret.

I can't let Tamano torment my sweet mate like this. Jinta needs my help, and soon.

I hoist Jinta into my arms and carry him bridal style

through the halls. "Come on, Sunshine. I'm getting you out of here, and I'm going to help you." I kiss his forehead. "I promise."

The light of dawn glows on the horizon when I pull up to my apartment building. The bite on my arm healed and no longer hurts, and Jinta slumbers beside me. He looks so peaceful. I don't want to wake him up, not when I'm unsure when we'll have another peaceful moment. I did this to him. I gave him this curse. What was I supposed to do, let him die? That was out of the question.

Maybe I'm the one who should have died. This life of mine is too dark and twisted for someone as bright and beautiful as him.

While I'm stewing in thought, Jinta's eyelashes flutter as he wakes. I brush my knuckles over his cheek. "Hey."

A pleased, sleepy sound escapes him. His brow furrows in confusion as he glances around the car. "Wait. Why are we here?" Before I can answer, he grimaces like he's tasted something foul. He touches the edge of his mouth and dried blood flakes onto his fingers. Awareness brightens his wide eyes, all traces of sleepiness gone. The panic sets in, quickening his breathing, making his eyes gloss over.

"Hey, Jinta—"

He lurches from the car and stumbles out onto the pavement. He's still wearing his hospital gown, but the streets are empty at this hour. "Just give me—" He doesn't finish his sentence, marching into the building. He rushes through the empty lobby and leans on the wall while he waits for the elevator.

"You didn't kill anyone," I assure him.

Jinta looks up at me, breath hitching. "R-really?" When I nod, he exhales raggedly, blinking fast. "But I remember an old woman. I... I was going to—" He swallows hard, skin blanching.

The elevator dings. Sweeping an arm around his shoulder, I guide him inside and hit the button for my floor. "But you didn't. I found you, and I stopped you."

Jinta grabs my arm, nearly pulling it off my shoulder. I wince when he inspects the hole he tore into my sleeve, then fixes wide, accusatory eyes on mine. "Did I do this?"

Shit. "Yes?" When horror makes him gasp, I try and smile. "Kinda kinky if you ask me."

Jinta blows out a breath, shutting his eyes tight like he's in pain. "Oh, god..." He leans on the wall and sucks in a breath. "I completely lost it. I'm so sorry. I couldn't stop her. The kitsune needed blood." He's babbling, lips trembling and eyes glazing over.

"Hey."

Jinta shoves past and into the foyer. The moment we're inside, he strips off the gown and tosses it on the floor, then walks naked into our bedroom. I pursue him down the hall and find him in the en suite bathroom, rinsing his mouth in the sink and spitting. He curses when the water runs red. "Fuck! I could have killed someone!" Shoulders heaving, he clutches the sink.

I lean hopelessly in the doorway while he grapples with what he's done. "But you didn't. I wouldn't let you do that."

Jinta spins around, eyes damp. "You won't always be there to stop me."

"Maybe not. That's why we need to get it under control. Drinking my blood calmed you down. Maybe that's the key."

Shaking his head, Jinta walks past me to the bedroom. He wrenches open the dresser and puts on some sweats, not bothering with underwear, then sits at the edge of the bed. "I can't do this... I'm not strong enough. Not good enough. I'm..." He cuts off with a choking sound, head bowed.

I kneel at his feet and take his cold hands. "Shut up. You can do this. If the kitsune wants blood, she can have mine. I don't care. It's a temporary solution to a problem we can solve."

Jinta sucks in a shuddery breath, his eyes clenched shut. "Should j-just lock me up where I can't hurt anyone. Let her have me."

A growl rumbles up my throat. I grip his cheeks. "Look

at me, Sunshine." Tears cling to his eyelashes when he opens his watery eyes. "You're mine," I say on a growl. "No one else can have you. Not another man. Not another wolf. Not a kitsune. We clear?"

His lips crash against mine, tasting of salt and cherry blossoms. I open for his tongue without thinking twice, sucking on it, my cock throbbing when he moans into my mouth. He grips the nape of my neck, curling his fingers into my hair and hauling me closer. Right where I want to be.

Maybe I can't chase away all his doubts, but I can make him feel good, make sure he knows beyond all doubt how much I need him. Dropping my hands to his hips, I pull on his sweats, and he lifts his ass high enough so I can tug them down.

His cock bobs in front of my face, already hard and needy. I stick my tongue out and run it up the length of him, swirling my tongue around his head. Jinta squirms, gripping at my hair. "Fuck, baby. Please."

When he begs, I want to give him the world. Parting my lips, I swallow him down in one fluid motion. He hits the back of my throat and cries out above me. Hollowing my cheeks, I suck him hard from base to tip, dipping my tongue in his slit. His earthy taste and whimpers of pleasure make my cock kick against my trousers, but I ignore it and focus on him.

Slipping my hand between his legs, I roll his balls, delighted by how full they feel. Pulling off, I kiss his crown, then stick out my tongue to lap away precum. "Fuck. Love the way you taste. Gonna cum for me already?"

Jinta nods, pupils blown out and cheeks flushed. "Need this. Need you, baby, please."

I suck on him hard, growling, and Jinta groans at the vibrations. Grasping the rock-hard base of his cock, I press a kiss to the weeping head of his dick. "Take what you need. Fuck my mouth." I want him to lose himself in pleasure. I want to see him let go as he fucks my mouth and floods it with his cum. Wetting my finger, I pet his hole until he softens for me, then thrust inside as I swallow his cock.

"Fuck, baby!" Jinta cries. When I suck him down my throat, Jinta lets go with a hoarse sound and starts to buck beneath me. He grips my hair hard, pulling strands. I bob my head faster, trying to match his frantic pace. When he fills my throat a few times, I gag a bit but keep going, working my finger in and out until I find that spot he loves.

"Shit!" Jinta claws at my scalp. "Gonna cum!"

I massage his prostate, moaning around his cock when he clenches around me, his body wound tight. Jinta cums with a desperate groan, spilling onto my tongue in hot, thick pulses that feel like they'll never stop. All the while, I milk his prostate until I'm certain I've stroked and sucked him to utter satisfaction.

My boxers are wet. *Shit*. I came just from servicing him. That's a first. Nobody's pleasure has ever gotten to me as much as his. Once I've sucked him clean, I tuck him back in his pants, then crawl up his body. When I kiss him, I part my lips and let him taste himself on my tongue. He shivers beneath me, grabbing handfuls of my ass and squeezing. Panting, Jinta slumps into the sheets, his eyes closed and face flushed. Totally wrung out.

I grin my satisfaction. "Feel better?"

A dopey smile lights up his face. "Oh, yeah. Definitely." He sinks his fingers in my hair, stroking. I close my eyes, relishing the feel of his fingernails over my scalp. He chuckles. "Look at you. Leaning into my touch like a puppy."

I slap his ass. "Not a puppy. Get some sleep. Take tomorrow off and stay close by. We're going to fix this. I promise."

Jinta sighs softly, eyes closing. "Okay..."

It's a promise I really hope I can keep. For his sake.

Jinta is still sleeping off the stress of yesterday when I wake up, so I kiss his cheek and leave him in bed. I change my clothes, grab an onigiri from the fridge, and jog downstairs to meet Ren. Ren drives me to the headquarters like usual. Two beefy bodyguards sit on either side of me, faces stern.

I frown. "Where's Goto?" He's usually on guard duty.

One of my guards lifts his shoulder. "Not sure, boss. We haven't been able to get in touch with him since Tadaomi died."

That's odd. Come to think of it, I haven't seen him since I killed his brother.

"How's things, boss?" Ren asks, lips quirking playfully. "Is Jinta feeling better?"

"Yeah." For now, anyway.

Ren grimaces when she hits a wall of traffic. "Damn it. We should have left earlier." We're suspended in a traffic limbo for over a minute.

Bored, I pull out my phone and swipe mindlessly. "What's the hold-up?" I ask.

Ren rolls down the window and peers out. "Looks like there was a wreck or something. I see some ambulances."

The distant rumble of a motorbike gets closer and louder. A black bike with two riders appears briefly in the rearview mirror. Ren suddenly screams, "Get down!"

Twin blasts of gunfire shatter the window behind me. Blazing pain slices into my shoulder. People in the street begin to scream. My guard pounces on me and shoves me down into the seat, then grunts in pain. His weight crashes down on my back, and something hot and wet drips into my hair. Two more blasts make my ears ring, and another window shatters, the one in the front. God. I hope Ren is okay. Fear makes my heart race. The moment the gunfire stops, I scramble out from under the dead guard and fall outside. The bike bearing the two gunmen has already disappeared from view.

"Ren?" I tug on the driver's side door. Ren leans into view, face pale and eyes wide. She jumps out. "Are you okay?" I try to grab her arms to check for a wound, but burning pain in my shoulder makes me wince and touch the wetness seeping through my shirt.

"I'm fine! Shit. Raiden, your shoulder!"

"It's just a graze." Burns like hell, but nowhere near as bad as it would be if I'd been shot, and it won't heal. Must have been silver. "What about the guards?"

We run to either side of the car. The guard who shielded me folds in on himself, a bloody hole through the back of his head. The other guard grunts in agony. I jog around to where Ren is. She leans into the vehicle and opens the guard's shirt. She gasps. "Raiden. Look."

I lean over, and my stomach twists. The bullet wound in his chest has turned black at the edges, and the blackness seeps into his veins. Aconite poison. He'll be dead in seconds once the poison reaches his heart. "It's okay," Ren says, voice shaking. "You're going to be okay." She rubs the guard's shoulder as his eyes roll back and spit foams in the corners of his mouth. His heart skips, then stops completely.

With a shuddery sigh, Ren leans her forehead on his still shoulder.

Rage burns through the shock. Snarling, I lash out and

scrape my claws over the roof. "Fuck!"

Those bikers were the Blades of the Onryō, and this was an attempt on my life. My guards are dead because of me. They were somebody's friends, brothers, husbands, sons. I smack the roof of my car again, squeezing my eyes shut. If Namikawa were alive, would he have let this happen?

"Fucking hunters," I growl.

Ren shakes her head. "Only one was a hunter."

I whirl around to face her. "What?"

Ren's hands curl into fists at her sides. "Right before the driver opened fire, his sleeve slid down. He had tattoos. I recognized them. There was a wolf fighting a dragon. That was Ishida's tattoo. That bastard betrayed us!"

The realization sparks in my gut, and fury blazes inside me. "That son of a bitch..."

Goto Ishida joined the Blades of the Onryō to get back at me for killing his brother, and he almost put a bullet in my skull.

Fuck. This is bad.

CHAPTER 5

Jinta

When I wake up, the bed is cold. Raiden's left for his day at the Namikawa-kai headquarters. My fever is completely gone, and my stomach is settled, but only because I gorged on my poor boyfriend's blood. A shiver rattles my spine. I'm almost relieved I don't remember anything.

In the bathroom, I brush my teeth and wash my face. A cold breeze tickles my neck as I bend over and spit into the sink.

When I look up, the bathroom is... gone. I'm standing in a black void. Panic squeezes my chest. "T-Tamano? If this is you, cut it out, please!" I cringe. I shouldn't say please to a jerk like her, but she *is* a goddess, and my mom taught me manners.

An anguished shout comes from behind me, making me jump. I spin around, and my jaws lock around a piece of sweet, juicy flesh. Blood fills my mouth, and I hunger for more. It's so sweet.

Must have more. All of it. I will drink my prey dry!

"Jinta, stop!"

My heart plumets into my stomach. Raiden's eyes are full of anguish, jaw tightly clenched as he fights back a scream. It's... it's *his* flesh. I'm hurting him. *No. No! I have to stop this. Have to let go!* My jaws are locked in place as I suck and suck down mouthfuls of his life's essence. Power flows through me, singing in my veins. It's like the giddy floaty feeling after one too many shots of sake but without the haze of drunkenness. It feels... good.

"You like it, don't you?" Tamano's cold voice ghosts over the hairs on my nape. "Just admit it. The power you wield feels good, doesn't it?"

My eyes mist over with tears as Raiden sucks in a shaky breath, squinting down at me through eyes narrowed with pain.

Reaching out, Tamano slides her finger through the blood sliding down Raiden's arm and licks it clean. "Delicious... and so potent, too. All kitsune must prey upon humans to grow our strength. Feed off their fear. Their misery. And yes, sometimes even their blood. But shifter blood makes us especially strong. You can be strong, too.

You'll never be weak again. Never be a burden. Next time you find weak and vulnerable prey, do not hesitate," she whispers in my ear. "Become the predator you're meant to be. He'll leave you behind unless you can prove you're worthy."

"No!" I snarl and tear myself away from Raiden. The abyss shatters around me, and I'm standing in the bathroom, back against the wall. Cold sweat trickles down my body. I suck in a gulp of air and try to calm my racing heart. I could have seriously hurt Raiden. I'd lost all control. Why did he forgive me? He shouldn't have. He should've locked me up somewhere I can't hurt anyone.

My phone rings in the bedroom. On shaky knees, I make my way to the bedside table. It's my boss. "Hello?"

"Onodera!" I jump at the urgency in his voice.

Oh, no. What now?

"Y-Yes, sir?"

"There was a shooting in Asakusa."

Shootings are so rare in Tokyo. I can count on one hand the shootings that happened last year. Gun laws are so strict that the penalty for possessing a gun, let alone firing a bullet, isn't worth the risk of getting caught. Raiden's gang doesn't own guns, not that they need them, for that very reason. This is huge news.

"Get your ass to the crime scene. Question witnesses. I want a story by this evening!"

"Yes, sir!"

After dressing, I grab my bag and tear from the apartment. A packed train ride later, and I'm jogging through the streets of Asakusa toward the crime scene. A crowd has gathered around the yellow tape, trying to see what's going on, and police stand guard to ward away anyone who gets too close.

Pulling out my camera, press badge swinging from my neck, I approach the crowd. I excuse myself and squeeze past people to get a better look. The police have sectioned off a big black *Mercedes*, all the windows shattered, blood spattered on the pavement. My heart falls into my stomach. That car belongs to Raiden. I'd know it anywhere. My gorge rises, and my hands shake so badly I almost drop my camera.

All thoughts of a story fly from my head as I rush up to a police officer. "Excuse me! Was anyone injured?"

"Two passengers were killed," he answers.

"And the owner of the vehicle?"

"We have no information yet."

Fuck. Why wouldn't Raiden tell me someone fired into his car? Unless... if it was hunters and they shot him with aconite, then maybe he's too badly injured to get in touch with me? The thought turns my blood to ice. Memories of the last time he was shot with aconite bombard me. My stomach churns.

Squeezing through the crowd, I lean against a streetlamp and pull out my phone. Raiden doesn't answer when I call.

I try Ren, and she's unresponsive as well.

"Raiden? Can you hear me?" I ask through our bond. A minute passes without a reply. I've got to see him and make sure he and Ren are okay. After collecting a few brief statements from witnesses, I learn, apparently, two masked bikers drove up to the car and fired into the windows. They think it was organized crime. Then I run from the crime scene and borrow a bike from a rack by the train station. In only minutes, I've biked to Raiden's apartment.

"Did you see Raiden?" I ask the doorman.

His eyes double in size, no doubt at my breathless, harried appearance. "No, sorry."

"He hasn't come home at all?" I grip the counter hard, heart racing.

The doorman gives a solemn shake of his head.

Fuck…

I have a seat and text Raiden, telling him where I am and that I'm looking for him. My phone buzzes. Please, please…

Yes! It's from Raiden. He's texted me an address, a license plate number, and added,

> **Raiden:** *There's a car coming to my building. Check the license before getting in!! Meet me at this address. Make sure you aren't followed!*

What the hell is going on?

In seconds, a car pulls up. I double-check the license plate, then hop in. Three beefy, stone-faced Namikawa-kai are in the vehicle.

"What's going on?" I ask.

"The boss will tell you," the driver says, stepping on the gas and driving fast, honking at people to get out of the way.

"Is he okay?"

"Yes."

Blowing out a breath, I slump in my seat. I have more questions, but my guards aren't the chattiest people in the world. I'd rather hear from my mate himself, anyway.

We arrive in a sleepy neighborhood and pull up outside an older apartment building that looks like it's seen better days, judging by the graffiti and overgrown vines. Lots of families walk the streets, bringing their kids home from school. The guard buzzes an apartment number three times, and then a voice I recognize as Raiden's growls, "Who is it?"

The guard says, "The black wolf hunts the fox at dawn."

We're buzzed in, and the guard leads me to an elevator. The elevator ascends, and I try to get my breathing under control. Fear and anger leave me shaking from head to toe, and I have to gnash my teeth to keep it all inside.

This fucking way of life is going to be the death of Raiden, and I can't lose him. I can't be without him. We arrive on the fifth floor, and the guard leads me to an apartment door. He knocks four times. Several locks click, and the door opens.

I squeeze through the door before it's fully open and collide with a hard chest that smells of sweet, citrusy yuzu. "Raiden!" I choke out, and my arms fly around him. Clutching him to me, I suck his scent into my lungs. Finally, I can breathe. He's here. He's alive. Thank god.

"Stand guard," Raiden's low voice says, and the guards grunt their assent. Raiden locks the door, and then his arms are around me, holding me tight. "Hey, Sunshine." The beautiful rumble of his voice makes my throat ache with emotion. I hadn't realized how terrified I was that I'd never hear his voice again until now.

"Jinta," Raiden begins, but he's cut off as I surge forward and kiss him, grabbing his face in both my hands to pull him close. My name becomes a gravelly moan that makes my cock kick against my trousers. I thrust my tongue into his mouth, a desperate sound escaping me when he twists his tongue around mine. Sharp teeth nip my lower lip, biting down.

I slide my hands up his back to his broad shoulders, and Raiden suddenly winces. I freeze, panting as I break our kiss. "What was that?" I run my hand over his shoulder again, and he tenses up.

"It's nothing." He leans back in, but I tug open the buttons on his shirt and yank it to the side.

My breath hitches when I notice the bandages around

his shoulder. "You're hurt," I whisper, horrified.

Raiden scowls, averting his gaze. "It's a scratch."

Fury heats my blood. "Just a—" I shove him away from me and cross the room. I want to destroy this dingy little apartment room. A furious snarl escapes me.

"Hey." The floorboards creak as he approaches me. He grabs my shoulder.

I smack his hand away. "You could have been killed!" Anguish mixes with my fury, bringing scorching tears to my eyes.

Raiden's lips thin, and he folds his arms. "But I wasn't."

How can he be so cavalier about this? "Why didn't you tell me you'd been attacked? I had to find out there'd been a shooting from my boss! Your car was completely wrecked. I couldn't reach you!" My lips shake, and I blink fast to try and fight back my tears. Fear for him makes my throat ache.

Sighing, Raiden scrubs a hand over his jaw. "I contacted you as soon as I could. We had to make arrangements. Ren's in hiding. I needed to make sure it was safe before I could see you."

"What happened?" I snap. "Nobody would tell me anything!"

Sighing, Raiden rakes a hand through his hair. "One of my men was caught meeting with Takada. I had to set an example."

"You killed him."

Raiden doesn't look at me. "I had to. But his brother wasn't quite so understanding. Ren recognized his tattoo on one of the bikers who attacked the car."

That makes no sense. Pacing, I fold my arms close to my chest. "What does that mean?"

"He joined up with the Blades and carried out a hit on us to get back at me."

My stomach churns, and I hug myself tighter. "So, what now?"

Raiden's eyes are steely with determination. "We hit them back."

I lurch to a stop. "You can't! You'll just set off a cycle of retaliation!"

"What do you want me to do?" Raiden slams his fist down on the kitchen counter, making me jump. "They killed two of my men! They almost killed me and Ren! If I let them get away with this, the whole city will think the Namikawa-kai is weak."

"Let them!" My voice matches his in volume as my desperation swells. "Let the whole fucking organization burn down. Let Takada, the hunters, and Namikawa's people kill each other. Isn't that what you wanted? A way out?"

Raiden shakes his head vehemently. "I can't do that. Those are *my* people. I'm the boss now. They need me!"

I want to shake this man. I want to fall on my knees and beg him, *beg him,* to walk away from this life before he gets himself killed. "And I'm your boyfriend! *I* need you. I need you more than anyone else ever will. Don't do this to me. Don't make me watch you be killed. I can't. I won't stick around for that."

Raiden's eyes are wide. "You'll leave?" There's a dangerous undercurrent beneath the fear in his voice.

I glare at him, blinking away the tears misting my vision. "If that's what it takes to make you walk away from this life, then yeah. I will."

His fingers curl at his sides. "You'd make me choose?"

I cross my arms and stare him down. "I would."

Shaking his head, Raiden grinds his teeth together. "Don't."

A laugh escapes me at the absurdity of it all. Our lives are completely fucked.

"What?" Concern dimples Raiden's brow.

"Maybe you just don't want to leave. Maybe you like it. The violence. Maybe you wouldn't be satisfied with a normal life." With me, but I can't bring myself to say that part aloud. The anger in my voice softens, betraying my insecurities. "Is that it?"

Icy silence is my only answer. I don't know how to interpret it. Is he quiet because he's shocked I'd think that way about him? Or, and my stomach twists at the thought, is it because he agrees with me? Maybe he's realized that he would never be happy with a normal life. Maybe he enjoys the power and control that comes with being the boss. But I would hate him for it if he broke my heart like that.

My stomach knots with anxiety. Our worlds are so different. How is it possible that he'll be happy with me? I couldn't make my last boyfriend happy enough to stay loyal, or my parents. Why would Raiden be any different?

Turning away with a shaky sigh, I make for the door.

"Where're you going?" Raiden's voice is wary.

"Back to my old apartment."

"You won't be safe there."

"I don't care." I throw off the chain on the top lock.

Raiden slams his hand against the door. "Well, I do," he growls in my ear. His body is so close to mine the heat of him seeps into my back. Grabbing my wrist, he spins me around. My back hits the door, and Raiden looms over me, fangs sharp, eyes dark.

"Let go," I say without any venom. All my fury evaporates and instead, I'm just tired.

Lifting a hand, he drags his thumb over the wetness on my cheek. "Like hell I'm letting you walk out of here pissed at me." When I try to look away, he grips my chin tight and forces me to meet his heated gaze. "I'm not giving you the chance to disappear on me, Sunshine." He leans in, breath hot on my ear, nose rubbing against my cheek. He growls into my ear, "Wolves don't like it when their prey runs away. You try and run from me, and I'll burn the world down to get you back."

The threat in his voice is very real, but so is the meaning in his words. He's choosing me. Maybe he can't leave the yakuza, but even so, he's telling me in his own way that I come first. Somehow, it's exactly what I needed to hear. I lunge forward, capturing his mouth with mine. A moan tears from me when Raiden slaps his hands against my ass and squeezes.

All the blood in my body goes straight to my cock. *Fuck. I need him. Now.* And when he starts yanking open my shirt and tearing at my belt, I know he feels the same. Piece by piece, our clothes hit the floor, leaving a trail to the sofa. With a shove, Raiden sends me sprawling onto the couch. Panting, I shuffle backwards so there's room for him. He stands over me, chest heaving, tattoos vibrant and bright, eyes black with longing.

With a pounce, he's on top of me, his naked body flush against me. "So fucking sexy," he growls, showering kisses down my neck to my collarbone. My fingers tremble when I touch the bandages on his shoulder. There's a slight dent in his skin, like a small chunk was taken out of him. *Fuck.*

I groan as he fists both our cocks and rocks his hips, rubbing our hard lengths together. My eyes roll back, toes curling.

"Love how hard you are," he purrs, voice low and breathless as he strokes us.

Grabbing the hair at the nape of his neck, I haul him down and crash my mouth against his. His lips swallow my whimpers and moans, which I'm grateful for. I don't want the guards outside to get an earful.

"Only way you're leaving me"—he pants between hungry kisses—"is if I die, or you do. Got it?"

I nod frantically, gasping as he sucks a bruising kiss into my neck.

"Say it," he commands, voice gravelly. "Tell me you're mine."

I arch into his fist. "Y-yours. I'm yours, baby."

The seams of his mouth curl with satisfaction. When his long fingers flex around my throat, my lips part around a shuddery moan. "That's my good boy," Raiden purrs into my ear. His palm slaps my hip, setting my skin ablaze. "Roll over."

I obey, biting my lip when my dick gets trapped between my body and the sofa. Precum leaks from my aching shaft and slicks the cushions. Raiden gets up, muscles in his ass flexing as he walks to the table and grabs a plastic bag, rifling through it. He waves some lube at me. "I stocked up. You and I are gonna be spending time here for a few days. Doesn't mean we can't have fun."

The sofa dips when he returns, kneeling between my spread legs. "Love this ass, Sunshine." He palms both globes appreciatively, squeezing until I whimper. He spreads me so wide I moan when I feel myself gape open for him. "Fuck," Raiden murmurs. "Your tight little hole is so sexy."

The cap snicks, and there's a spurting sound. A slick finger circles my hole.

"Put your fingers in me, baby. Please." I push my hips back, eyes closing in bliss as I bear down on his finger until he slips inside me up to the first knuckle. When he swirls his finger, caressing my sensitive inner walls, I moan shamelessly and push back on him, needing him deeper.

"Feels so fucking good," Raiden croaks, pressing a second finger against me. When he slides inside, stretching me wider, I can't hold back my groan. I need more. Rolling my hips, I fuck myself on his fingers.

When he adds a third finger, pumping them in and out of me faster and faster, I just about lose my mind. "Need your cock," I whimper. "Now."

Raiden withdraws his fingers, and I whine in dismay at how empty I feel. A big hand slides down my back and settles just above my ass. The blunt head of his cock notches at my hole. I blow out a breath and make myself relax. Raiden exhales harshly when the tip of his cock slides in, and he grabs at my hip and squeezes. My eyes flutter shut, and I bite my lip to stifle my loud moan as he slams in, filling me up in one long, smooth glide.

"Fuck!" I shout, unable to hold back, slapping my hands down on the arm of the couch so I don't fall over as he pounds into me. His hips smack against my ass so hard I know I'll be sore tomorrow, but I don't care. Not when he feels so damn good inside me, thick and hard and hot. He tugs on my hair and wrenches my head back, fangs sharp when he nips the spot between my neck and shoulders.

I can't hold back my shameless moans any longer. He fills me up until my world narrows down to his cock, throbbing inside me.

"That's it," Raiden growls. "Don't hold back on me, Sunshine. Want everyone in the building to know who owns this hole."

With a tug on my hair, Raiden angles my head, and his lips crash against mine. I tangle my fingers in his hair, needing him closer, even though he's already as close as he can possibly be, balls smacking my ass with every hard thrust. It's never enough. I need him with an intensity that I know will never be satisfied. Our tongues tangle as he claims my mouth with the same frenzy he's fucking me with.

When he wraps his hand around me and tugs my cock hard and fast, my balls wrench up. I'm leaking so much precum Raiden doesn't even need lube as his hand glides up and down my length.

"Fuck, baby, almost there!" My orgasm sizzles at the base of my spine.

Raiden nips my ear while he pounds his cock in and out. "Fucking cum for me," he rasps, jerking my cock until my eyes are rolling back and I'm suspended over the precipice. "Want that tight ass strangling my dick."

A guttural groan is all I'm capable of as my cock erupts, ropes of cum shooting all over Raiden's fist and spattering the arm of the couch. I clench so hard around his cock that

I feel him throb inside me as he lets go with a hoarse shout, filling me.

Raiden slumps over me, forehead to my shoulder, and breath huffing fast against my skin. His warm lips flutter over my shoulder, caressing my skin with tender kisses. I sigh when Raiden curls a hand around my ass and squeezes. His cock twitches inside me as it begins to soften. He tries to pull out, but I clamp down around him, smiling when his lips part around a silent inhale.

"Fucking hell."

"I know." I sigh, floating on a cloud of bliss. All the tension suffocating me is gone.

Sliding his arms around me, Raiden lowers us both backwards until I'm in his lap, and his back is against the arm of the sofa. We catch our breath while he kisses his way up my shoulder to the hinge of my jaw. I turn my head, parting my lips, and moan softly when he claims my mouth.

Look, I know we can't always fuck away all our problems every time, but we just made a very compelling case as to why it works.

I squirm on his cock when the wetness inside starts to trickle out around him. "Feels good," I murmur, leaning back into his hard chest and reaching up to play with his damp hair.

He sucks a kiss into my shoulder. "I know. I wish I could stay inside you until I'm ready to go again."

A chuckle escapes me. "I'd love that, but I do need to type out a story and send it to my editor."

Raiden squeezes me, as if he doesn't want me to go. "Fine. I'll order groceries and make us dinner."

"Sounds good." I get up, and Raiden slips free from my body, leaving me feeling empty. I go to the bathroom and return with a wet cloth. I straddle his thick thighs and wipe him down, then he accepts the cloth and cleans me, wiping between my cheeks, then my oversensitive cock. When my breath hitches, he leans in and captures my mouth.

Bumping his forehead against mine, he says, "Everything I do, it's for you. For us." He kisses my fingers, then gives them a squeeze. "You're the reason. For everything." Soft brown eyes hold my gaze. "So wait for me. This won't be forever, and then we can go wherever you want. No more yakuza. No kitsune. No hunters. Just us. Okay?"

Love for him blooms in my chest, filling my body with heat. Touching my lips to his, I run my fingers through his hair. "Okay," I whisper, and it's a promise I hope we can both keep.

CHAPTER 6

Raiden

"I've been meaning to ask. Is this your father?" Jinta offers me his phone and goes back to eating my homemade Pad Thai.

Setting down my chopsticks, I accept the phone he hands me and zoom in on the picture. My stomach lurches when I recognize the face staring back at me from the screen. His black hair has gone gray, and his face is lined and weathered, but I'd recognize those murky brown eyes and stern mouth anywhere.

"Yeah," I grunt. "Guessing he got arrested?"

Jinta nods. "That picture is a few years old. He was arrested for possessing illegal drugs, but he was released a year ago."

Sounds like dear old Dad picked up a few new vices after he bailed on us like a coward. I hope he's tormented by what he did, but somehow, I doubt it.

"Why the sudden curiosity?" I stir my noodles around my plate.

"I was supposed to write an article about an attack against the Horikoshi-gumi. They were in town visiting. Hunters took out some of their top men."

I nod, recognizing the name. "They're based in Osaka, right?"

Grabbing some pork with his chopsticks, Jinta chews, humming his approval. My wolf growls low in my chest, happy that we've pleased him. "Yup. Your dad escaped. He's a wanted man."

Something in my stomach gives a painful twist. All these years, and he was only a short plane ride away. I wonder if the woman he destroyed his mating with is still with him.

"Oh, no. You're making that face." Jinta's pouting when I look up.

"So're you," I counter, poking his bottom lip. "What face?"

Jinta sighs. "Like a kicked puppy."

"Not a puppy." I pick up some of my crispy pork and feed it to him.

Swallowing, Jinta rubs my forearm. "Should I not have told you?"

A part of me wishes he hadn't. I never wanted to see that

son of a bitch's face again. The past still has such a grip over me, and memories I'd buried down deep try to gnaw their way back to the surface. "It's fine."

"I mean, at least we know where he is, who he runs with. The Horikoshi-gumi will have info on him. We can track him down and find out how he cured himself of the kitsune curse."

I scowl before I can stop myself. "We don't need anything from him."

Jinta furrows his brow. "I'm sorry if I upset you."

Leaning over, I kiss his cheek. "You didn't. I'm fine." The lie is sour in my throat.

Jinta does the dishes and puts the leftovers away while I brush my teeth and get ready for bed. I spit in the sink, then look up and find my reflection staring back at me. He looks like me. My father. Older. Harsher. But like me.

Will I be where he is a few years from now? Evading the police, running around with the yakuza, the lines of a hard life wrinkling my face. Am I destined to be a yakuza thug for the rest of my life? Grimacing, I turn my back on the mirror and walk out.

In the bedroom, I strip down to my underwear. The bedroom is much smaller than the one back in the penthouse, but my people splurged on a good bed and appliances throughout the house. The Namikawa-kai own the building, and we've used this place as a hidey-hole in the past before. One of many we've got around the city.

After a few minutes, Jinta joins me in bed. "Goodnight," he says.

"Goodnight." I flick off the lamp, plunging the room into darkness. As the dark presses in on me, unease stirs beneath my skin. I can't sleep. Worry churns in my stomach. I could be seeing my father again soon. There are no pleasant memories I have of that man. Well, maybe that's not true. He was nice. Sometimes. He liked to take me golfing at one of the resorts Namikawa owned.

It was when we'd come home that things would sour. Mom would get on him about the drinking or the long hours he spent working for Namikawa. He'd find something to complain about at dinner. Their fights got worse and worse. I still remember when he hit her for the first time. It's seared into my memory. I don't even remember what they were fighting about. Just that suddenly, he'd swung, hitting her so hard she'd fallen down.

I'd felt sick. Bile had bubbled up into my throat. I'd gone to bed that night and cried, ashamed I hadn't protected my mother, furious that he'd put a hand on her like that. I promised myself if I ever found my mate, I'd never raise a hand against them. I'd kill for them instead.

The way I wished someone had just fucking killed my father the moment he laid his hands on my mother. I wish I'd just done it myself.

I'm not a weak little boy anymore. I'm not helpless.

So why does the mere memory of my father make me

feel so damn small again? Like I'm just nothing.

"Baby? You okay?"

My breath catches. I realize I've been breathing hard, gripping the sheets tight in my fist. "Fine," I mumble, curling my knees up toward my chest.

The sheets rustle, and Jinta's warm, slender body nestles against my back. His arms wrap around me, his cheek pressing against my shoulder. Beneath the blankets, he rubs his foot along my calf. The tension bleeds from my body, and I grip his arm and squeeze tight.

Somehow, I've got to get out of this life.

Before I hurt the only man who's ever told me he loves me.

The next morning, I call a meeting to discuss the shooting with my pack. Jinta stays in the apartment and works from home. I leave my guards with him, but I hate leaving him alone, even if he's safer in the apartment than with me. I was so tense this morning nothing would relax me. Not until I fucked Jinta over the counter. Felt his tight hot body clenching around me while I pounded him. Heard him moan my name. Smelled his cum as he spilled all over my chest. Sex with my mate always relaxes me, and I can tell it's good for him, too.

Fuck. I still feel awful when I remember how badly I scared him yesterday. The way he shook in my arms when he saw me after the shooting. I'm such an asshole for making him worry about me like that. He'd be so much happier without me. So much safer.

Grimacing, I shake away the thought as I step out of the elevator and make my way to Namikawa's old office where I've summoned my top-ranking members.

My men won't arrive for several minutes, so I dial a number into my phone and wait.

"This is Tozawa." The leader of the Horikoshi-gumi has a deep, rumbling voice.

"Tozawa, this is Raiden Noboru. I heard about the attack on your organization the other day. My condolences."

He grunts. "You're moving up in the world, Wolf. Last time Namikawa spoke to me, you were just a debt collector. Watch your back. The world is less tolerant of us than it has ever been."

"How many were killed?"

"Dozens, first in Tokyo, then in Osaka." Anger makes his voice deepen to a growl.

"And... what about Kenta Noboru? Do you know where he is?"

"Ah. Your father."

I almost correct him. That bastard isn't my father. I don't want him knowing that my father's abandonment still has a hold over me.

"He ratted us out to the Blades. It won't be long before we find him and make him answer for his crimes."

"You sure it was him?"

He grunts. "He has no honor, no sense of loyalty. It was him, I'm sure of it."

He's sure of it, but it doesn't sound like he has any tangible proof it was my father. Whatever. It doesn't matter.

"I hope you'll find him," I say. "That's all. Just wanted to know if you knew his whereabouts."

"Even if I did, Noboru, this is pack business."

"Understood." I hang up, unsure about how I feel. Should I try and track him down?

No. Fuck that. We'll lift the curse without that bastard's help.

There's a knock at my door, and I welcome my pack members in. Ren sits beside me, and I survey the room. There's a lot of tense faces looking back at me. "This attack against the Namikawa-kai will not go unpunished," I promise my pack. "The Blades of the Onryō want to take over the city while we're still recovering from Namikawa's death. I deeply regret the loss of Matsumoto and Takahara. They will be avenged. Mark my words."

"If Namikawa were still alive, none of this would have happened!" one of my men, Kirishima, erupts.

My hands curl into fists as my men throw Kirishima shocked and angered looks. Keeping my voice calm, I growl, "Watch your tongue."

His face is bright red, eyes blazing as he snarls, "He wouldn't have waited for the hunters to strike before declaring war! He would have done so immediately! Because of your inaction, our friends are dead!"

Ren glares at him. "Don't speak to the boss that way."

Another one of my men shakes his head in disgust. "Kirishima has a point. At least Namikawa wasn't fucking a human."

My blood pressure rises. Now that just won't stand. "Keep Jinta out of this," I say, voice low with fury.

"Humans make our kind weak. He's turned you soft. This pack will be a laughingstock if anyone finds out! You're a disgrace!"

I don't have to take this shit. That's the nice thing about being the boss. I pull myself to my full height and bare my fangs. "If you have a problem, then challenge me!" My voice thunders through the room. For several seconds, nobody speaks. Willing my fangs to shrink back to their normal length, I growl, "Ishida and the Blades will pay for attacking us. They think we're weak? We'll show them how wrong they are."

Ren clears her throat. "The boss of the Atsushi-kai contacted me a few moments ago."

Atsushi and his clan have been allies of ours for some time. They know our secret and though they are a human clan, they have never given us trouble for being shifters.

She says, "The Blades were skulking around his

pachinko parlor."

"What? Why?" It makes no sense for the Blades to target Atsushi and his gang. Hunters never target humans.

"No clue, but he needs our numbers. He thinks they are planning an attack."

Then this is the opportunity to hit them back. Jinta will be pissed at me for this. My wolf whines at the idea of upsetting our mate further, but this has to be done. As if sensing my distress, Ren meets my gaze. I look away and address my pack. "Ready yourselves. Meet me at Atsushi's pachinko parlor in an hour."

My men bow. "Yes, boss!" One by one, my men file out of the room.

A frown creases Ren's brow. "Hey..."

I tense, knowing exactly what she's going to say. "Don't."

"You should sit this out." When I jerk my head no, she sighs. "We need you strong and healthy, not bleeding out. And so does Jinta."

"If I'm not there on the frontlines, more people will start to doubt me."

"And if you get hurt, Jinta will be devastated!"

Guilt tears into me with fang and claw because, damn it, she's right. The last thing I ever want is to hurt him, but I've got a whole pack depending on me to lead them into this coming war and out the other side.

"You're going to have to choose. Jinta or the

Namikawa-kai. You will only ever have one fated mate."

Anger sparks within me. "No." The word is a growl. I can have both. I'll prove it. "Jinta is a grown-up. He knows the risks that come with being with me. As long as my world and his remain separate—"

Ren shakes her head. "You really think that's possible?"

"What would you have me do?" I shout. "I can't just leave the pack to frolic off into the sunset with Jinta! This is the only life I know!"

The look on her face can only be described as disappointed. Wordlessly, she turns and walks out.

Once Ren leaves, I cross to the window and look out over the streets of the city—my city.

I should feel like the emperor himself. Powerful, untouchable.

Instead, I feel like there's a blade aimed at me from the shadows, waiting to strike.

The only question is, will the attack come from the hunters or from within my own pack?

Chapter 7

Jinta

Raiden won't answer his phone.

I finished my article about the killing of the Horikoshi-gumi, sent it off to my editor for printing in the morning edition, and spent the afternoon typing out a story about the shooting. Raiden gave me enough information over breakfast this morning that even without attending the press conference, I'm sure I'll have enough information for an engaging story.

Now that I have nothing else to do but sit around and wait, worry gnaws at me. I know I'm supposed to be on the down-low after the attack, but so is Raiden, and he can apparently go wherever he wants. So why can't I?

"Because he doesn't trust you not to get hurt."

I jump as the otherworldly voice whispers in my ear.

"You're weak. Far too weak to be his mate. You're nothing but a burden to him."

Gnashing my teeth, I sit up and snap, "Would you cut it out?"

Tamano-no-Mae looks very out of place in this dingy apartment with her flowing red kimono and sandals. Despite the abundance of sunlight in the room, she casts no shadow, telling me she isn't really here. Her red lips curl into a sneer. "It's the truth, dear. Maybe not one you wished to hear, but the truth does sometimes hurt."

"Raiden does trust me. He's just being overprotective." I try and focus on my laptop screen. Annoyance rises in me when I can still feel her eyes on me. "Seriously, what's your problem with him? You try and make me kill him. You belittle how he feels about me. What, are you jealous or something?" I probably shouldn't tease an ancient and powerful kitsune, but I woke up and chose violence today, apparently.

Her eyes blacken with anger. *Huh. I guess I struck a nerve.* "You *are* jealous!" I squawk. "What happened? Get dumped?"

Her hair begins to bristle, face twisting in fury. "You insolent little—"

A pounding noise makes me jump. Someone's banging on the door.

When I look back, Tamano is gone. That's too bad. I felt

like I was getting close to an answer. I guess I should've had more tact, but it's kind of hard for me to sympathize with the evil spirit who wants to kill my boyfriend for unknown reasons.

Darting across the room, I look through the peephole. Horror freezes my insides.

"Holy shit." I wrench open the door, and Raiden practically falls inside, held upright by Ren and another yakuza member. "What happened?" My voice borders on hysterical as I race after them toward the sofa. They lower Raiden onto the couch.

"Another hunter attack, this time in Shinjuku. We went to aid the Atsushi-kai," Ren says, but I barely hear her. Blood soaks Raiden's shirt, which is torn in places. His hair glistens with what I think is sweat until a line of crimson trickles down his forehead.

"I thought you said you and the Takada-kai were the only yakuza shifters in the city."

"We are. I don't know why the hunters targeted them. It makes no sense!"

"Is he okay?" My lips shake, and I can't feel my hands or feet. Everything's gone numb.

"He's healing, just slowly. Silver got into his bloodstream, but no poison." Ren accepts a damp cloth the other yakuza hands her, and she starts wiping away blood. Shaking too much to stand, I collapse next to the sofa and clasp Raiden's hand. My heart throbs, eyes stinging.

"You bastard," I whisper through a throat tight with anguish. "Screw you for making me worry like this..."

Ren's sorrowful stare weighs on me. "He'll be okay."

I bear down on my inner cheek so I don't lose it, tasting blood. This isn't fucking okay. He shouldn't be bleeding out yet again. I told him... I fucking *begged* him not to retaliate, and he did it anyway. Why won't he just listen?

"Isn't it obvious?" Tamano looms over the sofa, a smirk on her red lips as she runs her hand over Raiden's chest, fingers coming away red. "He likes it. Likes the power. Likes the danger."

My teeth sharpen to fangs, and I yank my hand away from Raiden's as I sprout claws. Maybe she's right. If, *when,* we're able to start a life together safely... will Raiden even want to leave this life behind? I know he's implied he wants a normal life, but I can't imagine him working a normal job. Can't imagine him being satisfied with me.

Raiden stirs with a grimace, easing open an eye. "Fuck... what happened?"

"The silver weakened you," Ren says. "You passed out, and we brought you back to the safehouse."

Raiden sits up slowly. "Were you followed?"

Ren shakes her head. "Are you okay?" She reaches out and yelps in pain.

"Jinta!" Raiden exclaims.

I look down, and my heart lurches. I'm gripping Ren's wrist tight, claws driving into her skin. I don't care. Nobody touches my mate. I bare my fangs and snarl, "Back away." Fur ripples over my arms.

Ren gasps in pain. "H-hey. Easy. I wasn't going to—"

A roar tears from my throat, silencing her. "Don't fucking touch him!"

"Jinta, enough!" Raiden's voice snaps me out of my furious trance. The red haze descending over my eyes disappears. I yank my hand away from Ren's wrist, horrified as the skin darkens into a violent bruise. What the hell just happened to me? "I... I'm so sorry!" Clutching my clawed hand to my chest, I stumble back and bump into the wall. Oh my god. I wanted to kill her.

Ren watches as the bruises on her arm disappear. She glares at me. "I thought you both were supposed to be handling the curse."

When Raiden glances at me, he hastily looks away. "Go stand guard. I need to, uh..." He jerks a shoulder at me.

Ren looks between us, and whatever fury she sees on my face makes her cough. "Right. Okay. We'll just be... outside." She and the other yakuza leave. The door closes behind them, and in the frigid silence, it's like the slam of a dungeon door in some dank, dark prison. My anguish holds me captive, barely allowing me a full breath.

Raiden folds his arms defensively. "Hey, this isn't as bad as it looks. You should see the other guy."

"I told you not to retaliate." I barely recognize my voice as it shakes with anger and devastation. "But you just had to, didn't you?"

A muscle ticks in Raiden's jaw. "Yes, I did. I told you, we can't afford to look weak. My own men are starting to question me! If the pack falls apart, how are we going to fight off the hunters *and* Takada's people? We need to be unified!"

"Or we could just leave and go find your father! But no, you just won't do that, will you?"

Raiden lurches to his feet, lips in a tight line as he glares at me. "We don't need anything from that bastard. I'll figure out a way to help you myself!"

I want to rip my damn hair out. "Before or after I kill Ren or whoever else in your pack tries to touch you! Or—or maybe after I've drained an entire hospital dry! Would that be better for you?"

The low furious rumble of his voice hurts my heart when he says, "There has to be another way to lift the curse."

A scowl tugs at my mouth. "Do you know of one?"

"No."

"Then what other options do we have? I understand how you feel, but—"

"No, you don't!" he snaps, his harsh words make me flinch. "I never wanted a goddamn thing to do with that son of a bitch. He tore my family apart. Drove my mother into a deep depression. If he hadn't left, I never would have been forced into joining the Namikawa-kai. That fucker ruined my life. I want nothing to do with him."

"But—"

Shaking his head, Raiden turns his back. "Find him yourself."

He storms off like a teenager. What the hell? He's never walked out on me before. I bound after him as he stomps into the bedroom. Raiden yanks off his tie, then chucks his bloody shirt into the hamper in the corner.

When I say his name, he ignores me. Finally, I snap, "Would you quit behaving like a child?"

Raiden whips around, eyes blazing. "Yeah, you know why that is? I was never allowed to *be* a child. He stole that from me, and so did my mother. They fucked me up, so if you've got a problem, take it up with them."

Anger heats my blood and makes my cheeks burn hot. "I do have a problem. I'm possessed by a kitsune, and unless we can cure it, I could kill people! Is that what you want?" Throwing my hands in the air, I pace to the other end of the bedroom. "Do you like it, Raiden? The fighting? The killing?" When he doesn't respond, I whip around and find his arms wound across his chest and his gaze far away and vacant. My mouth goes dry, and a bitter laugh escapes me. "You do, don't you?"

Raiden closes his eyes and gives a heavy shrug of his shoulders. "And if I did? I spent all my life feeling totally powerless under Namikawa. Trapped. I don't feel that way anymore. Is that such a bad thing?"

No. I can't hold that against him, even if hearing him admit it breaks a dam inside me, flooding me with all the insecurities I've been trying to hold back. "Do you..." I swallow hard. "Do you even want a normal life with me? Is that something you'll ever be happy with?"

A sigh falls from his lips. Scraping a hand over his unshaven jaw, Raiden looks away. "I don't know if that's something I deserve." In the quiet that falls like a guillotine between us, he finally looks at me, and my own uncertainties darken his eyes.

My throat aches when I ask, "Then why are we doing this?" I don't know what *this* is. Fighting for our future? Trying to be in a relationship? Both?

Raiden just gives a hopeless shake of his head. "I'm yakuza, Jinta. This is the only life I know. There's a chance it will always be that way. Is that something you can handle?"

I take in his bloodied appearance, and my heart seizes. I don't think I can. Who in their right mind would be able to handle seeing the man they love get hurt time and again? So much could go wrong. He could be killed by hunters, other yakuza, or cops. Get arrested and thrown in jail. My lungs tighten, cutting off oxygen. I need to get out. Get away. Just for a little while. Turning my back, I make for the door.

"Where're you going?" His voice is panicked.

"Out. I have to be alone."

"Jinta—" The clump of his boots pursues me to the door.

"Don't!" I bark, whirling on him.

Raiden freezes in place, eyes wild, hands in fists at his sides. He doesn't move, but it looks like it's costing him a great deal of effort.

Blinking fast, I let the door slam in Raiden's devastated face.

I roam the streets for an hour, directionless and lost in a fog. In all the chaos, no guards followed me. I finally have breathing room, yet my chest is tight with anxiety. Craving some quiet, I leave the bustling main streets behind and find myself walking among rows of quaint, tightly packed houses on a peaceful residential street. The road is only a single lane, and plenty of people on bikes ride past. The sun warms my shoulders while birds twitter. It's a beautiful day, and I wish I was in the right headspace to enjoy it.

This isn't the first fight we've had, and it isn't even our worst one, but fear twists around my heart. What if he chooses the yakuza life over me? What if he decides we're through?

My anxious thoughts make no sense, but all I can remember is the big fight my ex-boyfriend Takahiro and I had. It plays on a loop, tormenting me. He'd been angry because I was away studying in Tokyo. I'd made him feel like he came secondary to my studies. Then, when I came home for Christmas to surprise him, I'd found him having sex with my brother.

Raiden wouldn't leave. He wouldn't. He's made it clear how committed he is to me. Even though I've done nothing to deserve his devotion. But what if—

My head starts to spin. My feet trip over each other, and I lunge to catch myself on the wall. A pit yawns in my chest.

"Raiden will leave. He'll choose his pack over you. You heard him." Tamano's voice croons in my ear.

"Shut up..." I cover my ears and close my eyes. "Just shut up!" Fur thickens on my arms, and the copper tang of blood bursts in my mouth as my fangs cut my lip. My breathing grows short and ragged. Someone dings their bicycle bell. Children scream and laugh as they chase each other through the streets. Fuck, everything is *so loud.*

"Shut up," I snarl, and lunge.

The child screams as I grab his little wrist between my claws. He wails, a chubby little thing with plump, soft flesh.

My phone buzzes and jerks me from the haze of fury.

I yank my hand back. "I... I'm so sorry!" But the little kid is already running away, crying. What the fuck is wrong with me?

My phone rings again. Snarling, I yank it from my pocket. It's Ren. Relief rushes through me. I need someone to talk to. "Hey. I'm really sorry about earlier. Are you okay? Did I..." I swallow hard, remorse making my eyes sting. "Did I hurt you?"

Her tinkling laugh soothes the ache in my chest. "No! I'm a werewolf. I healed. You weren't in control. But don't worry. Raiden is going to come up with a solution."

I scoff before I can stop myself. "No, he won't. Not as long as the solution means tracking down his father."

"Did he say that?"

"Yup." Bitterness seeps into my voice.

Ren sighs softly. "I'm sorry. Sounds like he's being pig-headed."

I scoff. "Yeah, really." More than that. He was hurting at the very idea of seeing his father again. I could feel echoes of his pain beneath the anger through our bond. A perk of being a kitsune, I guess. "I don't want to put him through something that's going to hurt him. But I can't do this on my own. I'm not familiar with the magical underworld like he is."

"I know someone who is."

"Really, who?"

She's pointedly silent.

"Oh. You?"

"You got it!"

"Any ideas where I can start?"

She hums thoughtfully. Behind me, tires rumble along the road. There's a black car driving along the narrow street, sunlight reflecting on the windows.

Ren snaps her fingers. "I've got it! So, there's this witch. A foreigner from the UK. He runs a cute little English-style pub in Kabukicho. In the past, we've used his magic to help track down traitors who cheat the pack. We can go there together if—"

The doors to the car fly open. Two men storm out, clad in furs, faces hidden by demonic masks straight out of a Noh play. They lunge for me, grabbing my arms so hard they cut off circulation. My phone clatters from my hand.

"Hey!" I struggle, kicking at them. "Let go of me! Get off me!" Their grip is like iron as they drag me toward the car. Something sharp pierces my neck, and a fire burns its way through my veins. The stink of silver makes my nostrils sting.

My vision darkens as I collapse into the back seat, boneless and weak.

"Raiden..." I surrender to the darkness.

Sometime later, I open my eyes. We're still in the car, and my cheek is sticking to the leather seat. My neck throbs where I was injected. Zip ties cut into my wrists, keeping them bound behind my back. I'm all the way in the back seat of the van. The big guys who grabbed me occupy the seats in front of me. I can't see the driver.

"Where're you taking me?" My voice comes out a dry croak.

A voice says from the front, "You're my present to the hunters."

Between the front seats, all I can see of the driver is his eyes in the rearview mirror. I don't recognize him, but the contempt in his gaze where our eyes lock makes me think he knows me. I can't see any tattoos to indicate who these men are affiliated with.

"Who are you?"

"Unimportant, mincemeat," the driver snaps. "Noboru's going to know the exact pain I felt when he killed my brother after the hunters have butchered you."

Wait. This guy must be Ishida. The brother of the guy who tried to join Takada's side. The horror of my situation makes my stomach twist. "Why not just kill me? Why take me to the Blades?" I ask, trying to keep the fear out of my voice.

His eyes narrow in the mirror. "Because I want to. Makes things more interesting, doesn't it? The hunters will kill you. Noboru will come to your rescue. The hunters will take him out."

My breath quickens. "Don't do this. Just kill me. Just—"

Ishida barks a laugh. "Just shut up. Don't worry. You'll see your sweet little boyfriend soon." Ishida focuses on the road, but he occasionally steals glances at me in the rearview mirror. I focus on keeping my breathing slow and calm.

Stay focused. I have got to escape. If I don't, Raiden will get hurt or—

My eyes prickle. God. I can't lose him.

Ishida drives us to Minato. The streets become emptier as we drive, arriving in an area full of warehouses. My heart sinks as I realize how secluded we are. We drive past a chain-link fence and toward a warehouse with shattered windows and overgrown weeds climbing up the sides of the building. I have no clue what to expect once we're inside that building, but I can't imagine I'm in for a friendly reception.

Ishida stops the car around the back of the building. I have a view of the Rainbow Bridge over the river. I wish I could appreciate the view. Ishida marches over to my door and yanks it open. "Out. Now!"

Heart pounding, I step out on trembling legs and make my way slowly toward the building. Ishida grabs my arm and makes me walk faster. "Hey! He's here!" Ishida barks, voice echoing through the yard. The doors slide open with a rusty screech, revealing a dark interior. Ishida shoves me inside.

Grabbing my nape, Ishida leads me deeper into the

warehouse. Over my shoulder, two men guard the door. They wear all black, the lower halves of their faces concealed by demonic masks so only their unfriendly eyes are visible. Their most striking feature is the wolfskins draped over their shoulders. *Shit.* These must be the Blades of the Onryō.

I yelp as Ishida shoves me onto my knees. There are more hunters lurking in the shadows, talking amongst their numbers in low voices. I count over twenty, maybe more of them deeper within the building. Footsteps echo in the vast space, getting closer to me. A low, raspy chuckle makes me shiver.

"Hello, little fox. It's good to see you again," a mockingly cheerful voice says, one I recognize. A man, tall and slender with long gangly limbs, comes to stand in front of me. He wears black wolf furs with the head of a wolf still attached and hanging over his face. The sight pulls a shiver of disgust from me. The furs remind me of Raiden in his wolf form. He tugs the hood back, revealing a face I recognize at once.

His name is Akira, leader of the Blades. We met once before when he infiltrated Raiden's ceremony. At the time, I had no idea who he was, not until he called and revealed himself to Raiden. The scar over his left eye and the one that hooks the side of his mouth should have been a giveaway of who he really was. No werewolves have scars. They heal too quickly.

"Thank you for bringing him to me, Ishida."

Ishida just shrugs, jaw tight with anger. "Didn't do it for you, hunter scum. Just make sure I get to be the one to put a bullet in Noboru's head. That bastard deserves it."

Akira hums thoughtfully, making Ishida scowl. "I will consider it. In the meantime, be a good dog and behave yourself."

Face reddening with indignation, Ishida stomps over to sit on a crate.

Those murky, baggy eyes light up when I meet his gaze. "It's been years since I've laid eyes upon a kitsune."

Despite the nerves racking my insides, I toss him a sunny smile. "Look while you have a chance. When my mate finds out where I am, he'll gouge your eyes out."

A big grin splits Akira's face, and he barks out a laugh. "I would like to see him try! It will be an honor to skin the Wolf of Asakusa." He picks disdainfully at the furs he's wearing. "My own are getting patchy. I need a new coat."

Disgust makes me gnash my teeth. "What did Raiden ever do to you?"

Akira rolls his shoulders. "Isn't it obvious, little fox? He's a werewolf. His kind have no place in this world. They taint the natural order of things and threaten humanity. If we don't exterminate the animals now, they'll take over."

That's it? Anger makes my fingers curl. "I can't speak for all werewolves, but Raiden and his pack help keep Tokyo safe. They hunt down criminals who evade justice. There's plenty of reason to hate yakuza, I'll give you that. But what about werewolves who aren't yakuza? Ordinary citizens like anyone else?"

A sneer wrinkles Akira's face. "Werewolves are not ordinary citizens. They can never be. Their very nature makes them a threat to humanity's superiority. The Blades will not rest until we've cleansed the rot from all of Japan."

"So, you're just a bigot. Got it." Swallowing around the dryness in my throat, I ask, "And what do you want from me?"

"Isn't it obvious, little fox? You're bait. That filthy mate of yours is awfully protective of you, isn't he? He'll come running to your rescue, but it will be far too late by the time he finds you, of course." A chuckle escapes his smiling lips, baggy eyes expanding with excitement.

"Why? What are you going to do to me?" I'm not sure I even want to know.

"An exorcism. Sit tight and wait for the priestess. The ritual must be done once the moon has reached its zenith."

Within me, Tamano-no-Mae shivers with dread. *"No,"* she whispers. *"Not an exorcism! You must escape, or we will both die!"*

"Will I... survive?"

Akira gives a fake sympathetic tut. "Unfortunately, the exorcism is quite... complicated. Neither you nor your filthy parasite will survive. But Noboru won't have to know that sad little detail. Not until he finds your corpse, of course."

Dread tightens my chest, but only some of it is for me. *Fuck.* I can't put Raiden through that pain. He'll blame himself for the rest of his life—*if* he survives the encounter with the hunters.

"In the meantime..." Akira's eyes light up. "Let's have some fun!"

Searing pain cracks across my jaw as Akira swings at me. I topple onto my side, eyes watering as a bone-deep ache racks my jaw. Howls of malicious laughter echo through the warehouse as the hunters cheer their boss on. I draw my knees to my chest to protect myself, but I grunt when Akira kicks me in the shoulder, rolling me onto my back.

"Look at how weak you are!" Akira jeers, face split in a sadistic grin. "This is the host of an almighty kitsune? How pitiful! You're nothing!"

I gnaw on my lower lip to stifle my yell as Akira presses his boot into my temple, crushing my head against the ground while the hunters laugh.

"What a disappointment you are." Lip curling, Akira turns away.

Fury rises within me. I've got to figure out a way to escape, and it's got to be before the moon rises. Or I'll never see Raiden again.

CHAPTER 8

Raiden

"Have you heard from him?" I snap into the phone. My boots are going to set the carpet on fire and burn down the whole building from all my damn pacing.

"No, I'm sorry," Ren replies. "I can't get in touch with him."

Biting back a scream of frustration, I slam a hand against the window. "And what about the guys you sent out to find him?"

"I just called. Nothing yet."

Fuck. Fury mixes with terror. It's been six hours since Ren overheard Jinta being attacked. What's happened to him? Where could he have gone, and which one of my countless fucking enemies has him? I've got my pick of the damn litter. Hunters, Takada-kai, Ishida.

"Call me the minute you hear anything!" I end the call and toss my phone onto the sofa. "Fuck!"

I shouldn't have lost my cool this morning. Should have run after him and told him I was sorry, that I'd do whatever he wants, even if it meant seeing my father again. Blowing out a breath, I knock my forehead against the cool glass. The city sprawls below me, a labyrinth of places to hide. Jinta could be anywhere, and I have no idea where to start. A knot forms in my throat.

"I'm so sorry, Sunshine."

My phone vibrates, and my heart leaps, but my hope fades when it isn't Jinta, Ren, or anyone else I know messaging me. An unknown number texted me and sent a couple of pictures. The message reads,

> **Unknown:** *Wolf. Come to the spot in the picture below.*

It's a satellite image from a maps app, showing the piers in the Minato area, with the exact address visible in the search bar.

> **Unknown:** *Hurry. Your mate is lonely without you. -A*

Akira. It's him. Has to be. Ishida kidnapped my mate and gave him to the damn hunters. Tasting sour bile, I worry I'll be sick as my stomach cramps. There's another picture, and my heart speeds up.

In the image, Jinta lies on the ground, a boot pressing into his cheek and grinding his head into the pavement. A trickle of blood runs from one nostril, and there's a cut above his brow, and his lip is split. The phone shakes in my grip, and I can't look away from his wide brown eyes. They're full of pain... and fear.

A snarl builds in my chest. My fangs lengthen. Fur sprouts on my arms and cheeks, ears tapering into points.

These bastards put their hands on my mate. Made him bleed.

I will burn their world to the ground.

They want a war? They fucking have it.

My roar of fury rattles the windows. In seconds, dozens of my pack members have filled the vast office. I brace my hands on my desk. A photograph of Namikawa looms over my head. No matter what I do, I feel like a pretender.

"The hunters have Jinta." Whispers spread among my pack. "Ishida betrayed us yet again." I can't keep the fury out of my voice. My claws scrape into the wooden surface of the desk. "Ishida needs to pay for what he's done. This is the chance we've been waiting for to run the hunters out of our city."

"Boss, you want us to risk our lives for a human?"

"Humans have been nothing but trouble!" another shouts.

My pack exchange looks full of apprehension and downright reluctance. They barely know Jinta, but they do know Ishida. Why should they risk their lives to help save a stranger, especially when it means turning on one of their own? Desperation claws at me. I can't do this by myself. Blowing out a breath, I add, "If the hunters aren't stopped tonight, they'll drive us out of the city. If you won't do this for my mate, then do this for your families, for everything you've built here in Tokyo."

That finally seems to get through to them. Determination lights up eyes, and low growls rumble in the air. But a handful of others step away from the group. One of them says, "Namikawa never would have gotten us into a war with hunters or asked us to sacrifice ourselves for a human."

It's like I've been slapped. Curling my lip, I snap, "Leave if you want, but don't think about showing your faces here again. You'll be exiled. Anyone who takes you in will become an enemy of this pack."

One of them rips his Namikawa-kai pin from his lapel and chucks it on the floor. "You've disgraced this pack, Noboru. You'll never be worthy of Namikawa's legacy."

"Then get out," I bite out the words as my hands curl on the desk.

One storms out, then another, and another. Fifteen, in total, turn their backs on me, leaving a sizable gap in the room. Fury boils my blood, but I make myself breathe in and out. I should've expected this. Being with Jinta was always going to be controversial, even though it shouldn't be at all.

"Boss?" Ren grips my arm. Her expression is grim, eyes blazing. "What do we do?"

I clear my mind of the cowards who turned their backs on me. They don't matter. The only one who matters is Jinta, but with my pack divided, we don't stand a chance against the hunters.

"We need backup."

"Who can we go to?" she asks. "The Atsushi-kai are allies, but they're scattered after Atsushi was killed."

It still makes no sense to me that the hunters targeted them. The Atsushi-kai aren't werewolves. So why attack them?

It doesn't matter right now. There's only one other person who could help us—but not without a price.

My stomach churns as I open my phone and look at the picture of my mate. His eyes plead for help as blood weeps from his wounds.

My fingers tremble as I type in a number and hit call.

How much am I willing to sacrifice to save Jinta? The answer is simple.

Everything.

Even my very soul.

I ride for Minato Ward. Tokyo Tower glows orange against a periwinkle sky. I blow smoke out the open window, drumming my fingers on the wheel constantly. I hate how jittery I feel. Smoking doesn't relax me, and I've gone through half a pack since this morning. My stomach churns sickeningly, and my heart thuds against my chest.

I've avoided coming back to this spot for as long as I can, and now here I am, walking willingly into a snake's den to save a pack plotting to overthrow me. There's a sour taste in my mouth when I park outside the fancy restaurant.

I chuck my cigarette out the window and step out of the car. Inside, the restaurant is still as classy as I remember it. A sparkling chandelier twinkles over the dining room. Servers carry huge cuts of beef with sides of mashed potatoes and vegetables to tables or pour expensive bottles of wine for guests.

I tell the host I have a reservation, and she leads the way through the restaurant. My stomach tightens when I realize I know where we're going. To our usual table, private and secluded.

"Right through this curtain," the host says, motioning at the curtain sectioning off an intimate dining room.

Taking in a breath, I reach out to part the curtain. Voices come from beyond. I recognize Takada's gravelly voice, and the other, a man's voice, is vaguely familiar. Ah. Must be Hirano Kasamatsu, Takada's second-in-command. I concentrate on their voices, my supernatural hearing filtering out the noise so I can eavesdrop.

"—gone soft, Hirano," Takada growls.

"This is only going to backfire on you. You have to know that!" Kasamatsu's voice is sharp with anger.

What's he talking about? Maybe whatever deal Takada wants to strike with me?

"Expanding our territory will make our pack stronger. There's good real estate in Shinjuku just waiting to be snatched up, and with our rivals out of the way, we'll have no one to compete with."

He's got a point. Why would Kasamatsu be so opposed about this?

"You have no honor, Saito!"

Kasamatsu must be talking about something other than Takada's interest in real estate. What else has Takada done? I don't want to know, and he wouldn't tell me if I asked.

"Shut up and get out!" Takada erupts. "Go and wait for me in the car. If you have problems with the way I run things, maybe I'll have to consider someone else for your position. Keep that in mind!"

Kasamatsu yanks back the curtain and storms out. He stumbles to a halt at the sight of me, then drops into a bow. "Noboru." I bow back, but he says nothing more as he storms past. I don't know what that was about, but I don't care. Time to deal with Takada. I open the curtain and walk in.

"Brings back nice memories, huh, Noboru?" Takada sinks into the chair opposite me. His usual spot. I squeeze my fists together. If he wants to make me feel like a helpless kid again by making me sit in my old spot, he's going to be disappointed.

"I'm not staying," I say.

Takada crosses one ankle over the other. "That's a shame. You always loved their ribs. Ate it right off my fork like a little baby bird."

Fury pounds in my ears as the humiliating memories claw at me.

"It's overpriced." I grip the back of my chair.

Takada narrows his eyes, the only hint of his annoyance, then shrugs. "Suit yourself."

"Let's get to the point," I say, staring him in the eyes. "Hunters took my mate. My pack isn't thrilled about going toe to toe with hunters for a guy they barely know."

Sucking on his cigarette, Takada blows smoke over his shoulders. "And so you come to me for help. I'm flattered."

My hands curl, claws biting into wood as a smirk tugs at Takada's mouth, but I rein in my temper. I've got to do this for Jinta, for my pack.

"And why in the fuck do you think I'd help you out of the goodness of my heart? Don't get me wrong, I love killing hunters as much as any other guy. But I don't make a habit of doing something for nothing."

Swallowing hard, I hold his gaze. "If you would do this for me, I... I'd be in your debt." And even as my pride screams in protest, I bow over the table.

A rusty smoker's laugh crawls from Takada's throat. "Oh? Now this is interesting. Spill."

I already have my damn answer.

To save my pack, to save Jinta, there's nothing I wouldn't do.

"You and I will share the Taito Ward's profits. We can be business partners."

A thoughtful purr answers me. "That does sound nice, but I'm afraid that's still not worth the risk of facing a whole pack of hunters."

I have to swallow hard as bile rises in my throat. "That's not all." Looking up beneath my lashes at him, I say, "You'll have me."

Takada's expression remains unchanged as smoke curls from his nostrils, but his pupils expand, and his scent shifts, becoming spicy with arousal. "I'm afraid I'm not sure what you mean, Noboru."

Gritting my teeth, I squeeze out the words, "I'll be yours. However you want me."

Takada bares his teeth in a smile that makes my skin crawl. He takes his sweet time answering me, making it damn hard to breathe through the knot in my chest. Takada blows out a cloud of smoke, then rubs the cigarette out on the ashtray. "That is a... very generous offer, Noboru." His voice smolders with lust.

If I keep my word to Takada, Jinta will never forgive me. I'll be Takada's pet for the rest of my life. But if I say no, then my pack dies. Jinta dies. Is my life really worth Jinta's, my pack's? No. It isn't. The right thing, the selfless thing, is to put the yakuza first. Like I've done my entire fucking life.

"Am I sensing some hesitation, Noboru?" When Takada's fingers crawl over my cheek, my entire body seizes up. "Do you really think the human will make you happy? That you'll ever be content with, what? Some white picket fences. A normal job. Come on, now. I know you. Better than your precious human ever will. You'll only disappoint him when you can't be the picture-perfect mate he wants. But you don't have to change for me, Noboru. I will never ask that of you." His breath ghosts over my mouth.

He's right. I'll never make Jinta happy, and I'll only disappoint him. Or worse, get him killed.

"Let him go," Takada breathes, eyes closing, nose brushing mine. "Be mine, and I will help you save your pack."

I seize his hand and squeeze. Bones crunch. Takada doubles over the table with a strangled shout, baring his teeth at me as he seethes through the agony of having his fingers broken in my grasp.

"Do we have a deal?" I snarl at him.

Panting through his pain, Takada nods. "We do."

"You stick to your side of this arrangement, or all bets are off." I drop his hand like it's something slimy and foul, wiping my palm on my pants. "If you think this arrangement means you'll own me, you're wrong. You will never be my mate."

Rising, I turn my back on Takada and march from the room, away from the shadow of the naïve boy I once was. I'm not some broken boy he can string along and abuse anymore. I have no intention of following through on my end of the deal. I could never let Takada touch me again. Maybe once I could have been selfless enough but not now.

I've given away my heart and soul to Jinta Onodera, entrusted it to his safekeeping. Nothing will ever change that.

Takada has never taken no for an answer. He'll come for me once I have deceived him.

There won't be anywhere in Tokyo that's safe for me.

CHAPTER 9

Jinta

My whole body hurts. I'm sure one of my ribs is broken. The slightest breath makes pain spasm through my body.

With a chuckle, Akira tosses his phone into the air and catches it with a smack in his palm. "Wonderful. He's on his way. It's a shame he'll be too late."

Fear makes my heart skip. *Raiden*. He's coming. Escape is impossible. The hunters are going to use me as bait to kill the man I love.

"Don't do this," I croak, wincing as pain racks my aching jaw. "Please."

Ignoring me, Akira checks the time. "When did the priestess say she was coming?"

"She should be here any minute, boss," one of the hunters answers.

Tamano-no-Mae appears beside me, painted lips in a thin line. "You have got to get out of here."

"Really? I hadn't thought about that!" I mutter.

"That priestess will do a purification ritual. The ritual will tear me from your body. The damage to your soul will be too great to withstand. You will die, and I will be at the whims of the hunters in my spirit form."

"You don't think they'll purify you?"

She scoffs. "If Akira stoops low enough to work with werewolves, then who is to say he won't covet my powers for himself?"

That's a nasty thought. The last thing Raiden and the pack need is an overpowered hunter.

I swallow hard with apprehension, though my throat is so dry it feels like it's full of sand. There's a hole in the ceiling, revealing the overcast sky. Moonlight illuminates the edges of the clouds. Outside, tires crunch as a car pulls up to the warehouse. The hunters throw open the warehouse doors, and a priestess enters, hair tied back with a red ribbon, red hakama swishing around her legs. She's armed with a staff, paper streamers swaying as she marches toward us.

Tamano shivers beside me, hissing, "You must delay the ritual or you will die, and my fate will be in Akira's hands."

"How?" I snap, panic-stricken.

"Must I hold your hand? Do you want to see your mate again, or not? Then fight back!"

Through the open doors, another car arrives in the yard. One that I recognize. Saito Takada slams the door and marches toward the warehouse. More cars pull up, and groups of Takada-kai file out and join their alpha. As Takada's dark eyes find mine, his lip curls in contempt, but he ignores me and goes straight to Akira.

"Get out of here, Takada," Akira says, as if he's waving away a fly. "This has nothing to do with you!"

Huh? How do they know each other?

"Except it does. You're operating in my ward, after all. Nothing happens in Minato without my say-so. I see you have Noboru's little human pet. Is Noboru coming?" Takada asks, lighting up a cigarette.

Akira clenches his jaw. "Yes," he grits out. "He'll be here soon." Akira throws me a snide smile. "Wolves are nothing if not predictable creatures. Threaten their mates, and they become careless with rage."

Takada grunts around his cigarette, not sounding convinced. "He won't be an easy kill. I'm more than happy to lend my assistance. Noboru and I have... history."

My heart sinks. *Shit*. How will Raiden and his pack stand against both Takada *and* the hunters?

Akira's brow twitches, then he huffs. "Very well. But save me the killing blow, Takada." Akira chuckles, touching the pistol in his belt.

This is bizarre. Akira is awfully agreeable with Takada.

Takada's gaze snaps to me and he approaches. "Not looking so hot, human. Will Noboru still fawn over you when he sees that fucked-up face of yours?"

Rage heats my blood as I glare at the man who broke Raiden's trust when he was only a kid. Takada groomed him, made him think his twisted abuse was love, then dumped Raiden when he wouldn't be the monster Takada wanted.

I grin despite the stinging split in my lip, because fuck him. "Sure he will. But he'll completely rearrange yours. You won't be able to stop him. We both know he's stronger than you."

A muscle jumps in Takada's jaw. I think I've found a way to bide time. It'll hurt, but dying will hurt worse. Lip curling above his cigarette, Takada squats down to my level and peers down his nose at me. "He's strong because I made him strong. But you... everyday he spends with you, he gets softer, weaker. Once you're dead, he'll realize you were nothing but a burden to him."

A scoff escapes me. Behind my back, I grow my nail out to a claw and begin sawing at the zip ties binding my wrists. "And, what? You really think he'll go back to you? He's not a child you can manipulate anymore. He's a grown man, and he knows what real love looks like."

"Noboru doesn't know the first thing about love. Men like him and me, we can't love. Any love we have is for clan and pack, and that will always come first, human." An ugly grin splits Takada's narrow face. His teeth are sharp and yellow from nicotine. "He doesn't know how to love, but he sure knows how to fuck. I taught him that, you know?"

A red haze descends over my eyes as my stomach roils in disgust.

"Has he ever let you fuck him, human?" When I don't reply, he laughs. "Of course not. But he let me. Does it burn you up, human? Knowing I was his first? That I've burrowed in under his skin before you ever could and ruined him for any other man? He begged me for it. Sometimes, I still remember the way he screamed when I made him bleed. Gets me off every single time."

My hands shake as I fist them, nails digging into my palms. Yeah. It does burn me up. I wish I had been his first. I wish this disgusting man had never put his hands on Raiden, never hurt him so terribly.

But if I have my way, Takada will never hurt Raiden again.

Takada huffs with satisfaction. "Face it, you never would have been enough for him. He would've grown sick of you eventually. Raiden needs the thrill that comes with this way of life. You never could have made him happy."

Over Takada's shoulder, the priestess comes toward me. "Step aside, please. We must begin the ritual," she says.

Breathing hard, I hang my head. "Maybe you're right," I mutter, hating how his words cut into me. The zip tie breaks in two.

Takada tuts. "Aww. What's the matter, human? I strike a nerve? I'll take good care of him after you're—"

I snap my head up and slam it into his chin. Yelping, Takada stumbles back and loses his footing, falling flat on his ass. Fury surges through me, and I pounce. The hunters and Takada-kai members shout as I swing at Takada. My fist strikes the ground as he rolls out of the way. The pavement rips the skin from my knuckles, and searing pain racks my hand.

"Piece of shit!" Takada kicks at me.

His foot plows into my injured rib, and pain spasms through me as I tumble over. Takada charges, preparing another kick. I throw up my arms and absorb the blow, which reverberates through my wrist down to the bone.

With a snarl of rage, Takada stamps. I roll out of the way of his foot and get my feet under me, propelling myself up. He charges, and I launch myself into his attack. I'm shorter than him, so it's easier to get my arms around his middle and hit him in the stomach again and again. My fist pommels his hard stomach, and when he grunts above me, adrenaline rushes through me.

With a roar, Takada brings his weight down on me, and we drop to the ground. Takada yanks my arm behind my back, making me holler as he twists it at an unnatural angle. My shoulder cracks and waves of agony ripple up my arm. Takada pins my neck with his knee, crushing me to the ground. I struggle as my air gets choked off.

The priestess circles us, pouring salt on the ground around us.

"Don't let her!" Tamano shouts, but it's hopeless. I can't get Takada off me. He's too strong.

"Clear the circle, please!" the priestess commands.

Snarling, Takada plows his fist into my head. My ears ring, blacking out my vision for a few seconds as I struggle to remain conscious.

"Hurry the hell up!" Akira roars.

The priestess lifts her staff and begins to chant, low and guttural, as she walks the perimeter of the salt circle. Sucking in a gulp of air, I lurch to my feet and try to run. Instead, I crash into an invisible barrier. Panic claws at my chest. *Shit! There's no way out!* No matter which way I go, an invisible wall where the salt circle is cuts me off. The hunters jeer and laugh. Takada blows out smoke, eyes intent upon me.

The priestess waves her staff, shaking the streamers over my head. Pain erupts through my chest. My knees give out, and I collapse, too weak and stricken with pain to stand. A fire burns beneath my skin, so hot it feels like it will consume me from the inside out.

"It's over!" Tamano wails, slamming her fists against the invisible wall. "Forgive me, my love!"

I have no idea who she's talking to, but through the pain, all I can think about is Raiden. Will he forgive me for dying, for hurting him so deeply? There was so much I wanted to do with him, so many places we could have seen. Our lives together had just begun.

"Raiden? Where are you? Hurry. Please. I need you."

I choke as black mist pours from my throat, taking the shape of a spectral fox.

My vision blackens at the edges, the darkness coming for me.

With the last of my strength, I call out across our bond, *"Raiden!"*

A deafening crash shakes the warehouse to its foundation. Metal screams as it bends. Alarmed shouts echo through the room. The pain gripping me suddenly fades completely. Heaving in a breath, I roll over onto my stomach. There's a black car in the middle of what remains of the warehouse doors. My heart skips a beat as the red thread around my finger thrums with power.

Raiden leaps from the car. His eyes are black with fury, fangs bared, black fur rippling over his arms and face. He's half-shifted, his powerful body straining against the restraints of his clothes. He stares right through the hunters and I can finally breathe again when those predatory eyes collide with mine.

I've never been happier to see anyone in my life.

"You came..." My voice is hushed, reverent.

A confident smirk tips Raiden's mouth, but only I know him well enough to notice the relief that soothes the feral rage in his eyes. "Of course I did. You called for me, didn't you?"

"Nobody move, he's mine!" Ishida shouts, and the gun bucks as he fires.

Raiden stumbles with a snarl as the bullet pierces his shoulder.

Something deep inside me wakes up with a low, furious growl. Raiden's citrusy blood floods my nose, and fury rises from within me.

"Now, attack!" Takada roars, and his men come streaming in through the warehouse doors, charging side by side with Raiden's people.

The kitsune roars deep within my soul, baying for blood and death.

Chapter 10

My relief at seeing Jinta only lasts seconds before rage heats my blood.

There's cuts on his face, bruises marring his fair skin.

One of the hunters has a familiar scent I recognize from my ceremony. Akira, the bastard who threatened to put a sword through Jinta.

Akira shouts, "Attack! Now! Priestess, finish the damn ritual!"

The hunters draw their weapons, a mixture of pistols, silver baseball bats, and katana.

"I thought about showing some of you mercy," I say, voice thickening to a low, furious growl as my body swells out of my clothes, black fur rippling over my skin. My head snaps side to side as my face reforms into a snout fitted with fangs. "But you hurt my mate. All bets are fucking off. You touch my mate, and you get the Wolf of fucking Asakusa!" My roar fills the warehouse, and I spread my arms wide to show my claws.

"Fuck you, Noboru!" Ishida shouts. His gun blasts again, and a bullet sears its way under my skin. It doesn't hurt like I thought it would. No. Instead, my body heals rapidly, pushing the bullet out and cleansing the poison before it can spread through my blood. Guess this form is immune to what would normally kill my kind in minutes.

Akira draws a katana. "He can't heal if he's dead! Kill that fucking thing!"

Takada's men have already started to shift. Takada's eyes lock on mine. His knuckles are bloody, and Jinta's cherry blossom scent is all over him. If I didn't need his help, I'd shred him to pieces.

Howls echo from behind me, and my wolves charge toward the hunters in a wave of fang and claw, Ren's white wolf leading the hunt. Gunfire blasts, wolves shriek in agony as bullets burn their flesh. The hunters clash with my pack and Takada's wolves, cutting off my path to Jinta.

A snarl escapes me as Ishida turns and runs toward the back of the warehouse, leaving the wolves and hunters to fight it out. There's no way to get to him. The coward escaped, but I won't stop hunting until I've found him and made him answer for his betrayal.

With a bellow, Akira charges toward me. His sword swings through the air. I grab it in one huge claw. The silver burns my flesh like I've touched a hot branding iron, but it's tolerable. I yank him in close and drive my fangs into his sword arm and crunch. His shrill scream is music to my damn ears as I bite down, fangs piercing the bone.

Akira lunges for another blade in his belt, the metal flashing as he stabs at me. The blade bites deep into my shoulder as I swerve my head at the last minute. He could have taken my eye out with that thing. I send him flying across the room, then rip out the blade and throw it somewhere else.

Hunters surround me, their blades slicing into my flesh. There's too many of them. When I tear one off, another is on me. They cut at my ankles, making me stumble and fall. When I hit the ground, they swarm me, kicking, stabbing.

A sword tears across my forehead, and blood blinds me, staining the world in crimson hues.

The thread around my finger connecting me to Jinta thrums with terror.

"No, no, no! Raiden, hang on!" Jinta cries through the thread connecting us.

The thread vibrates and burns hot like it's been set aflame. Fury pumps through our bond, bestial and raw.

"Don't. Touch. Him." The words are a furious snarl, barely recognizable as Jinta's.

A roar shakes the warehouse to its foundation. The

hunters attacking me freeze, stumbling off me in a panic as they shout in alarm. Wiping blood from my eyes with a furry fist, I whirl toward Jinta.

But Jinta is gone. In his place is a monstrosity of a fox as big as a damn horse, nothing even like Namikawa's kitsune form or even Jinta's regular form. His fur is pure white, with red markings that streak through his fur. His eyes blaze a furious crimson.

Jinta's kitsune is beautiful and terrifying.

Snout wrinkled in a snarl, the kitsune hurls himself against the invisible barrier. Cracks appear in thin air, spreading through the barrier as Jinta smashes against the wards holding him again and again. Blood smears his forehead.

"What the hell..." Takada whispers, shooting me a shocked, furious look. "He's a damn kitsune! When the fuck were you going to tell me?"

"It wasn't your damned business!"

"The hell it isn't!" Takada rounds on me, face twisted in fury. "That thing is going to kill us all!"

I shout, "Jinta, stop!"

The kitsune snarls, *Must. Protect. Fight. Kill!*

A chill runs down my spine. That isn't Jinta's voice. It's the voice of a feral animal who will slaughter friend and foe alike to protect me.

"Ready yourselves!" Akira howls, drawing his pistol.

The kitsune hurls himself through the barrier and

charges in a white blur. Gunfire makes my ears ring, and I cry out in horror as blood bursts from various parts of the kitsune's body.

Nothing slows the beast down. He pounces upon a group of hunters, seizes one in his jaws, and shakes her around like she's nothing but a chew toy. Blood spatters the hunters pinned beneath him. Then he throws her broken, mangled body into the wall. With a furious roar, he conjures bright blue orbs of foxfire.

"Get back!" Takada bellows, but it's too late.

The foxfire blasts through the air, roasting the flesh and fur of any wolves it touches, consuming hunters' bodies in seconds. The screams and the stench of burning meat make my stomach roil.

Takada's wolves howl in anguish as fire melts the skin from their bones. The kitsune clones itself, making wolves and hunters alike become distracted by fighting off three different versions of himself, and then he vanishes before my eyes.

In a flash of white, he appears behind me and presses himself against me. His big, bushy tails wrap around me. A growl rumbles through his body, reverberating through my own chest. Changing back to my human form, I grab at his fur.

"Jinta. Hey. Sunshine, listen to me. You need to calm down!"

"Get that thing away from the boss!" one of my men

shouts, and my wolves charge toward me.

I bellow, "No! Stay back!"

But it's too late. I can only watch, frozen, as the kitsune leaps upon my own wolves, slashing at them, shredding them with his fangs. Their screams of horror and agony sear themselves into my memory.

That thing isn't Jinta. He's been turned into a monster that can't differentiate friends from foes. He became a monster to protect *me*.

I'm the reason my own people are being torn to pieces right now.

Ren barks as she charges, leaping toward him.

With a snap of his jaws, Jinta grabs her out of the air and crunches down. Ren howls in agony as blood stains her white fur.

"Jinta, no!" I roar, terrified I'm going to watch my mate slaughter my friend.

Snarling, Jinta hurls Ren across the room, and she smashes into a shipping crate with a yelp of pain.

I hate to abandon my pack, but if I stay, the kitsune will kill them all in my name. Drawing in a deep breath, I bellow, "Jinta!"

The kitsune whirls toward me, eyes blazing, snout wrinkled in fury.

"Let's go!" I start to run, tearing toward the exit.

"Noboru!" Takada roars. "Get back here and fight!"

A snarl splits the air. The kitsune leaps, slamming down

on the ground in front of me. One of his many tails coils around me. The kitsune bunches his muscles and springs into the air, completely weightless as he flies up toward the roof. The wind roars in my ears as the kitsune soars up through the hole in the roof and higher still, up among the clouds.

The city falls away below us, and my stomach lurches with the sudden urge to vomit. I swallow frantically and close my eyes, trying to gird my stomach. We stop ascending and drift among the clouds. The kitsune lifts his tail, and I let out an embarrassingly shrill scream as he suddenly drops me.

"Fuck, shit!" I crash onto his fluffy back and immediately grab handfuls of his dense fur.

The wind billows around us as the kitsune flies over the city and toward the distant mountains. My stomach swoops as the kitsune dives. I hide my face in the kitsune's white fur and nearly lose my damn dinner when we land with a bump on solid ground.

Feeling like my heart and bowels exchanged places, I slide off the kitsune's back and touch the forest floor. The woods around us are dark and quiet and oddly familiar. The kitsune rubs against me and leads the way. I follow at his side, and the trees eventually clear, revealing a familiar traditional home.

This home used to belong to Namikawa, but he left it to my grandfather, who then left it to me in his will. I haven't been to this house since before Namikawa and my grandfather died. We should be safe here.

I approach the door and find the spare key hidden in a potted plant. I turn toward the kitsune and shiver under those intense red eyes. The fury has left, but the kitsune hasn't shifted back.

"Gonna change back?" I ask him.

The kitsune grumbles and paws at the dirt.

I let us both inside, my bare feet slapping the wood and leaving bloody smears behind. The scent of tatami brings back memories of gathering here with Namikawa and the others, sitting beside my grandfather. I glance toward the tatami room and almost expect to see him kneeling there, a cup of green tea steaming by his hand. Rubbing my chest, I shake away the image. My feelings for the old man are... complicated, but I miss him.

The stairs creak as I climb them. Jinta's claws click over the wood as he follows me up to the second floor where the bedrooms are. My eyes getting heavier by the second, I slide open a door and find a couple of futons on the floor. The room smells like dust, but no one has been here in a long time.

Exhausted, I crash down into the futons. The mattresses dip as the kitsune settles in behind me. His tails wrap around me, and his nose bumps against the back of my neck, the coldness of it making me shiver.

When I close my eyes, the screams and agonized howls

come back to me. Images of the kitsune shaking hunters and wolves in his jaws, *my* wolves, make my heart race. Tonight went nothing like it was supposed to. I allowed my own men to abduct Jinta. Allowed him to kill them. His desire to protect me turned him into a monster.

I've turned him into a monster.

And if I can't get him the hell out of this life, I'm going to watch my sunshine be consumed by the darkness of my world.

Chapter 11

Jinta

I wake in the night, and it takes me a moment to figure out where I am. Flickers of memory tease me. I was flying, I think. But wait. What happened before that? Images flash. There was a warehouse. Takada and Akira's hunters. Raiden arrived.

My heart skips. That's right. Raiden came, and dozens of hunters hurled themselves on him. Cold terror had gripped me. I'd tried to escape the barrier, but no matter how hard I'd hit it, I'd been unable to get free.

For a heart-stopping moment, I'd been sure I was about to watch as Raiden was killed trying to save me. Fury had burned me up inside and—

Gunfire. Screams of hunters. Agonized howls of wolves.

Blood gushing in my mouth and down my throat. Bone crunching between my jaws.

Cold sweat breaks out over my body. I lurch upright, a hand over my mouth as bile rises in my throat. *Oh, fuck. What have I done?* I'd completely lost control, and I... I'd killed people. My hand starts to shake, my heart thumping out of control. Not even Raiden's sweet yuzu scent can soothe me. Carefully, I untangle myself from where I'm wrapped around his body, hoping I don't wake him.

Desperate for air, I go downstairs, and once I'm outside, I sit on the stoop. The night is cool and quiet. My chest is tight, and I struggle to suck in a full breath to calm my racing heart. Pulling my legs to my chest, I hide my face behind my knees. A whimper escapes me, and I clench my jaw tight to hold in my despair.

I became a monster. No better than Tamano-no-Mae when she'd slaughtered all those poor people Namikawa had forced Raiden to capture. The moment I'd scented Raiden's blood, felt his agony through the bond, I'd lost all control. What if it happens again? Who else will I hurt?

A low, musical laugh makes me freeze. I can feel the kitsune's presence, looming like a dark cloud above me. "If you were stronger, you could control it."

I squeeze my knees tighter to me. "Shut up."

"Why do you feel so bad? Don't you enjoy feeling powerful?"

My jaw creaks as I tighten it in anger. "You've turned me

into a monster. Maybe I should have died if this was what I was going to become."

She scoffs. There's the sound of a fan snapping open, then a flapping sound as she fans herself. "I did this? You insult me. If I'd been in control of the kitsune, not a soul in that warehouse would still be alive. Besides, I can't take full control while I am confined to your body, unfortunately. Or else I would have done so already. Do you think I like being stuck in your head, human? Listening to you pine over your mate like the main character of a romance manga?"

Heat flames my cheeks. "I do not pine over him."

Fanning herself with a bored expression, she continues, "Your feelings of inadequacy, of weakness—that is what made you lose control. You have no confidence."

Snorting, I prop my chin on my knee. "Gee. I wonder why? Could it be the lady in my head shit-talking me all the time?" As if I need her to tell me I think the worst of myself. Even though I have a partner who sees the best in me, I still struggle to see what Raiden does.

"As do I," Tamano chimes in, making me scowl when I realize she heard my thoughts. "He's a fine mate. Strong. Handsome. You do not deserve him."

My fingers curl. "And you do? Make up your mind. Do you want to kill him, or are you jealous?"

She *hmphs* and turns her pale face to the moon above. "Why would I ever want another mate? I have always been better off alone. Men are tools to use and throw aside. That is all they're good for."

I huff, amused. "Oh, really? So you've never loved anyone? Not once?"

Tamano turns her face away, shoulders rising toward her ears. I can tell I've struck a nerve. "Of course I have. It was a mistake."

I lean back on the heels of my hands and stretch out my feet so they dangle off the steps of the porch. "Who was he?"

"None of your concern," she snaps.

I'm too curious to let things lie. "Look, I get it. My last boyfriend cheated on me. I was pretty sure I wanted nothing to do with guys again. Ever." Am I seriously talking about boys with the ancient kitsune possessing my soul? My life. Whatever. I'm going with it. "But I met Raiden, and our connection was just... instantaneous. He's great. So maybe there's another guy out there for you."

"Do not speak of things you know nothing about!" She whirls on me, black eyes narrowed, fangs sharp. "You do not need to rub your mating bond in my face, human. There is no one out there for me. The only one for me died long, long ago."

I wince. Man. Do I always have to put my foot in my mouth? "Oh. I'm sorry." I scratch my head and look away from Tamano's tense frame, her red robes swaying in the night breeze. "Do you... want to talk about it?"

"Talk, talk, talk..." she mutters. "What is there to talk about?"

"Clearly a lot, if you're still upset about it."

She's quiet, arms folded to her chest. I figure I've pushed her too far, so I look away. She'll probably vanish in a few seconds. Claws click over the wood. I jolt, eyes opening. There's a fox with red streaks in her fur sitting on the porch beside me, nine tails curled delicately around her legs. She's a beautiful fox.

"His name was Konoe." Tamano's voice echoes in my mind, making me jump. *"He was one of Emperor Toba's many sons, back when I still walked the earth countless years ago. In the village where I lived among humans, people paid for my services, whether that was cursing a home, tricking their enemies, or other forms of mischief. However, one human came to me and offered me a great sum of money to assassinate the emperor."*

I stay silent, but I think I can see where she's going with this.

The kitsune turns her pointed snout toward the moon. *"I'd come to seduce the emperor, but it was his son who captured my heart. The instant we locked eyes, I knew I would never desire another man again. That he would be the only one I would ever care for. I became his lover, and we spent many days together, getting to know each other to the very depths of our souls. Even when he found out what I truly was, he did not reject me. He planned for us to marry, but his father forbade it. He had arranged a marriage for him with another woman, one he deemed worthy of his heir."*

Even though she's a fox and only so many emotions can show on her face, her voice shakes with anger and pain. I think I know why she chose this form to tell her story. It's easier, like hiding herself behind a shield.

"I poisoned the emperor so that we could be together."

I sigh, knowing this story doesn't have a happy ending. "That didn't happen, though."

The fox's small body shivers as she lets out a sound like a broken sigh. My chest tightens. *"The emperor's illness exposed me for what I really was. I had to flee, but Konoe had no time to accompany me. Hunters from the palace tracked me down and slew my mortal body. Konoe found me in the woods and wept. I wish I could have consoled him, told him that I was right there beside him in spirit. He took his own life. A priest confined my spirit within the Sessho-seki, and I was unable to pass on and join Konoe in death. For years, I waited for us to be reunited, and the longer we were separated, the more furious I became."*

"And when Namikawa broke the Sessho-seki..."

Her eyes narrow, snout wrinkling in anger. *"Namikawa promised we would be reunited, but only if I would serve his pack. In my fury, I demanded a sacrifice in exchange."*

Understanding makes me wince. "You had Namikawa abduct one-half of couples and fated pairs and tear them apart. The way you and Konoe were torn apart."

A growl rumbles from the kitsune beside me. *"You sound so incensed, human. But tell me this. How is it fair that so many got to be happy while I was left to suffer for so long without my love? If I can't be happy with my mate, then why should anyone else?"*

"I can understand. If I were separated from Raiden, I'd be devastated, too, but hurting others the way you've been hurt isn't the answer."

She snaps her fangs in my direction. *"Save your moral superiority for someone else, human. My kind do not follow the same codes and conducts as your race. Even after one hundred years passed, still, Konoe and I remained apart. I lost myself in fury and craved only blood, death, and suffering."*

"Do you still?"

The fox nods. *"Of course. Until I am reunited with Konoe, I will do whatever it takes to return to him. If I have to take your body, I will take it for myself. If I must kill, then I will kill!"*

"Sheesh. Take it easy. So all this time, you've been jealous of me and Raiden, is that it?"

She nods. *"Yes."*

Well, I appreciate her honesty. "I guess I can understand being jealous." I'd be pissed, too, if I'd been separated from Raiden. And while I won't ever forgive what she did under Namikawa's influence, tonight has only proven that I'm capable of the same violence as Tamano. I flew into a rage when Raiden was just *hurt*. But losing him? What would I do then? A shiver rattles my backbone.

"But you want to go back to him, don't you? So why were you talking earlier like you wanted nothing to do with guys?"

She growls lowly. *"Because I will never see him again. You will use me to destroy your enemies, the same as Namikawa, and you will never let me go. Why give up such immense power?"*

"No!" I blurt. The fox looks up at me, ears twitching. "I'm not going to keep you imprisoned inside my body, Tamano. I'm not Namikawa. I'd never do that. I want you to be free, too. But only when I'm sure you won't hurt anyone."

She narrows her red eyes. *"You expect me to believe that?"*

"No. I don't. Namikawa lied to you and used you. But I won't do that to you. As long as releasing you won't result in bloodshed, I'll help you get home to Konoe. I promise."

She gazes up at me with something like hope in her wide eyes. *"Truly?"*

I give her fluffy head a pat before I can remind myself she's a deity, not a cute fuzzy fox. "Yeah. Really."

She shakes off my hand and glares up at the moon. *"I'll believe it when I see it, human."*

"So make me a promise, okay?"

She curls her lip but doesn't argue.

I hold out my hand. "I'll set you free when the time

comes, but you have to stop acting like we're enemies. No more mocking me. No more trying to take control and hurt people. We both want the same thing. So let's work together until then, okay?"

Tamano's fur bristles as she growls, and then she huffs. When she sticks out her small paw, I shake it. *"Very well, human. But go back on your word, and I will make you and everyone you love regret it."*

I'd be lying if I said I trusted Tamano completely. She and I got off to a rocky start, but we're both in the same boat here. I'm going to do everything I can to lift this curse, for my sake as well as Tamano's.

Chapter 12

When I open my eyes, Jinta's side of the bed is empty. The tinkling of shower water against porcelain faintly carries from down the hall. Golden dawn light streams in through the windows and pools on the bed. The world outside is quiet except for birdsong. It's like having our own little corner of the world, but I know it can't last.

My phone rings, and I curse when I recognize the number. "Takada."

His voice is low and furious when he says, "You lied to me, Noboru."

A vein pulses in my temple as I grunt, "Did not. Just didn't tell you shit that wasn't your damn business."

"An out-of-control kitsune is my fucking business!"

Jinta wasn't himself last night. I know that because I know him, but I can't expect my pack or Takada to see things the way I do. Fact is, they watched Jinta kill their allies as well as their enemies. They will demand repercussions. And if they try and hurt Jinta... I'll kill them all. And where will that leave me? A pariah among my own pack. That's the very last thing I need, especially with hunters gunning for us.

"Jinta and I are trying to lift the curse, Takada. It's going to take time."

"Well, hurry the fuck up. If you want my pack's help, then you will get that thing under control. Our deal is off the table until I'm sure the kitsune is a weapon in our arsenal rather than a ticking time bomb. Got it?" He hangs up before I can respond.

This isn't good. I need Takada's pack if we're going to stand against the hunters. Slumping over, I tangle my fingers in my hair, growling. *Fuck*. How can I keep my pack together *and* keep Jinta safe? If it comes down to it, I'll choose Jinta. Always. Even though I know he deserves better. Lifting my head, I gaze out the window as the sun shines through the emerald leaves of a tree, branches rasping against the glass in the breeze.

The simplest thing... would be to send Jinta far away once he's cured. Away from the pack, the hunters, and me. Pain spasms through my chest, tearing a gasp from me. I grip my chest, grinding my teeth against the pitiful whimper that tries to escape me.

Mate. Mine. Ours.

My wolf despises the idea, and so do I. But what other option is there?

Fuck this. I can't torture myself with these thoughts right now. I'm not giving Jinta up, not without a fight. Kicking off the blankets, I cross the room and grab some lube I stashed in the dresser during my last visit here, then I follow Jinta's cherry blossom scent down the hall to the bathroom.

I need my mate. Need to feel him against me. His mouth hot and pliant against mine. Hear his soft cries, my name a breathless groan on his tongue. Want to bury myself in his arms, in the desperate clutch of his body.

I slide the door open and step into the bathroom. A gentle mist hangs in the air, and the shower door is fogged up, only allowing a tease of Jinta's lithe body through the glass. My bare feet slap over the floor as I approach. Jinta's silhouette freezes on the other side of the glass. I reach for the door.

It opens, and my breath catches as Jinta's gentle eyes find mine. His brown hair is almost black when wet, clinging to his round face. Water sluices down his high cheekbones and drips off the tip of his button nose. His lips are damp and pink. Wordlessly, I go to him, and he twines his slender arms around me. Long fingertips glide up my back to curl in the hair at my nape.

My heart thuds hard as Jinta molds himself to me, his cheek to my pec right over my heart. I want him closer. I've never needed someone so close, even though he's as close as he can possibly get. I've never *let* myself feel this way for anyone. It's terrifying because if I lost him, I don't think I could recover from it. It would break me irreparably.

A shiver racks Jinta's body, and a breath like a sob catches in his throat. Burying my fingers in his hair, I give a gentle tug and make him look up at me. Jinta's lip wobbles, and my heart cracks in two when his eyes take on a damp sheen.

"I... I'm sorry," he croaks. "So sorry. I-I don't know what happened. I c-couldn't control it, baby. I swear, that wasn't me. I wasn't—"

I sway us beneath the warm shower spray. "I got it," I murmur into his wet hair. "I know."

"Your p-pack. They'll be so angry. I don't want to turn them against you."

"Fuck them," I rasp as a growl rises in my throat. "Hear me? Fuck all of them."

Jinta shakes his head, shoulders hitching when he hiccups. "Don't. You can't isolate them from you. You need them, o-otherwise how will you fight the Blades and Takada?"

Encircling his face within hands, I lift his head. "I need *you,* Sunshine."

Lips thinning, Jinta brushes my hands away. "I'm not

worth this, Raiden. I'm *not.* The pack has to stay strong. We can't face the Blades and Takada alone. Maybe we can, I don't know, keep our distance. O-or I could leave and go to Osaka and try to find your father."

My hands shoot out and grab his wrists, tugging him closer. I'm not ready for this. Even though I told myself this morning that I have to let him go, I can't. Not yet. Not until I've exhausted every other possible solution. "No. We'll think of something."

"Like what?" His tone is accusatory.

"I don't know! Anything!"

A part of me shivers at the idea that if he leaves, I'll never see him again. It's what should happen, but fuck if I don't hate it. Jinta nods, then wipes his eyes. I never knew my heart could break for another person's tears. I've never cared about seeing other people get hurt before. After years in this life, I've become desensitized to it. Jinta Onodera is the exception to every rule I've put in place to protect my heart.

Leaning down, I kiss his forehead, then drop kisses to each of his cheekbones. Flicking out my tongue, I catch a hint of salt on his skin before the shower washes it away. I slide my hands down his warm, wet skin, blood heating as he sighs. He's hard when I take him in hand, stroking and squeezing. A gasp escapes him, head tipping back against the shower wall. My wolf growls as he bares his throat, and I lunge in, nipping at the pale skin, cock kicking hard as his moan vibrates low in his throat against my lips.

Jinta grabs at my hair and tugs, crashing our lips together. A groan tears from me, and I grip both his hands and pin them over his head. "Don't do a thing," I pant against his lips. "I'm here. Gonna make you feel good, forget everything else. Leave all of this to me. Yeah?" Sliding my hand down, I grip both our hard cocks and rub. Jinta's eyes flutter closed, lips parting as he moans with me. "Let me take care of you."

I want to be responsible for his pleasure. Need to remind myself I can do so much more than just cause pain. I need Jinta to entrust everything to me. His body, his pleasure, his soul.

Biting his supple lip, Jinta rolls his head back. "I'm all yours." He flexes his hips, pushing into my touch, rubbing our cocks together.

Mine. My blood burns hot with need, and I lunge in, mashing my mouth against his. He's so pliant, parting his lips against mine, groaning when I plunge my tongue inside to tease his. My hand works our cocks, and I bite on his lip, growling.

"That's it," I grunt out the words. "Fuck my fist. Tell me what you want, Sunshine. Tell me, and I'll worship this gorgeous, perfect body of yours till you cum screaming my name."

"I-I—fuck!" Jinta's panting, eyes closed in bliss as he thrusts faster and faster. "I w-want to feel you."

I flick my tongue over his earlobe and say, "Tell me where."

Chest heaving against mine, Jinta chokes out, "Your mouth. Want it on my cock."

I smack a kiss to his panting lips, bucking my hips and grinning when he cries out. "Good boy." Gliding my hands down his hips, I dig my fingers into the soft mounds of his ass. When I glance up, Jinta's got a curious frown on his face, like he wants to ask me something.

"What?"

He shakes his head. "Nothing." He arches his hips, urging me on. I can't refuse him anything. Not my body, not my heart, or my soul. On my knees before him, I part my lips and guide his cock to my mouth. When I wrap my lips around the head, Jinta grabs at my hair, knees shaking. I lap at the underside of his cock, moaning around my mouthful. I love the taste of him and can't imagine I'll ever get sick of the sounds he makes when I suck him off.

When I bring him to the back of my throat, my nose buried in his pubes, Jinta lets out a whimper. "R-Raiden... fuck. That feels so good. Want to... can I..."

I pull off with a lewd slurp and pump him in my hand, squeezing out a bead of pearly precum, and lap it up. "I'm yours, aren't I? You can do whatever you want to me."

Jinta throws back his head, mouth falling open as he squeezes my hair so hard it almost hurts. "Want to fuck your mouth. Need it."

"Choke me with your cock," I rasp, then suck him back down to the root.

A hoarse cry escapes Jinta, and he lets go, pumping his hips shallowly at first. When I slip my hand beneath his hard balls and rub my fingertip against his clenched hole, Jinta snaps his hips forward, and I gag around him. "Yes! Put your fingers in me. Make me ready."

I love how bossy he is. Jinta's shy, so seeing him let go, knowing I'm the cause of it, is such a damn treat. Grabbing the lube I'd put on one of the shelves, I slick my fingers up then press one against his hole, cock twitching when he bears down on my finger, and I slip inside up to the first knuckle.

"More. Please. Give me another." Jinta's voice is hoarse and breathless. He thrusts into my mouth, then pushes his hips back against my finger.

I work another inside, moaning around his cock when his heat encases around my fingers. He feels so fucking good, every single time. I pump my fingers in and out of his blissful heat while I wrap my lips around his throbbing cock and suck hard. When he rewards me with a breathless curse, I massage that soft spot inside him that makes his legs tremble and his breath catch.

"Oh, fuck, Raiden, I—I'm going to cum if you keep doing that."

I smirk around my mouthful. I'd love for him to flood my mouth and let me drink every drop. But he's not begging and babbling yet, which tells me I haven't earned his release. When my third finger stretches his hole, Jinta's whole body shudders. His body clenches around my fingers, and my eyes roll back, knowing how good he'll feel wrapped around my cock. In my mouth, Jinta's shaft pulses, precum spilling onto my tongue. He's close, and hell, so am I. I need him.

"Fuuuck, baby. Need you inside me. Now." Jinta's voice is strained, and his stomach muscles are clenched.

I pull off his leaking cock and take him in my hand. Jinta grabs my shoulders hard, biting his lip. "How do you want me, Sunshine? I'm all yours."

"Fucking ruin me." There's a desperation in his voice I've never heard before, and those three words sever my self-control. I'm on my feet, crushing my mouth to his. While I slick up my cock with lube, I push my tongue past his swollen lips, knowing he'll taste himself in my mouth.

Hooking my arm beneath his knee, I hoist his leg up high. Grabbing my cock, I position myself at his entrance, snarling through gritted teeth as I slide home in one smooth motion. A broken sound escapes Jinta as I bottom out, grabbing frantically at my shoulders, nails biting into my skin.

"Gonna lift you," I warn him, and when he nods emphatically, I hook my other arm under his left knee. "Ready?"

"Yes!" He jumps a little when I lift him and winds his

arms around my neck, back against the wall, my arms supporting his knees. He wraps his legs around my waist and squeezes. Once I'm sure he's secure, I drive into his exquisite heat, draw out slow, then sink back in until I'm as deep as I can possibly go. *Fuck.* He feels so good. Always does. Never gonna get over the way he sucks me right into his needy body.

Jinta throws back his head, grunting out a breathless, "More. Don't hold back. Need you to—fuck!" He claws at my back as I slam in, my pelvis smacking the back of his ass. I don't give him time to recover, growling in bliss as I watch him take every inch of my cock.

"This what you wanted?" My voice is practically a snarl as I take him hard and fast, fucking him against the shower wall. "Want me to fuck you so hard you forget your own name?"

"Yes!" he cries. "Need it. Just like this. Make me forget everything but you."

So that's what this is about. He wants to forget last night ever happened. That he was taken. The things he did. The pain he endured. *Fuck.* This is why I've never let myself get close to someone. I can bear my own pain. But I can't bear his. I never want to experience the fear I felt yesterday when I realized he was gone. Not ever again.

Lunging in, I capture his mouth with mine, swallowing his cries as I let loose and fuck him with everything I have. Because I need it, too. I need to remind him that he's mine.

Need to remind myself that he's here with me, my cock buried so deep inside the warm clutch of his body that our souls are practically touching.

"Nobody's taking you from me again." I pant against his mouth as I pound into him relentlessly. "Hear me? You're mine, and I protect what's mine." I couldn't protect him, not this time, but I will find Ishida, and I will make him regret ever trying to take my sunshine away.

Jinta's arms fly around my back, teeth nipping at my shoulder. His body tenses up, his hole strangling my aching cock. "Gonna cum, baby. Need to. Please make me cum. *Please.*" He practically growls out the final plea.

My balls wrench up as I let go, giving him everything I have until he rewards me with a ragged shout, his hot velvety walls squeezing my cock so hard my eyes fucking roll back. Jinta shudders, hips jerking as his cock pulses, spilling thick ropes of cum all over his chest and stomach.

I'm so close, balls painfully hard, cock throbbing with the need to spill inside him. My movements become erratic, my whole body seizing up. I crumple into his neck, grunting, panting into his skin. Jinta bites down on my earlobe and whispers, "That's it, baby. Let go for me. Cum for me."

A feral snarl escapes me as my hips jerk forward one more time, grinding against his ass. My orgasm erupts from me in thick, heavy spurts so intense I can't even make a sound as pleasure courses up and down my cock. I snap my hips again and again, gripping his ass hard enough to bruise, until I've emptied every last drop into his body. Every muscle threatens to go completely lax, so, carefully, I lower us down to the floor of the tub and let Jinta sit in my lap.

Water courses down on us as we catch our breath, my spent cock still cradled in Jinta's body. The heat from the shower, coupled with the bliss of my orgasm, is almost enough to make me black out right on the spot. My heart clenches when Jinta nuzzles into my chest, lips fluttering over my skin, rubbing my chest gently.

I close my eyes and kiss his wet hair. "I'm sorry I let them take you." I turn my face away even though he can't see me, embarrassed as my voice thickens.

Jinta slips his arms around my neck, planting a tender kiss against my chest. "I thought I'd... that I'd have to watch you die," he admits, his own voice shaking.

Squeezing my eyes shut, I hold him close. I never want to feel that terror again. "Nah. Not me. I'm hard to kill." Bringing his hand to my lips, I kiss his knuckles. "We're gonna make them regret fucking with us. Every single one of them."

It's a vow I'm going to see through to the very end.

CHAPTER 13

Jinta

"We should find my father." Raiden sounds like he tasted something foul as he picks at his rice. He's scowling when I look up from my untouched food, but he meets my gaze, resignation souring his face. I want to reach out and stroke away the lines in his brows.

"Ren was telling me about some mage who might be able to track him down."

Raiden frowns, then understanding brightens his eyes. "Yeah. Charlie. He'd be a good place to start."

As happy as I am that he's on board, I can't imagine he'll want to accompany me. I take a sip of green tea. Ever since I tasted Raiden's blood, my stomach has finally settled enough to eat regular food again. "So, he'll hopefully tell us where your dad is, and then I'll go and—"

Raiden sets his bowl down. "I'm going with you."

Hope flickers in my heart. "Really?" When he nods, a determined set to his jaw, it flickers and fans into a flame that warms every part of me.

"I've got a score to settle with my old man. If I don't show up, that bastard will think I'm afraid of him. Besides, I'd be a real ass if I let you do this alone." He curls his hand over mine, and affection makes my heart skip.

"Yeah, you would be." I grin and lift his hand, kissing his knuckles then the stub of his pinky finger.

The distant rumble of an approaching car gets louder and louder, the engine cutting off in our driveway.

Unease prickles over my skin. "Are we expecting some-one?" But Raiden's tense shoulders and narrowed eyes are all the answers I need.

"Stay." Keeping low, Raiden creeps to the window and peers out. "Shit."

"What is it?" I lower my voice instinctively, get down on all fours, and crawl to the window. Who in the hell would be out here at Namikawa's old house, and why? Mouth dry, I peek my head up just high enough to peer over the window ledge.

There's a big black car in the driveway. My pulse races as the doors open and shut. Four men climb out and march toward the house, their voices loud and disgruntled. Their bodies are tense, faces full of anger.

"Those aren't my guys." Raiden ducks down out of sight, claws scraping the floorboards.

"Takada-kai," I whisper, fear making my stomach churn.

"Hey, Noboru!" One of the men booms, voice echoing through the countryside. "You in there with the monster that slaughtered our comrades? Come the hell out!"

Fuck. Chills break out over my skin. They're here because of me. Because of what I did. They aren't here to talk. That much is clear. If Raiden gets hurt because of me—oh god. Will I lose control again? Somehow, I've got to de-escalate things.

The porch creaks, and I jump when a heavy fist slams into the door. "Open up! We can smell you inside!"

Raiden growls. "Hide."

I grab his arm. "No, I'm not leaving you!"

"Just do it. I don't want you losing control and blaming yourself for what you do!" he hisses, shoving me toward the stairs.

"If you don't leave, neither do I!" I snap, then I bolt the door. Grabbing his hand, I tug him up and toward the back of the house. Kicks hit the door behind us. We slip out the back door just as the yakuza storm into the house.

"They're trying to escape, don't let them!" Furious snarls pursue us, claws scrabbling over wood floors.

Gripping Raiden's hand, I try to steer him toward the front of the house. "We need to get to their car!" We can get away without even engaging them in a fight. Raiden tugs me around the side of the house toward the vehicle. The back door crashes open, and wolves pelt after us, claws kicking up dirt as they rush toward us.

"Go ahead and get the car started. I'll hold them off!" Raiden shoves me ahead before I can protest. His black wolf bursts from his clothes and charges toward the four wolves pursuing us. Panic tries to freeze me, every instinct screaming to help him.

Behind us, another car swerves into the driveway. *Shit.* They brought reinforcements. Four more men storm from the car and rush toward us.

"Got'cha!" A weight comes crashing down on top of me. A rough hand seizes my neck and pulls hard. "Where's that big monstrous form of yours now?" The yakuza sneers in my face before he swings me around and hurls me into a tree. My vision whites out as my skull strikes the bark, and pain spasms through my back. The four of them close in on me.

"This is for every comrade you fucking slaughtered!" The toe of a boot slams into my stomach, sending the contents burning up my throat and out my mouth in a sour rush. I cough, choking on foul bile, and I yelp as a kick cracks across my face. My lip splits, nose crunching, blood gushing down the back of my throat.

All I can do is curl into a ball, so racked by pain that I can't move. Blood pools beneath me from my nose. My eyes roll when I'm kicked onto my back. A man straddles me, drawing back his fist. I sluggishly lift my arm, but his punch snaps my head back. When he wraps clawed hands around my neck and squeezes, panic tightens my chest. My air is cut off, and no matter how much I kick and thrash, I can't get this asshole off of me.

"Jinta, no!" Raiden screams. "Get off him! Get the fuck off him!"

"Watch, Noboru, watch as we kill your precious little mate!"

"Get off me! Jinta, hang on, I—" Raiden yelps in pain. The scent of his blood scorches my nose.

A tide of fury rises in me, eclipsing even the pain.

No, fuck, no. I need to get to the car. I don't want to fight or kill anyone... but the kitsune does. Fur ripples over my arms. My fangs sharpen. Claws pierce my palms. They hurt my mate. Made him bleed. *They will fucking pay for it!*

The kitsune roars within my soul. My body grows, tails sprouting from my spine. A growl swells in my throat, rumbling like thunder. The wolves attacking Raiden whirl around, furious snarls dying to whimpers. One of them has Raiden's ankle between their fangs. Another has their paw on his skull.

Mate. Must protect him. Must kill.

They spilled his blood. I will spill theirs!

I spring, soaring through the air toward the wolves clustered around my mate. A swipe from my claws bowls two off their feet and sends them flying. Snapping my jaws, I grab another between my teeth and crunch down, breaking his neck between my jaws. I hurl the corpse into his friend, leaving him prone beneath the body of his comrade.

The two I threw off charge at me in a blur of fur and fangs. Their teeth pierce my flesh, but it feels like the bite of little needles. It's laughable. With a snarl, Raiden leaps on one of the wolves and wrestles him away from me, tackling him.

I swipe, claws flaying away the flesh on a white wolf's snout and staining his fur crimson. Yelping, he paws at the blood blinding him, and I attack. As I will it, a geyser of foxfire erupts beneath his paws. The wolf screams as his flesh and fur burns off his bones.

Only one remains. Tail tucked, he takes off into the trees. *Prey to be hunted, caught, and devoured!* The world blurs around me as I shoot after him in pursuit. I leap through the air and crash to the ground in front of him. His paws scrabble in the dirt as he tries to flee, but he's not fast enough. I snare him in my jaws and bite down, splintering his ribs between my teeth, flooding my mouth with his sweet blood.

More. I need more. With every piece of flesh I consume, my power grows. I will kill anyone who threatens my mate. Consume the world with my foxfire. Flood the streets of Tokyo with blood.

"Jinta!"

A sweet, citrusy aroma penetrates the haze of bloodlust. A wave of calm washes over me, tearing me from my shifted state. A foul taste floods my mouth, making my throat prickle. My stomach lurches, and I cough, spitting blood and flesh and fur from my mouth.

What... what the hell did I *do?* I open my eyes.

A scene of carnage straight from a damn horror movie makes the air freeze in my lungs. Wolves lie broken and bloody, bodies mangled, innards sprawled over the blood-soaked grass. My lungs tighten.

Oh, god... I did that. I did all of this. My vision spins as I lift my hands, caked with blood and stinking of gore.

A voice comes from far away, but my ears ring too loudly. I can't hear it.

"Get away from me," I whimper, teeth chattering so bad I can hardly get the words out. Falling backwards onto my rear, I crawl away from Raiden as he reaches toward me. What if I'd lost control and hurt him? What if it was his blood staining my hands, his blood coating my throat? My vision fogs as horrified tears burn my eyes.

I'm a monster.

Raiden heaves me off the ground and holds me against his chest. His citrusy scent is awash in blood and gore, but I huddle into the warmth of his body. I suck in a ragged gulp, and his big hands stroke my back.

"I got you, Sunshine. You're okay." Raiden's voice

shakes, and he squeezes me tight against his body. "Nobody's going to hurt you again."

But what if I hurt him next? Or someone close to him? Who will protect him from *me*?

Raiden kisses my hair, chest shuddering against me. "I'm so sorry," he whispers, voice ragged. He's never sounded so gutted before.

Wrapped in the sanctuary of his arms, I close my eyes and finally know peace.

CHAPTER 14

Raiden

It's been fifteen minutes, and my hands won't stop shaking.

I grip the wheel tight, eyes constantly darting between the road to Tokyo and Jinta. He's curled in the passenger seat, eyes closed as he rests. I got him dressed and helped him clean the blood off his face. His wounds have healed. He's *fine*.

Fuck.

My eyes burn, a lump rising in my throat. Squeezing the wheel until it creaks, I try and battle my emotions into submission. I can't fall apart. Not now. But my mind torments me, forcing me to imagine all the horrible ways that attack against Jinta could have ended. The wolves had held me down. I wasn't able to break free and get to him. If he hadn't shifted, Jinta could have been—*fuck*. I could have lost him.

A strangled scream tries to escape, but I fight it down by boring my teeth into my inner cheek. My people are right. I'm nothing but a shadow of what Namikawa was. I hated the man, but I'll be the first to acknowledge the respect and power he commanded. Because he wanted this life, wanted to be a leader. And I don't. Never have, never will.

I can't control my own men. I can't control Jinta's kitsune. My pack will turn on me one by one, and if the hunters and Takada-kai don't kill us, we'll consume ourselves from the inside out. Something's got to give.

The scenery blurs by, and I lose track of time until Tokyo's skyscrapers come into view. I wish I could take Jinta and go far away from Tokyo, run away from the responsibilities awaiting me. But I can't. I've got to keep the pack from falling apart before our enemies take advantage of the cracks in our armor.

My phone rings on the dashboard. I swipe to answer. "Ren, what's going on?"

"We did it."

Finally, some good news. "You found him?" My wolf infuses my words with a growl, the urge to hunt rising within me.

"He's waiting for you in the usual spot."

My fingers curl on the wheel. My lips lift, fangs sharp.

"On my way."

I slam on the gas and drive straight for the piers. Jinta still dozes when I put the car in park, exhausted from the chaos of the past couple of days. I hate to wake him up. Reaching out, I brush my knuckles over his cheek, but he looks too sweet in his sleep. He deserves to rest.

Closing the door softly behind me, I leave Jinta in the car and make for the warehouse ahead. Namikawa used the place to *question* people, usually those who crossed him. Often, that was me. Just the sight of this building makes an icy trickle of some old, primal fear run down my spine. A remnant left over from the last time I was here. It wasn't long ago that he held me here against my will. Compelled me to put a knife in my hand and cut off my own finger.

I was Namikawa's dog. That isn't who I am anymore. I'm the boss now, and I will never allow anyone else to own me. Takada's deal crawls into my mind, and I shake it out. *Focus.* Behind me, more of my people park and make for the warehouse. I summoned them here during the drive over. They need to learn what happens to anyone who crosses me.

The doors screech when I open them, taunting me with memories I've tried to forget. Zip ties cutting into my wrists. Sweat cold on my body. Chest tight with dread. The pain that never seemed to end. With effort, I swallow it all down. No. I will not be broken down by my past. I have risen above it. I'm better, stronger, than I ever was before.

In the center of a room full of shipping crates is a chair. Blood has soaked into the wood. My blood. This time, I'm not the one in the chair. Ishida is, hands bound tight behind his back, skin clammy with sweat, frantic eyes darting around the room as he looks for a way out. But there is none. I would know. My pain in this place was never-ending.

And his will be, too.

Ren glances my way and murmurs, "Are you okay? I know being here isn't easy, but I wasn't sure where else to—"

"I'm fine." My tone makes it clear that's the end of the conversation. I need it to be. The room is full of my people. I can't afford even a hint of weakness. I must be the boss. Untouchable and powerful. Later, I can numb my wounds with sake and fall asleep in my mate's arms.

But now? Now, I make this bastard pay for hurting my sunshine.

Ishida shakes, rattling the chair. "Hey, come on, boss. I didn't even hurt Jinta! I swear! Ask him yourself!"

"Quiet." The fury in my voice drains the blood from Ishida's face. "You keep his name out of your mouth. You don't even *think* about him."

A line of sweat streaks down Ishida's forehead and drips off his chin. His fear shrouds the air with a sour reek that makes my lip curl. I turn my back and take a few items off a metal table by his chair. A bamboo cutting board. A dagger. Bandage and string. When I face him, Ishida's lips are quivering. Sweat soaks through his shirt, which strains against his heaving chest.

I set down the board and place the knife, bandage, and string on the surface. I draw the blade and walk around behind him. Ishida whimpers when I slice through the zip ties, immediately rubbing his wrists. I chuck the knife onto the ground at his feet.

"Pick it up."

Namikawa said those words to me once, and I had to obey. Now, I'm the one giving the orders. I'm in control for fucking *once*. Adrenaline rushes through me, speeding up my heart. It feels fucking good. When Ishida only stares, eyes bulging, I slap him across the face so hard he stumbles to the side.

"Pick it up," I snarl.

Panting, Ishida picks up the blade. "Y-yes, boss."

"Kneel."

He obeys like a mindless servant, kneeling before me.

"You know what to do."

Ishida swallows hard, eyes glossy with panic. The knife shakes in his trembling fist. He's helpless the way I was helpless. *Hey. Rather him than me.* Bored, I light up a cigarette while I wait for him to grow the balls to do as he's told.

Ishida presses his trembling lips together. "You'll just kill me anyway."

Blowing out smoke, I say, "True. But I'll make it quick and painless if you apologize first. Think about it, yeah?"

Indignation reddens Ishida's face. He glares up at me, drool trickling from the corner of his mouth as a callous grin possesses his face. "Oh, I'll think about it the next time I'm alone with your pretty little human pet, and he's on his knees choking on my—"

Suddenly, the cutting board is in my hands, and I'm swinging, smashing the board across his disgusting, smiling face. Ishida crumples, eyes rolling back. The blood has only just started flowing before the wounds heal. But it doesn't matter. I grab the knife and pounce, slamming my knee down on his wrist to pin his hand to the floor.

Nobody threatens my mate.

"Watch closely!" My voice bounces around the room. "All of you!" The wide, startled eyes of my people fall upon me. "And the next time you think about betraying me, I want you to remember this!"

I bring the blade down, slicing through flesh and bone until the blade hits the concrete floor. Ishida screams and screams, but it's silenced when I cram his own finger in his mouth, making him choke on it. The coppery tang of blood saturates the air, so pungent I can taste it. My people let out exclamations of shock, even a few curses.

Ishida gags around my fingers, eyes watering.

I yank my fingers free and squeeze his jaw shut. "Swallow."

Ishida makes a disgusted noise, tears rolling down his cheeks.

I slap him hard. "Swallow!"

Ishida's throat works furiously, but he gags. Rolling over, he vomits onto the ground, coughing and spitting.

"Pathetic." I slam my foot into his heaving stomach, making him roll onto his back. Fisting the sweat-dampened front of his shirt, I haul him in close and crack my fist across his nose. The bone snaps, and blood gushes down Ishida's face. Before the wound has a chance to heal, I strike him hard again and again. His blood smears my knuckles, hot and wet. My finger breaks on his jaw.

I drown in the smell of his blood, reveling in the fact that it's him and not me who's helpless and weak. For once, I'm in control, and I never want to be helpless again. For as long as I live, there will always be enemies breathing down my neck, trying to drag me back down into the mud at their feet. I'll never be able to have a normal life. Leaving the yakuza will be nothing but a death sentence to me and Jinta. The only way either of us can survive is if all of Tokyo knows my name and fears me.

"Raiden, stop!" Someone grabs my wrist and holds tight.

Sweat drips down my face, mixing with the spatters of Ishida's blood. Strands of hair hang in my face and stick to my forehead. The breath saws in and out of my lungs, and shudders rack my body. Ishida groans beneath me, his face a bloody swollen mess. He's still alive to threaten me and mine, and I won't stand for it.

The sweet aroma of cherry blossoms threatens to take the edge off my wild rage. Panic makes my chest hitch. Jinta's here. He saw me lose control. Bile burns my throat. Wetting my lips and tasting blood, I turn and encounter wide, frightened brown eyes.

Jinta drops my wrist and stumbles back, glassy eyes darting from me to Ishida's bloody face. "T-that's enough." His voice shakes, breathy with fear.

I wring out my hand, wincing as one of my disjointed fingers pops back into place. "He's still alive."

"I don't care." Jinta blinks hard, chest rising faster. "You've made your point."

The eyes of my people weigh on my shoulders. Whispers flicker through the room, tinged with unease. Even Ren looks disturbed. So, this is the kind of leader I am. Not one who rules with respect, but fear. I'm nothing like Namikawa. No. I'm more like Takada.

I went too far. Way too far. I thought this was what I wanted, to be feared and powerful, but one look in Jinta's petrified eyes and disgust makes my insides roil. I terrified him. But why? I've done way worse than beat a man bloody. I've killed people before, for *him,* for fuck's sake, and he never looked at me like I'm an out-of-control beast.

I reach for him with bloodied hands. "Jinta—"

He takes a step back. "Don't touch me."

His rejection hurts like a physical blow.

Without another word, Jinta turns and walks out. I can't breathe. It feels like I'm drowning. All I want is to chase after him and beg him on my hands and knees not to leave me, to swear I'll change. But if I went to him now and he told me he was disgusted with me and never wanted to see me again, I'd break.

I wipe my bloody hands on my trousers and force myself to turn away from the warehouse doors. I pick up the dagger and clean it with a handkerchief from my pocket. Then I approach Ren. "Take Jinta to Charlie's." I draw the blade across my palm and squeeze a few drops of blood into the tissue. "Bring this for the ritual."

Ren nods, and I ignore the worry creasing her brow. "Got it."

Once I've handed her the bloody tissue, I collapse into the chair by Ishida's battered body and don't move until everyone has left the room. Metal grinds against metal, and the doors close, leaving me alone.

I was wrong. I'm not powerful or untouchable. I'm still a prisoner, shackled by my own demons, and if I can't exorcise them, then I'm going to lose the only man who makes my wretched life worth living.

Chapter 15

Jinta

What's wrong with me?

Why can't I get Raiden's face out of my head?

Ren drives us through Tokyo's streets, but I'm far away from the car, my attention drifting in and out of focus. Sometimes, I'm in the back seat of the car. Then, I'm back in the warehouse, watching as Raiden twists himself into something I barely recognize.

A frustrated sigh escapes me, and I lean my forehead against the glass. Why is this getting to me? I've seen him kill people. It's as natural to the life he lives as stubbing my toe on every piece of furniture on my way to the bathroom at night is to me. I don't even like Ishida. Hell, I was glad to see him get what he deserved.

Until I looked at Raiden, and saw the wicked grin splitting his face in two. How free he'd looked as he towered over Ishida. I don't think I've seen him that happy, even when he's with me.

Raiden doesn't revel in killing or beating people up. He's not a sadist. It's simply part of a job description for him. Even if he was committing violence in my name, he still wouldn't enjoy it. And, as messed up as it is, I *like* that he wants to protect me, that he'd kill for me. Ever since we met, he's made me feel safe and cherished.

But this... this wasn't that. This was different. I could feel his emotions through our bond now that I'm a kitsune, and all I got from him was waves of adrenaline—and beneath it all, *fear.* Raiden was scared, and I don't know why.

"Are you okay?" Ren's soft voice makes me jump.

"Uh... yeah. Yeah, I'm fine." The false cheer makes my voice squeakier than usual.

Ren glares at me in the mirror. "I'm not stupid, Jinta. Come on. Talk to me."

I blow out a breath, shoulders slumping. "Raiden was scared back in the warehouse."

Ren nods, hands tightening around the wheel. "That warehouse holds a lot of bad memories for him. Namikawa would take him there as punishment."

A memory tugs at me, luring me back to the day I found Raiden sitting on the floor of his shower, hands bloodied and a finger missing. I swallow hard as a lump forms in my throat. "Namikawa's gone."

In the mirror, Ren's brows furrow, eyes glistening. "But I think his ghost still haunts Raiden. For so long, Raiden was under his control, and now, he's the one in charge. It must be a heady feeling, having that much power after years of taking orders. If I were him, I'd find it all so addictive."

That... actually makes sense when she puts it that way. The way he'd wailed on Ishida had seemed desperate. Like he was trying to assert himself over his own *ghosts*. When Namikawa was alive, Raiden would tell me how powerless he felt. How he'd never had a choice in joining the yakuza or serving Namikawa.

As he'd beaten Ishida, a shudder had rattled down my spine, but now, his savage grin makes more sense. He must have liked it. Not necessarily hurting Ishida but being the one *doing* the hurting rather than being hurt. Finally, he has the power and control that was denied to him.

"So why would he want to give up all that power to be with me?" Heartache makes my eyes sting. Raiden told me many times he disliked being yakuza, but that was back when he still served Namikawa. Now, he's the boss, a king on his throne. What do I have to offer that could possibly compare to that?

"Jinta," Ren whispers, voice sympathetic.

Sniffling. I wipe my eyes. "No, it's okay. Just keep driving." If I even try to think about Raiden choosing between me and the yakuza, I'll break down, and I don't know how I'll piece myself back together.

Kabukicho's iconic gate glows red as Ren and I walk the densely packed and narrow alleys. The only time I ever come here is when my colleagues and I go out for drinks with our boss. It's too busy for me, and I've gotten scammed at a bar or two before, which turned me off from the place.

Ren points to a bar with English flags waving above the windows. "That's Charlie's place, right there."

I can't deny I'm excited. I'm going to meet my first-ever wizard! Mage? Magician? Is he a warlock? I played too many RPGs during college. "What kind of magic does he do?" I ask, hardly able to contain my excitement. "Can he levitate things? Light things on fire? Oh! Is he a necromancer?"

Ren chuckles. "None of those. He's a hemomancer."

"A... what?"

"His spells are powered by blood."

I lurch to a stop. "Blood?" My excitement turns to disgust. "But isn't that dangerous?"

"Mostly to the wielder, honestly. They have to use their own blood to cast certain spells or rituals. Don't worry. Charlie's a nice guy."

The pub inside looks normal enough. People drink beers or eat European-inspired dishes. There's a soccer match on the television above the bar, as well. A foreign woman works the bar, pouring foamy beers and chatting with customers. Her curly hair is tied back with a bandana. She smacks her gum and grins. "How can I help you?" she asks in Japanese, though there's a hint of an English accent in her words.

"We're here to see Charlie," Ren says.

The woman jerks her shoulder toward the door behind the bar. "Downstairs and to the right, through the office."

Ren and I head down into the basement and stop outside an office door. Ren knocks.

A voice calls something in English, his European accent thick, but I don't understand a word. Ren looks just as puzzled. Clearing her throat, she says, "It's Ren."

The man says in Japanese, "Come on in!"

What lies beyond the door? Vials of potions? Shelves full of leather-bound books that can fly or curse you if you open them? An alchemy table? Heart racing, I step in after Ren.

It's a normal office. My shoulders slump. *Man. That could have been so cool.* There's a computer and keyboard. A desk stacked with boring paperwork. A screen full of security footage. Basic stuff. There's a man tapping away at the keyboard. He's got a shock of ginger hair beneath a green beanie, a smattering of freckles, a patchy beard, and piercings through his ears. He looks normal, too.

"Just a moment..." He hums, clicking the mouse. "And

done!" He spins his chair around toward us. "How may I help—oh!" His arm smacks into a tower of papers, which wobbles before scattering all over the floor. "I'm so sorry, just a—damn it! I need to get this place cleaned up!" he mutters, dropping to his knees.

"Do you need help?" Ren asks.

"Oh, no! Don't trouble yourself!" Charlie crawls under the desk and grabs fistfuls of papers. "Just let me—ow!" he cracks his head on the underside of the desk. I wince. "You know what, let's save this for later." He rises and flashes a smile. "Sorry about that. How may I help you?" His cheeks are bright red, almost the same shade as his hair.

Since Ren's too busy trying not to laugh, I say, "We're trying to locate someone."

"Someone you know?" Charlie asks.

I shake my head. "My boyfriend's father."

"Ah! He doesn't happen to be here, does he?"

Ren says, having composed herself, "No, but I brought this." She unfurls a balled-up tissue from her pocket. There's drops of dried blood on it and a faint citrusy scent. Raiden's blood. I tense.

"How did you get that?" I ask. My kitsune stirs with a low growl.

Alarm flashes in Ren's eyes. "He gave it voluntarily."

What's with me? I make myself relax. "Right. Of course." My kitsune seriously needs to chill.

"Perfect! That will do just fine." Charlie dashes forward

and gingerly accepts the tissue. "Right this way, please." He heads toward a locked door across the room. "Which key is it? This one? Ugh. I can never remember!" He yanks a ring full of keys from his belt and flips through several, muttering, until he unlocks one lock, then another, and another.

Seriously, what's behind that door? Oh! Maybe his alchemy lab or something.

I brush past Ren, eager for a look as Charlie holds the door for us.

I gasp, mouth falling ajar because *now we're talking!* "This is so cool!" I practically squeal. There's a shelf full of leather-bound books, bundles of herbs, various wild mushrooms growing in pots around the room, and an array of substances in glass jars. There's even an alchemy lab in the corner with beakers, mortar and pestle, among other things.

"Thank you!" Charlie's face goes red again. "It's my pride and joy."

Ren elbows me. "Hey. Where was this enthusiasm for werewolves?"

"I mean, werewolves are cute."

Ren gawks. "*Cute?* We're fearsome predators!"

Shit. Was that offensive? "Yeah! Yes, totally! But also, one time Raiden got drunk and shifted when he got home and demanded that I rub his belly for an hour. It was so—" I cough. "Anyway, Charlie, what do you need his blood for?"

Charlie's already bustling around, picking plants, sorting through bundles of herbs, and dumping whatever he needs on the alchemy table. "A person's blood reveals everything I need to know about them, including their lineage. In this instance, if people share DNA, I can combine blood magic with a locator spell."

"A locator spell?" I ask, wondering if it means what I think it does.

Pestle in hand, Charlie mashes up some herbs. "Yes. Using Raiden's blood, I can cast a spell to locate anyone he's related to."

"Wow, that's incredible!" We could find Raiden's father within hours.

"Where's his father?"

"Somewhere in Osaka," I say.

"All right. If he's still there, then I should be able to track his exact location. And what's his name? I need the name of who I'm locating for the spell to be as accurate as possible." Once I've told him Raiden's dad's name, Charlie rubs his hands together. "Got it. Here we go..." He adds the bloody tissue to the mixture in the mortar, grinds it up with the other ingredients at lightning speed, until it resembles a thick, nasty-looking paste.

My stomach churns. "You're not going to—"

Charlie tips the bowl and the paste plops wetly into his hand, then he crams the mixture in his mouth.

I almost gag. "Oh god. Yes, you did."

Grimacing, Charlie swallows the thick paste. Charlie dashes to a wooden box, which he searches through. "Come," he barks, rushing to a nearby table and unfurling a piece of parchment. It's a map of Osaka. He unfurls another map, one of Japan.

Charlie flicks open a switchblade, speaks in rapid Latin, then slices the palm of his hand. I wince as blood pours from the gash, dribbling over the parchment. The blood starts to *move*, trailing over the parchment like a slug. Charlie chants in Latin, and the only words I catch are "Kenta Noboru."

The blood spreads toward Osaka, getting closer and closer, until Charlie suddenly yelps in pain and clutches his head.

"Charlie?" I ask, reaching for him.

Groaning, he doubles over. "I'm... I'm okay," he grunts.

"What happened?" I ask. The blood has stopped moving. The little blob loses all consistency, seeps into the parchment, and doesn't go any further. "What's going on?"

Panting, Charlie gives his head a shake. "There must be some kind of protection ward around Noboru that prevents him from being tracked. I'm sorry. Whatever magic it is, it's powerful, and I can't risk trying to push through it."

Disappointment wells inside me. "Then, does that

mean we can't find him?"

Charlie frowns. "Unfortunately, yes."

I exhale, my shoulders slumping. No. This can't be where our search ends. "What about another relative? Maybe someone who might know where he is?"

Charlie hums thoughtfully. "I can't guarantee that this person will know where to find him, but I should be able to locate them unless they're warded, too. I just need a name."

I turn to Ren. "Can you think of anyone in Raiden's family?"

Ren's lips are thin. "Yes. Her name is Shoko Noboru."

"And she is?"

"Raiden's mother."

The woman who abandoned him and threw him to the yakuza. Anger flares within me, but we have no other options.

Ren adds, "Although she might have gone back to using her maiden name, which was..." She taps a finger to her forehead. "Ah, yes. Miyamoto."

"Shoko Miyamoto. Got it," Charlie says, then squeezes his hand, producing more blood. As the blood drips onto the map of Japan this time, he speaks in Latin and says Miyamoto's name. The blood drops come together and congeal into a blob, then trickle over the map, moving much faster this time. My heart skips as the blood flows along the map and stains the city of Hiroshima red.

Murmuring to himself, Charlie grabs another map and unfurls it, revealing a detailed map of Hiroshima. He repeats the ritual, spilling blood, chanting, and the blood flows, forming into a precise little dot over a specific area. I pull out my phone and open up a map app, check the physical map, and then zoom in on my phone's screen.

"She's in a hospital," I say.

"You're sure?" Ren asks.

I double-check. "Yeah. Positive. Unless... is the blood only showing where she's at this very moment? Will it change along with her location?"

Charlie shakes his head. "Maybe if this spell were done by an amateur, sure, but my magic is very precise. The blood will only show a place the person has a strong connection to, like a home. So she must have been a patient at this hospital for some time."

That doesn't sound good. "Can werewolves get sick?" I ask Ren.

"Not from human diseases, but there are some conditions that only affect our kind. Some can be fatal."

Nerves twist in my stomach. We've got to get to Hiroshima. There isn't any guarantee that she'll even know where to find Raiden's father, but she's our only lead, and we've got to chase it.

I just hope she doesn't die on us before we get there.

It's late by the time Ren and I get to her apartment. To-gether, we make some stir-fry for dinner. The door opens, and Raiden walks in just as we've set the table. My stom-ach twists when our eyes meet. Before I can greet him, Raiden breaks our stare and bends over to take off his shoes without so much as a hello. It's just as I feared, things are strained between us, and I don't know how to fix things.

"Welcome home," Ren says.

Raiden only grunts, then sits down opposite me. We dig in, though I only pick at my food. Raiden doesn't look at me and focuses on his food. Even though we're close enough for our feet to touch beneath the table, it feels like he's miles away from me, and I can't catch up to him.

"Jinta, did you want to tell Raiden about our appoint-ment with Charlie?" Ren suggests.

"Not really," I answer.

Raiden stops chewing but only briefly, a sour expression twisting his lips.

With an awkward cough, Ren launches into the details about what we learned from Charlie.

Raiden's expression turns dour. "So, my mother is our only lead."

Ren grimaces. "Unfortunately, yes."

Heaving a sigh, Raiden sets down his chopsticks. "Then

I'll have to go and speak to her. Who knows if she'll even have any answers for us? This might be a waste of our time."

"Or she'll tell you how to find your father, and Jinta can be cured of the curse," Ren adds.

Raiden dips his head in a reluctant nod. "Then I'll leave tomorrow."

My gut clenches. Is he going to invite me? I don't like that he's taking off without me. Old, ugly insecurities gnaw at me. I swallow hard around a sudden surge of nausea. "Thanks for the food." I clear my plate though I've barely touched my food, and then escape into the bathroom to wash my face and brush my teeth.

Tamano suddenly appears in the mirror, standing behind me.

"Finally!" She huffs. "I was wondering when your dull picture-perfect relationship would get interesting! I've always loved a good drama."

I almost bite my toothbrush in half. Spiting with force into the sink, I quickly rinse my mouth. "Shut up, Tamano." Maybe I should speak more politely to an ancient goddess, but I'm all out of fucks to give.

"I was starting to get jealous, you know," she says, leaning back against the bathroom wall. "I honestly don't understand why such a fine specimen is interested in the likes of you."

"Keep insulting me and my relationship. It really makes

me want to help you more," I snap, leaning on the sink as my anger threatens to boil over.

"You're worried, aren't you?"

I grit my teeth. "About what?" I feign ignorance.

"That he's straying. That you won't be enough to convince him to leave this life behind."

"Of course I won't be enough." What really bothers me is that it feels like he's distant, like he's... pushing me away. "Just because you're bitter about being away from your mate doesn't mean you get to mock our relationship." I level a glare at her.

Tamano snaps her fan shut and looks away.

My fingers curl at my sides. I'm fucking tired. So sick of doubting if I'm enough for Raiden, doubting if I'm strong enough to control the kitsune, then hearing other people doubt our bond and my own capabilities. I've been looked down on my whole life, by my family, by my brother.

A nine-tailed fox jumps up onto the sink. Her tails wrap around her legs, and she lowers her head. *"I'm... I'm sorry,"* Tamano says, though it sounds like she's swallowed poison. *"You're right, that was—it was cruel of me. I am a little jealous, I suppose. And it's hard being away from my mate. I wouldn't wish that upon you. If you're truly concerned that he's distancing himself from you, then you know what the solution is, right?"*

I swing my head in a no.

She bristles and snaps her fangs. *"Talk to him! Tell him*

how you feel. You can't fuck away all of your problems!"

"I know, I know!" I chuckle. "Okay. I will. Thanks." I ruffle her thick fur.

She turns away and glares at the wall, growling. *"Men. I swear…"*

The apartment is empty and quiet except for the gurgling of the dishwasher. It looks like Ren and Raiden have both gone to their rooms. However, as I pass by the balcony doors, Raiden's shadow pools on the hardwood. He's outside, powerful body framed by the light of a flickering streetlamp. Nerves flutter in my belly, so I take in a breath and ease open the glass door.

Raiden doesn't react as I come to stand beside him. He stares off ahead, his face blank, body tense. My heart aches with the urge to reach out and touch him, but I feel like there's a barrier between us that I can't breach. Like he'd push me away if I tried. Holding my breath, I press my shoulder into his. Raiden stiffens, then his shoulders relax.

What will he say? Will he push me away?

Steeling myself, I push the words out. "I'm coming with you to Hiroshima." It's not a question. Raiden is stuck with me. I can't let him meet the woman who abandoned him by himself. This must be hard enough on him already. "Or if you'd rather I didn't, at least take Ren with you. You don't need to do this alone."

Raiden shakes his head. "I'm not leaving you here alone. Not after what happened this morning."

Relief warms my heart. "So, you still want me around, huh?" I try and smile but it wobbles on my face. There's a needy, insecure part of me that needs to hear him say it. Raiden's breath hitches and wounded eyes find mine.

"Jinta," he begins, voice gutted.

"I just... this morning, seeing you with Ishida, it—" Emotion thickens my throat, and I scratch awkwardly at my neck. "You looked like you were enjoying yourself."

Raiden looks down into the streets, dark and empty this late at night. "I was." His confession is so soft I wouldn't have heard it without my preternatural senses. "I hate that you saw me like that."

My fingers twitch. All I want is to reach out and touch him. "It was a bit scary."

His brows furrowing, Raiden closes his eyes tight. "I'm sorry."

The remorse in his voice makes my heart ache. I grab his hand and squeeze tight, trying to find the nerve to ask my question. "Do you"—I almost choke on the words—"do you want to leave the yakuza, Raiden? Is a normal life really something you want? Just tell me."

His silence makes my stomach twist. Raiden wets his lips, lowering his gaze. "I... don't know."

I try not to wince, even though his words feel like a battering ram to my heart.

"I want you, Jinta. But I don't know if I can give you what you need. I don't know if I'll ever be *normal* enough for the life you want."

That makes sense. It does, really. Adjusting to a civilian life would be a challenge for him, but I think he could do it. It sounds like he's just doubtful. I lean over and press my lips to his shoulder, rubbing my hand up and down his arm. "I think you could do anything you set your mind to, baby."

Raiden huffs. "Wish I had your confidence."

I need him close, now. When he turns around, leaning back against the railing, I cage him in, hands gripping the railing on either side of his big body. "Say it?" I ask, wincing at how desperate I sound.

And because he knows me to my core, he doesn't have to ask what I need. His breath warms my lips, long lashes fanning his cheeks as his eyes close. "I'll always want you, Sunshine. I don't know what kind of life I want, but I want you by my side. Always."

My eyes sting, and my chest tightens. I bring my lips to his, cradling his face between my hands. Breath quickening, I swipe my tongue over his plush lower lip. He lets me in, and sweet relief sings through my veins. He still wants me, still needs me, and, god, I need him. I'll always need him. Our tongues tangle as I press myself against his body, his taste making me whimper.

Raiden's chest rises and falls fast against me, scent spicy with need. "No more talking. Not now. Just... keep touching me." There's an unspoken plea in his voice. He needs me to be in control for him now, and fuck, being needed so intensely makes my cock throb.

I capture his mouth, smooth my hands down his powerful chest, and I shiver at how hard his nipples are beneath the fabric. "I've got you, baby. I can do that."

I'm going to take such good care of him.

CHAPTER 16

Raiden

The mattress creaks beneath me, the sheets soft against my bare skin.

Jinta stands over the bed, lips flushed and swollen from our fervent kisses on the way to the bedroom, his eyes black with need. He drops his pants and boxers in one go, his long slender cock curling up toward his stomach, and tosses off his shirt. My cock pulses at the sight of all that pale, bare skin, his cute pink nipples hard and straining.

Jinta lunges for me, hands slamming into the mattress on either side of my head. His long legs tangle up with mine, and the hard length of him brushes over my leaking cock. Jinta swallows my ragged groan with his lips, teeth nipping, tongue thrusting. My whole body burns for him as I tug on his hair, and an urge I've never felt before rises within me. I want to submit to him.

"Yesterday, in the shower, I wanted to ask if you've ever bottomed before."

My heart skips. I haven't bottomed in years. The last person I bottomed for was Takada, and that was… I shudder. "I have," I say, swallowing hard. My arousal threatens to flag at the memories clawing at me. "With… him."

Jinta's eyes darken, and anger floods his sweet scent.

Takada groomed me and took me to his bed as soon as I was legal. Our time together turned me off from exploring my bisexuality for years. Later on in life when I was ready, I reclaimed the first time he tainted for me with better experiences. I no longer think of the night we spent together as my first time, or even as sex. It was cruelty, nothing more or less.

Wetting my lips, I avert my gaze from Jinta. "Not with anyone else since. It was too—it hurt." I just shake my head at a sudden loss for words. If I start talking, I'll open the lid on a box I've kept locked up for years. I'll drown in self-loathing. I can't let Jinta see me like that. He's seen the worst of me enough for today.

Panic squeezes my chest. Does Jinta want to top? I don't know if I can do that. Don't know the places my mind will take me. But what if I hurt him by saying no? What if he thinks the worst of me? What if—

"Baby." Jinta cradles my cheek. I open my eyes, not realizing I'd shut them—or that I'd started shaking and panting like a frightened animal. "We don't have to. Okay? You can say no to me, and I'll always respect that. I just wanted to make you feel as good as I do. You have a choice with me. I'd never..." Jinta's throat bobs, and his eyes glisten. "I'd never hurt you. Never."

My throat's tight. I feel like I'm going to break apart. Nobody has ever treated me the way he does, like I'm cherished—and I've hurt him. He's been hurt because of me. Could *still* get hurt, and it would be all my fault. Jinta is the only person I've never wanted to hurt, and I...

"M-might never be ready for that," I croak, breathing hard as I avert my gaze.

"That's okay," Jinta whispers, breath warm against my mouth. His thumb strokes over my cheek. "That's fine, I promise. I love what we do together. I love... I love you."

Fuck. My chest is going to splinter apart.

"Tell me what you need," Jinta implores me, kissing down my jaw, fingers stroking my hair.

"You," I choke out the words. "Just you. Only you."

A low growl rumbles through Jinta's chest. He slides a hand down my stomach and rubs my softening cock. "Is this okay?"

I arch beneath him. "Y-yeah."

Jinta pecks a kiss to my mouth, sucking on my lower lip when he rocks his hips. Our cocks rock against each other, and the air escapes me with a groan.

"What... what about this?" Jinta's panting as he takes us both in his hand and strokes.

My hips arch to meet his thrusts. "Fuck. This. *Yes.*"

We don't have lube, but that matters less and less as our precum quickly slicks things up between us. My hoarse grunts and Jinta's frantic pants fill the room as he strokes us faster and faster. My eyes roll back as I rock into his fist, fucking his hand.

We're being way too loud. I'm sure Ren can hear us. I grab Jinta's hair and tug him down into a sloppy kiss full of tangling tongues and muffled moans as we stroke each other off with increasing urgency.

Jinta curses softly, his breathing hitting my mouth is harsh, hot pants as he jacks us in his fist. "F-fuck, baby. You feel so good against me. Love your cock. The sounds you make. The way you say my name."

My head falls back against the pillow, a moan tearing from my throat as he squeezes the rock-hard base of my cock. "Fuck. Jinta. Close. Keep going. Don't stop, fuck, don't stop!" I grab the sheets and squeeze, tearing them when Jinta's long, hard cock grinds against mine again and again.

He's close, too, every hard stroke squeezing out little spurts of precum that drip onto my stomach. I need more. Sitting up, I suck on my fingers, then reach behind him. His head tips back, eyes closing in bliss when I rub my wet fingers over his hole, which softens under my caresses.

I push inside, find his prostate with ease, and start to stroke. Jinta's mouth falls open with a desperate, broken moan. I've never been so familiar with another person's body before, but I know Jinta's like I know my own. The connection we share is... terrifying. Everything. My greatest source of strength and joy.

"Raiden," Jinta whines my name as he ruts into our fists with abandon. "Fuck. I'm going to—"

I am, too. My thighs are quivering, my toes flex so hard they start to cramp, and the muscles in my legs burn. The breath tears from me, and I can't stay quiet even if I wanted to. My balls tighten, cock going agonizingly stiff.

White fur ripples over Jinta's body. "Mine," he growls, eyes flashing red. He lets loose, pumping his hips into our slick fists. "Gonna cover you with my cum. Make you smell like me. Come on, baby, cum for me."

The command in his growling voice tips me over the edge. "Fuuuck," I snarl as I start to shoot in long, heavy spurts all over our fists and my stomach.

Jinta stiffens above me, doubling over with the force of his orgasm. Powerful shudders rack his body, and through it all, he goes on stroking us, squeezing out every last drop, milking me damn dry.

I catch him in my arms, legs wrapping around his waist. Sinking my fingers in his damp hair, I pepper kisses over his neck and jaw. Our release smears between our bodies, but I don't care. The whole room smells like him, and me, and sex, and I wish I could bottle the scent of us. Jinta's hot, slick tongue glides over my chest. He circles my hard nipples, sharp teeth pinching my collarbone. Slipping his hand between us, he gathers our release and rubs it into my skin.

My spent cock twitches. "Fuck," I whisper. Jinta is marking me in the most primal way, ruled by his kitsune's instincts to claim me. I let him, basking in his eager kisses and hungry little licks, shivering as he rubs his spunk into my skin. Finally, soft lips claim mine.

He looks so beautiful above me as his kitsune comes out, turning his hair white and eyes red, snow-white fur on his cheeks, and two pointed ears twitching above his shock of white hair. A rusty chuckle escapes me. "Happy?"

He rumbles low in his chest. "Mine," he whispers, leaning down to nuzzle my cheek.

My throat tightens with emotion. "Yeah, Sunshine. Yours."

As Jinta settles down, his foxlike features melt away, but he goes on worshipping my chest, my neck, and my cheeks with little kitten licks. I smile, closing my eyes. He's so damn cute. He blinks sleepily, then his cheeks redden, and he peels his tongue off my skin. "I'm sorry! I don't know what came over me."

"I liked it. Your kitsune is a possessive bastard, huh?"

Jinta gives a nod, his cheeks flaming redder. "I was worried you were going to run off on me all day."

"Sorry." Guilt makes me wrap my arms around him, pulling him down against my chest. "I wouldn't do that. No matter how far I go, I'll come back for you. Promise." Sleep tugs at my mind. My body is so warm, muscles lax and tingling from my orgasm.

Jinta laughs softly. "Really?"

I stroke my hand down his back. "Yeah. Always." A yawn cracks my jaw.

Jinta peels his body off mine and mops up the seed on our bodies with a sheet. He tosses the soiled sheet on the ground, then flops back into my arms. "You, too," he whispers.

Shuttering my lids, I wrap my arms around him, holding my mate close as I finally find sanctuary in his arms.

First thing the next morning, I book us an afternoon flight to Hiroshima. Even though I don't anticipate us being there for longer than a few hours, I'm still nervous about leaving Ren and the pack alone with hunters and Taka-da-kai prowling about.

"I can hold down the fort while you're gone," she insists, practically shoving us out the door. "Just don't stay away for long."

"If she tells us where my dad is, I'm hoping we'll be back

in a couple of days. If we come back early, that means we didn't find him." My stomach twists with nerves. If my mother doesn't know where he is, we'll be shit out of luck if Jinta loses control again. Shaking my head to chase the thoughts away, I motion for Jinta to follow me. "Just stay in touch, okay? And let me know if anyone finds Ishida."

Jinta spins toward me, panic widening his eyes. "*What?*"

I sigh, realizing I forgot to tell him. "Ishida escaped the warehouse. Nobody knows where he is, but we're looking for him." If I'd just killed the bastard, this wouldn't be an issue, but I'd been too worried about how Jinta might react.

Ren pats my shoulder. "He'll be found. Don't worry about him. Just focus on your goal."

Before I can follow Jinta out the door, Ren suddenly blocks my path. "Hang on. There's something I wanted to ask you."

I motion for Jinta to go on ahead and Ren kicks the door closed after him. "Hit me."

She gives me a suspicious look I don't like. "You never explained how you were able to get Takada to aid us."

Shit. I really don't want to get into this with her now. "It's—"

"Don't you dare say it's nothing." Ren folds her arms. "You and I both know there's only one thing you could offer Takada that would get him to dance to your tune."

She's right on the damn money, unfortunately.

My silence must be all the confirmation she needed. "Shit..." she whispers, eyes widening. "Tell me you didn't agree to anything he wanted, Raiden. Please."

"I had to," I say, grinding out the words through my disgust.

"But you're not going to go through with it? Right?" She grabs my arms, squeezing. "Raiden, you can't. Jinta will be devastated. I'll never forgive you if you let that sick bastard touch you."

I wince at even the idea of causing Jinta pain. "Things won't get that far." They can't. I'm not selfless enough to sacrifice myself to Takada's perverse desires.

Ren shoves me back, shaking her head. "They had better not. I'll die before I let him hurt you again. Jinta doesn't know, does he?"

"He doesn't have to. He's got enough to worry about."

Jaw tight, Ren glares at me. "Don't you dare give up on finding a cure for the kitsune. Got it? Go to Hiroshima. Find your father and lift the curse. Promise me."

Hating that I've upset her, I wrench her into a hug, squeezing. "I will. Quit nagging me."

Her body relaxes against mine when I stroke her hair. "Keep me updated."

"Got it." With a final squeeze that makes her squeak, and me laugh, I let my best friend go.

I make myself breathe through my nerves and follow

Jinta downstairs. Ishida still hasn't been found. I have no idea where the little rat is, but if I had to guess, he's hiding out wherever the hunters are located. He knows if he ever sticks his face above ground, I'll smash it in myself.

We ride the train to Haneda Airport and get there in under an hour. From there, we proceed through security and go in search of our gate. On the plane, we find our seats, and Jinta grips my hand when the plane lifts off, and I chuckle. "Been a while since you've flown?" I guess.

He nods. "Not for a long time."

"Ever been to Hiroshima?" I ask.

Jinta laces his fingers through mine and squeezes. "No. I always wanted to try conger eel with rice! Oh, and we've got to try Momiji Manju!"

I snort. "Guess I need to feed you more."

Jinta grins. "Yes, please."

Fuck, he's so cute. "Do you want to stick with me or explore a bit?

"I don't want you to face your mom alone."

A laugh escapes me, though affection blooms warm in my chest. "Think I can handle a sick old woman."

"Of course you can." Jinta huffs, folding his arms with a pout. "That's not what I meant. It'll be hard for you to see her again, won't it?"

It will be. I feel sick at the very thought, but I'm ashamed to admit my mother still has such a hold over me. How will she react? Will she be angry? Surprised? That is, if she isn't comatose from whatever's left her bedridden in the hospital. What if we get all the way there, and she's comatose?

"It's okay," Jinta whispers, and I realize he must have felt echoes of my anxiety. "I'll be here." He brings my hand to his lips and kisses my fingers.

Relief blooms in my chest as I rest my cheek on his soft hair. "I know."

And I appreciate it more than I could ever say.

Chapter 17

Jinta

Hiroshima is a beautiful city. Despite the city's tragic past during World War II, it's blossomed into a stunning and vibrant city. I wish there was time to take in the sights, maybe even visit the Hiroshima Peace Memorial to pay respects to those who were killed so senselessly.

From the airport, we go straight to Minami Ward where the hospital is supposed to be. In the taxi, Raiden is stiff beside me, hands tightly clenched in his lap. The frantic beat of his heart drums in my ears. I haven't learned how to tune out all the extra noises I pick up on.

I wish I knew the right thing to say to ease all his worries, but I'm glad I came with him. He shouldn't have to face his mother alone after all the pain and trauma she's caused him. The taxi pulls up outside the hospital, and we get out. Raiden is silent beside me as we enter the building. Behind the desk, a lady in a surgeon's mask types away at a computer. I hang back while Raiden approaches the desk, speaking softly to the receptionist.

She nods a few times, eyes crinkling as she smiles behind her mask. Raiden motions for me to follow him, and we take the elevator up to the third floor. Beside me, Raiden's breathing hard, hands clenched at his sides. I reach out and poke his finger with my pinky. His hand relaxes enough for me to take it.

"It'll be okay," I tell him.

Raiden exhales through clenched teeth. "I know." He doesn't sound convinced. The elevator opens, and Raiden leads me through the quiet, winding halls until we arrive outside a door. Raiden's fingers shake when he reaches out and grasps the handle, and I hold on tight to his hand as we step into the room together. The room is small but cozy. A couple of big windows let in golden streams of sunlight. There's a painting on the wall, a vase of flowers of some kind, but not much else in the way of decorations.

It's so quiet. I hear the moment Raiden's breath catches. In the bed, Shoko Miyamoto lies beneath the blankets. There's a sour odor coming from her, a musk that makes my nose wrinkle. It's death, I realize. She's not dead, but she will be soon. Raiden blows out a breath, and the tension drains from him, face twisting into something that looks like pity.

"What's wrong with her?" I whisper.

Raiden swallows hard beside me. "We call it Lone Wolf Sickness. Wolves without a pack or a mate are at risk of getting it. It's the human equivalent of dying of a broken heart. We're pack animals, not meant to go through life alone. After Dad left, after she... abandoned me, she must have closed herself off from others completely." His voice wavers, and he clears his throat. "Her entire body is shutting down. She doesn't have long left."

Tamano materializes beside Shoko's bed. "I know all too well that kind of loneliness," she murmurs, pity furrowing her brow. "It's like a slow, agonizing death."

Shoko lies so still, I think she's sleeping, until she slowly opens her eyes. When she sees us, she slowly props herself up with what looks like a great effort. Raiden leaves my side and goes to her bedside. He adjusts her pillow, giving her something to support her. Side by side, I can see the resemblance between mother and son. Though her face is lined and wrinkled, Raiden has the shape of her eyes and her elegant bone structure.

"Hey, Mom," Raiden says, and his voice is softer than I've ever heard it. I imagined so many ways he might react, and anger was at the forefront of my mind. But it's hard to be angry when she's so feeble and sick.

Shoko's tired eyes well with tears at the sight of him. "It's really you..."

"Yeah. I'm here."

Her trembling lips form a smile. "Kenta. My love."

Raiden's breath catches audibly.

My heart sinks. She thinks Raiden is his father, her long-lost mate.

Shoko reaches out to touch his face. "I thought I'd never see you again." Tears spill down her wrinkled cheeks. "I've waited s-so long for you, my love. I've missed you."

Raiden blinks fast, then turns his face from my view, leaning into her touch. "I missed you, too." I've never heard such devastation in his voice.

Suddenly, I feel like I don't belong here. I want to stay and support Raiden, but I feel like an intruder witnessing something I have no right to see. As quietly as I can, I sit in a chair nearby and stare into my lap, trying to give them some privacy.

"I... I don't understand," Shoko whispers. "We were happy. Weren't we? Wasn't I a good wife? A good mate?"

Raiden clears his throat. "Y-yeah. 'Course you were."

"Then why did you leave me?" Anguish makes her voice shake.

There's a moment of silence filled with so much anguish I can barely breathe. Finally, Raiden says, voice hoarse, "I, uh... I was an idiot. A coward. I didn't realize how lucky I was to have you. But I'm back now. I'm here."

"You said I was your destiny."

"You are," Raiden whispers. "Always."

Shoko sighs, the sound as sweet and gentle as a warm spring breeze as it thaws the winter snow. I wish they could have a fresh start, a new beginning. But I know it can't be. Shoko will be gone from this world soon, and the only one who will miss her and mourn her loss is the son she abandoned. As much as I feel for her loneliness and pain, I can't forgive what she did to Raiden.

Raiden swallows audibly. "Whatever happened to our son, Shoko?"

There's a long pause. I look up as Shoko lowers her hands from Raiden's face and curls them in the blankets. "After you left, I..." In the sudden quiet, a bird sings a lonesome song outside the window. "I couldn't bear to stay in that house with the boy any longer. I had failed him in every way a mother could fail her child. Just as I failed you, dear."

"How do you know that?" Anger and heartache bleed into Raiden's voice. "Did he tell you that? How can you know what he felt?"

"Every time I looked at him, I saw you," she whispers, voice trembling. "You told me I was your destiny. That we were fated. And you tore our bond to shreds. I had no love left in me to give, not to myself, not to our son. I hated him. Hated how he reminded me of you. Hated that cold, empty house. Then, your organization came to collect, and you'd left me with nothing! Nothing but that boy. I gave him to the yakuza. To his grandfather."

"Why?" Raiden's voice shakes. "Why would you do that to me?"

She squeezes her shaking hands in her lap. "It was what was best for him. He would be well provided for, and he'd always loved his grandfather. I saved him from a miserable life with me."

"I needed—" Raiden's voice cracks down the middle, and he sucks in a harsh breath. "He didn't need the yakuza. He needed *you*. His mother. He'd just been abandoned, for god's sake, and you abandoned him again!" His voice shakes violently, thick with grief and anger. Raiden lurches from the bed and paces to the window, moving too fast for me to get a look at his face. Shoulders rising and falling fast, he grips the window ledge and hangs his head. "You destroyed him," he whispers.

Shoko exhales, and a tear spills down her cheek. Lips tight together, she dashes it away. "I did what I thought was best for the boy. There's no changing the past. He was better off anywhere than with me."

"That wasn't your choice to make!" Raiden shouts, whirling toward her. My heart seizes in my chest. His eyes are red and wet, his whole body shaking with grief and fury. In the sudden quiet, he pants harshly, sucking in gulps of air through trembling lips. God, I want to go to him and hold him, but I can't. I blink away the burn in my eyes and force myself not to intervene. Raiden has to battle his demons, and it's not a fight I can help him win.

A broken sound escapes Shoko, and she folds, hiding her face in her quaking hands. "Why did you leave me?" she asks between shuddery sobs that rack her body. "We were happy. I—I didn't know how to go through life without you!"

I can't help but feel glad she's so torn up about what she did, even though my heart hurts for them both. She should feel guilty, but Raiden's father is to blame for all of this. He tore their family apart and caused them both so much pain.

"I would have gone anywhere with you, Kenta." She wipes her streaming eyes. "Back to Osaka. We should have stayed there. We were so happy. Do you remember our secret spot where we'd meet, away from our families? You said it was the only place you felt safe, there with me. Not even the cops knew where to find you there. It was just us. Not our disapproving families. No yakuza. It was perfect."

Raiden scrubs a hand down his face. "I don't remember." His voice is wiped clean of emotion.

Shoko shakes her head. "How could you forget? Our little cabin near Kodai-ji Temple. You marked the trees with your claws so we could always find our way there."

My heart skips. Is it possible that Noboru is there?

Raiden pushes off from the window ledge. "I'm done here." He walks by me to the door.

"I'm sorry," Shoko says, and Raiden freezes. "For everything."

Raiden's hands clench at his sides. He doesn't speak, just walks out. I take in a deep breath, my entire body tense. That was brutal just watching, so I can't imagine how Raiden must be feeling. He needs me, but my feet are locked in place. Anger burns in my gut. I can't leave, not before I've spoken to Shoko.

Shoko's eyes narrow at me as I approach her bedside. Wetting my lips, I say, "I know your son. Raiden."

Her fingers tense in the blankets, balling the fabric. "Ah," is all she says.

Filling my lungs, I press on. "He's made a life for himself, despite the pain you caused him. He's strong. Brave. One of the best people I know. I love your son."

Surprise widens Shoko's eyes.

"I... I don't know how he feels about me, but I'm almost certain he loves me, too. Almost." Anger makes my fingers clench. "I say *almost* because he puts up these walls, and it can be hard to get close to him. It's hard for him to be open about how he feels. After what you did to him, I don't blame him at all. This amazing man doesn't think he's deserving of love. And that? That's all on you. You did that to him. You hurt him so badly, and I—"

My heart pounds, and I have to grit my teeth to rein in my anger. "I hate you for hurting him that way." My voice cracks on the words, eyes stinging. "You'll never get to see the amazing person he became all by himself... without you. That's your loss. I'm going to love him in all the ways you couldn't. He's going to know every day that he's wanted and loved and that he changed my life for the better. Because that, *that* is what he deserves!"

Shoko dips her head. "I see. Then I thank you for doing what I could not."

There's more I want to say, but the man I love is hurting, and he needs me.

Face red with anger, I turn my back on Shoko and walk out. Raiden isn't in the hallway, but his citrus scent lingers in the air. My phone buzzes before I can follow it. When I see the name on the screen, my pulse leaps. It's my father.

Do I answer or not? I have no idea what he could be calling about. The last time I saw him was for my brother Katsuki's birthday celebration, and that had ended with Katsuki kissing Raiden and me punching Katsuki. I wonder if he ever told them about that. I assume if he had, I wouldn't have heard the end of it. Maybe he was embarrassed his little brother whooped his ass for a change.

My stomach twists with dread. He'll probably just yell at me like he usually does. But what if it's an emergency? Before I can make up my mind, the call ends. Heaving a sigh, I stuff my phone back in my bag. If there's trouble, he'll call again. I'd rather not speak to him unless it's necessary.

Raiden's scent leads me from the building and out into the streets. Sniffing, I follow his scent around the corner in time to catch him walking down a narrow alley. In the alley, Raiden stands before a vending machine.

"Want anything?" he asks, not turning as I approach.

"What do they have?" I ask, just to make conversation. I lean over Raiden's shoulder.

He jerks his shoulders. "Sake. Some beer."

"I'm good."

Raiden feeds the machine some cash. I chance a glance at his face. It hurts to look at him. His shoulders are slouched as if burdened by an invisible weight, and his eyes are red-rimmed and dark. The machine grabs his drink, but halfway to the chute, it gets stuck. Raiden's lips thin, nostrils flaring. "Fucking piece of shit." He slams his fist on the glass. "Come on! Really?" He takes a few steps back and kicks the glass, rattling the machine.

"Hey, just leave it," I say, gripping his arm. "We can go somewhere else. There has to be a few bars around here."

Raiden yanks his arm out of my grip. He slams his boot into the glass again. "Fuck you, piece of junk!" His fist pounds the glass so hard that the glass cracks.

My hurt lurches. "Raiden, cut it out. You're going to hurt yourself! If you want a drink so badly, we can—"

Raiden whips around and shouts, "I don't want a fucking drink! I don't care about the stupid machine. I just... I—" He never finishes his sentence as his voice cracks down the middle. Anguish twists his face. His shoulders heave. He stumbles back into the wall, a hand curling over his face. Sobs tear from him in great wrenching gasps, shaking his entire body.

I... I don't know what to do. What to say. I've never seen him cry before, and it's one of the worst feelings of my life. Of course this isn't about a stupid vending machine. Raiden doesn't want a drink. He's just had his heart ripped from his chest. He confronted the woman who'd abandoned him, only to be abandoned a second time. He'd probably known what the outcome would be between him and his mother, but that doesn't mean it hurts any less. He wants her in his life, and she rejected him... again.

There's nothing I can say to make this less painful for him. No, *there, there,* or *don't cry* because that's toxic and terrible. I can't say, *it's okay, I'm here, I won't leave you like she did,* because what good is that? I'm not a replacement for his mother.

All I can really do is be there for him and offer him support in whatever way I can. Hoping he won't push me away, I touch his arm. Raiden doesn't shove me away, so I run my hand up to his shaking shoulder. Raiden turns to me, falls into my arms, and sobs so hard that my heart breaks to pieces. He clutches at my shoulders, fingers gripping at my shirt. He nestles his face into the crook of my neck, his breath hot and shaky against my skin.

Eyes stinging, I hold him tight, one hand protectively at the nape of his neck. I stroke his heaving shoulders, then down his back, trying to soothe him as best I can even though I can't find the perfect words. Raiden's shaking subsides, and he sucks in deep breaths, exhaling steadily into the crook of my neck.

Breathing hard, Raiden turns his back and wipes his face. Sniffing, he says, "You heard my mother, right? Some temple in Osaka. We gotta get there."

"We don't have to rush," I say, wishing he'd just slow down and give himself time to process things. "We can stay the night, and in the morning—"

Raiden shakes his head, combing shaky fingers through his hair. "No time. I'm sure the organization he betrayed is looking for him. We've got to get to Osaka and find my father before they do."

I want to argue, but I'm just too drained. "Okay. If you're sure." Raiden sweeps by me, head bowed from my view. "Baby," I begin, gripping his hand.

But words fail me when Raiden yanks his hand from my grasp. Even though he was so vulnerable with me, he feels even further away than before. His rejection shakes me to the core, but I shove my feelings down. I need to give him space and time. He'll come back to me. He always does.

Right?

CHAPTER 18

L ove only ends in heartbreak.

It's a lesson I thought I learned when my father cheated on my mother and I watched her break down, when my father put his suitcases by the door and left before I could say goodbye, and when my mother put a five-yen coin in my hand before she pushed me at Namikawa. Even after all these years, my mother never recovered from the loss of my father. The memory of his betrayal still haunts her.

I told myself I'd never let anyone close enough to hurt me the way they hurt each other. Yet here I am, fated to Jinta. A beautiful ray of sunshine destined to be strangled by the darkness of my way of life. This has to end.

"Raiden? We're here!" Jinta motions me out of the taxi.

"Sorry," I mumble, annoyed that I'd spaced out.

The airport terminal bustles with activity. All the smells and sounds rankle my wolf. I'll be lucky if I don't eat some screaming kid on the plane. By the time we clear security, I'm ready to crawl out of my damn skin. I want to be home in Tokyo with my pack, wrapped in the familiar scents of my den.

"Are you hungry?" Jinta asks.

Not really, but I should probably eat something now. "Maybe."

Jinta laughs. "How can you be *maybe* hungry? How about we stop in that restaurant over there? Their sushi looks good."

Shrugging, I drag my feet over to the restaurant. We have an hour and a half before our flight, so we've got time to kill. Once we're seated, we order. I swipe through my phone to occupy myself and to avoid looking at Jinta. Looking at him feels like a chisel is pounding into my chest, shattering my bones like glass.

I'm so fucking embarrassed he saw me break down like that. He shouldn't have had to see me at my worst. He says he loves me, but how can he? It makes no sense.

My phone buzzes, disrupting my thoughts. It's Ren. Grateful to have a distraction, I swipe. "Hey."

"Did you find your mother?" she asks.

"Yeah."

She huffs. "And? How'd it go?"

I shrug, then remember she can't see. "She told us about a secret place she and my father liked to visit."

"So you're not coming back?" There's a current of anxiety in her voice.

"Why, what's wrong?"

Across the table, Jinta looks up, body stiffening.

Ren says, "I don't know. All day today, I've felt like someone was following me."

My fingers squeeze my phone. "Really?"

"Yeah." She sighs. "I'd feel like someone was watching me, but every time I turned around, I never saw anyone. And earlier, when I came home from grocery shopping, my door was unlocked, but I swear I'd locked it!"

A low growl escapes me. "Tell me you're not still at your apartment."

"Duh. I'm not a dumbass, Raiden. I'm staying with my girlfriend in a whole other ward."

"Huh? You have a girlfriend?"

She groans. "Yes! If you'd listen when I talked to you, you'd know that."

That's good she's safe, or she should be, but my blood pressure has gone way up. Frustration tightens my jaw. *Fuck. I should be there.* "Sorry." Guilt makes me hang my head.

"No, don' be!" She laughs. "It sounds like you're close to finding your father. Stay on his trail, and let me know what happens!" A distant voice says something, I'm guessing her girlfriend. "Coming!" Ren calls. "We're having dinner now."

"So are we."

I can hear the fondness in her voice when she says, "Enjoy and don't worry, boss man. Say hi to Jinta for me."

Our sushi arrives just as I hang up. Jinta and I dig in, and I try to keep my mind off Ren and the pack.

During the flight to Osaka, Jinta fell asleep beside me, hair tousled, cheek smooshed against my shoulder.

Disgust claws at me. I want to push him away and run before I detonate in his face and ruin everything. I'm such a selfish bastard. Meeting me is the worst thing that could have happened to him, but he'll never leave me. Jinta will follow me into hell and back, and I would let him.

I've got to end this. Us. My eyes sting, and an ache rises in my throat. It has to happen. Before he realizes he's better off without me and leaves anyway. Like my parents. It will be easier if I leave first. At least that much is in my control.

A little voice whispers, *what's happening to me? Jinta loves me. He'd never leave me. Why am I thinking this?* But I ignore it, close my eyes, and try not to break down in the middle of a packed airplane.

The sun is going down by the time we land in Osaka. I rent a car from the airport and drive into the city. The temple my mother mentioned is way up in the mountains. That's a trip for a whole other day, so I book us a room for one night at a hotel. Tomorrow, I'll drive the car up into the mountains and find my father.

"Whoa. This room is so nice!" Jinta says, dropping his bag by the door and rushing into the luxury suite. There's a stunning view of the city beyond the windows.

"Can you call Ren and check in at home?" I shrug off my suit jacket and hang it up in the closet.

"My phone's dead." Jinta grabs his charger from his bag and goes in search of an outlet. He exhales nervously. "I hope my dad didn't try to call during the flight..."

Annoyance makes my brow twitch. "Why would he?" I look away when Jinta tries to meet my gaze.

"There was something he tried to call me about earlier at the hospital. I hope everything's okay."

I hang up my tie. "Why wouldn't it be?"

Jinta plugs his phone into an outlet. "I don't know. I just can't figure out why he'd call me unless something was wrong." Shrugging, he turns to face me and offers a smile that's tired but bright. My stomach fluttering, I pretend to adjust my jacket on its hanger in the closet. "I feel grimy from all the traveling. Want to take a bath with me?"

My blood heats at the thought, even if we don't do anything in the tub. I'd just enjoy being wrapped in his scent, feeling him against me—while I still can. "Sure."

"I'll get the water running."

The door closes behind Jinta, and water gushes into the tub. Fishing out my phone from my pocket, I sit on the bed and call Ren. She doesn't answer, but that's not surprising since it's so late. She's asleep by now. I text her, telling her we're in Osaka and to call me in the morning, then plug my phone in to charge.

"Raiden, the bath's ready!" Jinta calls.

Hopefully, a soak with Jinta will relax me. I strip in the bedroom, fold my clothes in one of the drawers, then join him in the bathroom. We rinse ourselves first in preparation for getting in the tub. As conflicted as I am, the sight of Jinta's pale, smooth skin obliterates all other thoughts. Once we're cleaned off, Jinta cautiously dips his foot in the bath, gasping as the hot water soaks his skin. A pleased sigh escapes him. "Feels great."

My eyes glide down his body from his slender shoulders to the supple globes of his ass to his thighs. He's absolute perfection. Jinta smiles when he meets my gaze, and his cheeks flush pink from the warmth of the bath. "Join me?" His offer sets my blood aflame.

I take his offered hand and we both sink into the blissfully hot bath. Jinta laughs softly, the sound music to my ears. "You look cute when you're relaxed."

I snort. "You're the cute one." No, he's more than that. He's beautiful. No ugly tattoos stain his pink skin, no scars from blades, claws, or bullets. Not yet. He's nearly been killed so many times. First by the kitsune, then when he was kidnapped by the hunters.

Once we lift the curse, then he has to rid himself of the curse that is Raiden Noboru. My whole family, we're just... cursed.

"Raiden?" Gentle fingers weave through my hair.

I lift my gaze, my head feeling suddenly too heavy to hold up. Jinta frowns at me. "What is it?"

I can't tell him how I feel. Not now. Right now, I just want to make him feel good. He deserves it after the horrible afternoon I put him through.

I claim his lips with a kiss, sweeping my tongue into his mouth to taste him. I encourage him to stand while I remain kneeling, bringing his half-hard cock close where I want him most. Pressing my mouth to the hard line of his hip, I lick the water clinging in little droplets to his skin.

Jinta strokes my hair. "Raiden, you don't have to. It's been a rough day. We can—" But he gasps when I squeeze his hard cock and start to stroke, relishing the way he twitches in my fist. I'm blessed to know his body so intimately. This man has given me so much. His trust. His love. And I deserve none of it.

"Let me," I croak, gazing up into his chocolate-brown eyes. "I want this."

No, I *need* this. Need to make him feel good, to tell him through actions how much our time together has meant.

He deserves to hear it in words, but I'm too broken to say those three words and mean them. Part of my curse, I guess.

My eyes sting as I nuzzle into his thigh, parting my lips to kiss and lick my way down his skin. When I flick my tongue over his cockhead, Jinta lets out a shuddery whine and tangles his fingers in my hair. This, this I can do. I can make him feel good. Sex is all I can offer. All I'm good for.

"R-Raiden," Jinta whispers, rocking his hips slowly. His cock slides deeper into my mouth, and I wrap my lips around him and suck from his head down to the base, worshipping every perfect inch of him. Closing my eyes, I lose myself in his taste, reaching around to fondle his ass in both hands. When my fingers brush over his hole, Jinta tugs on my hair and whimpers. The sound is muffled, like he's biting his lip. I want to look and appreciate how sexy he is, but I won't.

This isn't about me or my wants. This is all for him.

A groan escapes Jinta when the tip of my finger pops inside him. His hot, velvety walls wrap around my finger. No matter how many times we do this, being inside him will always feel as amazing as the first time. I stroke my finger in and out of him, massaging his prostate while I bob up and down on his cock.

"Yes. Fuck, baby. That feels so good." Jinta pants, his thighs quivering as he thrusts into my mouth.

His cock pulses in my mouth, dribbling precum onto

my tongue. The taste of him makes my own cock throb, but I ignore it. Taking in a breath through my nose, I swallow him down to the root while I work my finger in and out of his tight body. Jinta cries out as I deepthroat him, swallowing around him.

"O-oh, god," Jinta moans, hips lurching forward. "That's it. Always make me feel so good, baby."

My chest tightens, and my eyes winch shut. My throat thickens, and I have to pull off. I kiss the head of his cock, swiping my tongue over his slit to taste his precum, then kiss my way down his length until my face is hidden in his thigh. Throat clicking as I swallow, I wrap my arms around his waist and hold him tight.

Fuck. I can't do this. How am I supposed to let him go?

"Baby?" Jinta strokes my hair. "If you need to stop—"

"No," I croak. I won't leave him wanting. "Let's go to bed." I don't want him standing.

"Okay..."

I lead him to the bedroom, his hand in mine, and tug. Jinta falls down atop me, his mouth meeting mine in a kiss that steals the breath from my body. I lose myself in his soft lips, surrender to the hungry flick of his tongue when it strokes mine. I want to love him, body and soul, to tell him everything I can't say in words. If this is all I can give him, then it has to be as good as I can make it for him.

After I roll him over, I shuffle back between his knees and lift his legs up over my shoulders. I can't get over how sexy he looks, cock hard against his stomach, balls hugging the base of his shaft, pretty pink hole clenching under my hungry eyes. I need him, and I'll never stop.

Jinta arches beneath me with a hoarse cry as I lick his hole, then press the tip inside. His tight pucker softens with every slick glide of my tongue over his skin, and all the while, I stroke his cock. His fingernails scrape my scalp, and I groan in pain and pleasure as Jinta tugs on my hair—hard. His legs shift restlessly on my shoulders as he keens and thrashes.

When I sink my fingers inside his tight, hot body, Jinta's whole body stiffens. "Fuuuck," he whispers. "I'm so close. Make me cum. Please."

There isn't anything I wouldn't give him, except my heart. I don't have one to give, but if I did, he would've had it the moment we locked eyes across that packed dance floor and my wolf howled within my soul. I swallow his cock to the root and crook my fingers over his prostate. Jinta's hole spasms around my fingers, cock flexing as he floods my mouth. Every muscle in his body seizes up, head thrown back as he shouts his release. I savor every second of it, swallowing his cum.

Finally, he relaxes around my fingers and sinks into the bed, fingers grasping at the sheets. Dark eyes hazy with bliss find mine. "Come here," he whispers. I shouldn't, but I'm like the moon gravitating toward his sun. I can't stay away. I'm always pulled back to him time and again.

He pulls me down into a kiss, hands fumbling down my body. When he grasps my cock and strokes in the way only he knows how to please me, I break apart. His lips swallow my every pitiful sound as he strokes me. I'm beyond words. All I can do is fuck his fist, mouth falling open in a silent howl as I cum *hard*. My ears ring, and my eyes water as my body jerks again and again into the hot cradle of his hands.

Jinta kisses me through it, moaning with me as he brings me over the brink like his pleasure is mine.

My arms shaking, I reach out and haul him against me. I never want to let go. I have to. But not now. Not tonight. Just give me one more night with him, and then I'll let him go. I promise. It'll kill me, but I've got to. I won't be the eclipse that takes away his light.

As Jinta falls asleep in my arms, I stroke his hair and finally let a tear fall down my cheek.

Pressing my lips to his forehead, I whisper, "I'm sorry for everything."

CHAPTER 19

Jinta

When I wake, my bladder is close to bursting. Beyond the curtains, the barest light of dawn kisses the horizon, gently illuminating the room. Raiden sleeps beside me, face tucked into his pillow, hair askew. Quietly, I untangle myself from the bed and go into the bathroom. Once my business is concluded, I wash my hands. My face flushes hot when I glance at the tub.

Raiden was so attentive last night. He's always so focused on my pleasure, but last night felt... different. Like he was savoring me, worshipping me. There was this intensity and devotion coming off him in waves. It was amazing, and yet, something felt off about it. It almost felt like he was there, but not. With me physically, but his mind was miles away.

Worry makes my stomach churn. His meeting with his mother really messed him up. I'm unsure of how to help him except to give him space and time. I leave the bathroom, my bare feet whispering over the carpet. Raiden's phone screen lights up, vibrating quietly. It's a message from Ren.

Is she okay? Raiden seemed worried about her earlier. I should check just to make sure. I tap in his code, which is the year of my birthday, and open her message.

> **Ren:** *sorry I didn't get back to you earlier. I'm fine. I don't think I'm being followed anymore, but I'm still going to play it safe.*

> *No matter what happens to me or anyone else, do not accept Takada's offer. Keep looking for a cure and don't stop until you've exhausted all options.*

> *Nothing he promises is worth being his slave for the rest of your life. Call me later. Stay safe.*

Ice falls into my stomach. I reread her message about Takada again and again. What the hell is she talking about? Raiden never told me about a deal with Takada. Though, I was surprised when his pack and Raiden's fought side by side, I'd been too distracted to think much of it. Nausea roils through my stomach as I sit on the edge of the bed, fingers trembling around the phone.

Takada wouldn't do something for nothing, and I know exactly who he covets even more than the Taito Ward. I glance at Raiden bundled beneath the blankets behind me and have to fight the urge to wake him up and demand answers.

Terror rises inside me, constricting my chest. Raiden wouldn't accept whatever foul deal Takada has offered him, would he? But if it was to save me, to save his pack... I force myself to swallow the sour taste in my throat. I need to know what Takada offered him before I jump to conclusions.

Raiden wouldn't choose Takada over me. Right? I wrap my arms around myself and squeeze, urging myself to breathe as old wounds slowly reopen. Raiden isn't Takahiro. He wouldn't betray me like my ex-boyfriend did. He wouldn't sacrifice himself and leave me behind. I know this, so why is it so hard to trust that he'd choose me?

I need something to preoccupy myself, so at 7 A.M., I leave our room and go to the café across the street. I order a coffee for Raiden, a matcha with soy for myself, and a couple of pastries. We've got to get a move on and find Raiden's father soon, so we won't have time for a big breakfast.

Out the windows, the streets slowly fill with people. Being back in Osaka feels… strange. I grew up in this city, so it holds so many different memories. Some of them are good, but the rest are just bitter. This is where I grew up and went to school. I made friends and had crushes on guys in my class, fell in love with photography and journalism, and tried for years to fit myself into the mold my parents wanted as heir to their hospitality franchise. My brother happily accepted his duties and responsibilities in the business, but I struggled. I don't feel like the same person I was then. In some ways, I'm a better version of myself, but I still have so many doubts about my self-worth.

Maybe those feelings will always be there, like scars on my skin. The thought is depressing, but I may just have to learn to live with it. *Thanks, family, for the trauma and pain!*

Oh, that's right. My father tried to get in touch with me yesterday. My phone charged overnight so while I wait for my order, I take a seat and check my messages. Mom texted me while we were flying to Osaka.

Mom: *call me.*

Then there was a missed call early this morning.

Shit. Something must have happened.

Stepping outside so I don't disturb the peace and quiet, I return my mother's call. My heart races, and my stomach does flips. What's happened? It must be bad if she's trying to call me.

"Jinta!" my mother says, voice warm. "How are you, dear?"

"I'm okay. Sorry I couldn't return your call. I was busy. Work stuff." I tense, expecting a nasty comment about my job or my obligations to family.

Instead, she says, "That's... that's all right. I understand how busy life can sometimes be."

I blink, honestly stunned. For years, I tried to be their perfect son in the hopes they'd adore me as they did my brother. But when I refused to be who they wanted, they shut me out and no longer supported me in anything I wanted to do.

"How are you? Are you well?" she asks.

"I'm fine," I say. "Uh... is everything okay?"

Rather than answer, she says, "There's something your father and I need to discuss with you if you're available to chat sometime today."

Instantly, I'm on guard. Whenever they need to talk to me together, it's usually about how I've failed or disappointed them in some fashion. I should just decline. I don't owe them my time, not when they've never treated me like family. Besides, I'm supposed to be helping Raiden. "Maybe." I didn't want to be rude and say no, but I also don't want to accept her invitation. "I'm a bit busy today."

"Ah. I see," Mom says, disappointment plain in her voice. I wince. Can't anything I do be good enough? Why am I always such a fuckup? "Jinta... I know our relationship has been difficult lately." I almost scoff. "But even so, we're still your family, and we need you to be a man and step up."

Suddenly we're family when they need something from me? "Mom, I..." *Just say no!* I mentally scream the words. "I'll let you know if anything changes." I want to hit myself.

"I understand." Her voice is cold and clipped. "Let me know before tonight. Have a good day." She hangs up on me. Sighing, I shove my phone in my pocket. I'm twenty-two years old, but I still let my parents make me feel like an asshole for setting boundaries with them. Seriously, what was I expecting? That they'll realize I'm the son they never had and finally accept me?

Even I know that's never going to happen.

"Sir?" The barista holds out the paper bags with our pastries.

Caffeine and pastries acquired, I dart back across the street and ride the elevator back to our room.

What could have happened that's so bad they need *my* help? They've spent years making it clear they want nothing to do with me for turning my back on them. What if it's something bad? I can't imagine what would be so bad they'd turn to me for help. I'm sure my brother Katsuki knows, but I'd rather bite off my tongue than speak a word to him ever again after he kissed Raiden.

I swipe our room card. Inside, the bed is made and empty. For a moment, my heart stops dead. Did Raiden leave without me? No. No, why would he do that? Before I can panic, the tinkling of the bathroom sink registers in my ears. He's here. Everything is fine. Why am I so anxious? I'm not usually this doubtful.

Come on, Jinta. Cheer up. Focus on helping Raiden find his dad. Don't worry about everything else.

Right. Like that's going to happen.

I set Raiden's coffee on the table along with the mochi donuts I bought. Raiden comes out of the bathroom, fully dressed, handsome face clean shaven. The sight of him makes my stomach flutter—until I remember Ren's text. He's hiding something from me, and I'm too nervous to ask what it is.

I dredge up a smile. "Good morning."

He returns my greeting. "Thanks for the food." He presses a warm, damp kiss to my cheek but before I can melt into his tender touch, he's moving out of my reach. It's probably just me feeling insecure, but he seems distant. Raiden checks his phone while he eats his pastry and drinks his coffee.

"It's good, right?"

Raiden nods wordlessly.

Why am I so nervous? That wasn't exactly the most engaging conversation starter. Try something else. "Have you been to Osaka before?"

Raiden lowers his gaze. "My family would visit to see my grandparents on my mom's side. Don't remember much." He becomes interested in the crumbs from his donut, pushing them around his plate.

I'm not imagining things. He *is* distant. Worry claws at me. Trying to keep him engaged, I say, "I grew up here."

A little flicker of interest shines in his eyes before it's quickly extinguished. "Oh, right. Must have a lot of memories."

I laugh. It sounds fake to my own ears. "Yeah..."

The conversation dies. Neither of us can carry it.

"Think we should get a move on." He clears the table.

There's a pit in my stomach growing wider by the second as I watch him walk away from me. What's going on? Does this have anything to do with whatever deal he made with Takada, or the meeting with his mother, or what we did last night? There are too many possibilities. Unable to sit still, I follow Raiden out the door after we grab our bags.

While the skies were only a little overcast this morning, they've darkened considerably. The gray clouds only lower my spirits. I climb into the passenger seat with Raiden. Raiden says nothing as he starts the car, all his focus on the road. The scent of his distress is thick in the air, feeding my own misery. I want so badly to reach out to him, but I don't think he'd let me. The silence hangs between us as we drive through the streets. I can't take this. There has to be something I can say to cheer him up, but it's difficult when I don't know what's wrong.

"Raiden?"

He grunts curiously but keeps his eyes on the road.

Wetting my dry lips, I say, "It's going to be okay. We can find your father."

A pained look twists across Raiden's face, one I can't decipher.

"You were really brave facing your mother like that." Respect for him warms my voice. "I can't even face my family. It was hard, but you did it."

Raiden's throat bobs when he swallows, and my heart sinks when moisture gathers in his eyes. *Shit*. I need to change the subject. I look out the window, desperate for something to say, anything. Maybe the present is too painful, but what about the future?

"Hey. Once this is all over, let's go away together. How about Thailand? I've always wanted to go. It can be just us. No yakuza or hunters."

Suddenly, Raiden yanks on the wheel. I yelp in fear and surprise. Cars honk as Raiden cuts through the lane beside us and slams on the brakes when we reach the curb.

"Raiden! What the hell?" My heart is about to leap out of my throat, and my hands shake violently. Raiden's knuckles whiten over the wheel, and he sucks in ragged gulps of air. My fear only deepens when I notice how wide and glossy his eyes are. I've never seen him so panicked before.

"Can't," he rasps, sounding like he's choking. He slumps over, forehead to the wheel. "I can't think about a future."

I wince. Damn it. I only upset him more. "Okay," I say softly. "That's okay. We don't have to talk about anything if you don't want to. We can just drive." Raiden sucks in a ragged breath, hands shaking around the wheel. "Baby..." I touch his leg. His knee jerks violently.

"Don't," he croaks, his voice a desperate plea.

It feels like I've been punched in the stomach. "Okay."

I take in slow breaths to keep myself together. Raiden's harsh pants slowly shift, following the soothing rhythm of my breathing. Rain starts to fall, tapping against the windows. Raiden activates the windshield wipers. In the silence between us, the windshield wipers pulse like a heart.

"I've been thinking." His voice is monotonous, like he's utterly drained. His throat clicks when he swallows. Suddenly, I fear his next words more than anything else. Still, I wait, hanging on his every word. Willing him not to break my heart. "When this is over, maybe you should stay in Osaka."

My heart stumbles to a stop in my chest. I can't say a word. Maybe if I just hear him out, it won't be nearly as bad as I think it is. Maybe—

Raiden blows out a shaky breath. "Or somewhere else. Anywhere you want. The pack will look after you, give you whatever you need."

"Why?" I don't recognize my voice. I've never sounded so small, so hurt.

Raiden clenches his teeth hard, a muscle beating in his jaw. "Takada made me an offer."

My heart sinks into my stomach.

"He's going to let the Namikawa-kai survive. If I… if I give myself to him."

My worst fears have been confirmed. Raiden's going to sacrifice himself. Why? Why would he do this to us, to *me?* "Tell me you didn't accept." I look at him, unable to tear my gaze away as I struggle to read his expression.

"No. I didn't. But if I can't find my father and we can't lift the curse, then I… he'll want me to—" He cuts off, a disgusted expression on his face. "I can't do it. Not again. I can't let him put his hands on me. Maybe if I was stronger I could—But I can't. I'm not selfless enough."

A part of me is relieved to hear it, but I know the worst is yet to come. "So what are you going to do?" Anger rises slowly but surely because whatever he has decided, he's made his decision without me.

Raiden finally meets my gaze. "I'll get you out of Tokyo, and I'll face him with my pack. We won't survive. I'm sure of it. And if the kitsune curse isn't cured, you can't be there with us."

So, this is it. He's running away. My heart shatters to pieces in my chest.

"Jinta, I…" A sob chokes him. "This is for you. I'm

doing this for you."

Fury burns inside me. "Don't." My voice shakes with outrage.

"Jinta—"

"You asshole!" I erupt, my voice filling the car. I've never screamed like this before, so loudly it tears at my throat. *Fuck.* I can't even look at him. Ripping off my seat belt, I lurch from the car. Rain spatters my body, soaking through my clothes in fat, cold drops that chill me to the bone.

"Jinta!" Raiden pursues me into the downpour. He grabs my arm.

I rip my hand out of his grasp. "Don't touch me!"

Raiden stumbles back and drops his hand to his side where it trembles.

The rain pours down around us, the downpour deafening. I can't breathe around the ache in my throat. My eyes burn, wet from rain and tears. Raiden's lip wobbles, his eyes glossy with pain.

"Jinta." My name is a broken croak from his lips. "I was never any good for you. I have nothing to offer you, nothing except danger and death and pain. And you..." His voice breaks, face crumpling. "You're the one person I've ever wanted to protect. My sunshine. I want to be a better person. For you. But I'll never be. I'm too fucked up. My world is too dangerous. I can't be the reason you die or get hurt anymore."

I want to fall apart as his eyes fill with tears and his voice shakes with anguish.

But for once in my life, I'm just too hurt, too angry, to take any shit. Not from him, not from my family.

Something between a laugh and a sob escapes me. "You're scared." I understand, finally, and I know for a fact that he's putting up walls and shutting me out because of what happened yesterday with his mom.

Raiden balls his fists. "I'm not. Fear has nothing to do with it! I'm not good for you, I—"

"Seeing your mother again messed with your head." This is about his mother and how things ended between his parents. He can't push me away. My parents pushed me away, my brother, my ex-boyfriend. I won't be able to take it... not from him. "She made you doubt our bond. Your parents weren't fated, Raiden. They couldn't have been. I'd never hurt you like your mother was hurt. I'd never leave you."

"You have to!" Raiden shouts, voice shaking. "You have no future with me, if you don't leave, you'll—"

"Then tell me to leave!" Pain splits my heart in two, tears mixing with the rain coursing down my face. I make myself move toward him.

Please, don't push me away. Please, don't hurt me like this. Not you. It was never supposed to be you breaking my heart like this.

I tip my chin up and look him in the eyes, daring him to

fight for us. "If this is really what you want, then tell me, and I'll go. It's up to you." My voice shakes, and I struggle to catch my breath as silence descends on us.

Raiden opens his mouth, and a broken sound escapes him. His lips tremble and he closes his eyes tight, shoulders shaking.

I can't take it anymore. I grab his cold hands and hold them to my chest. "I know it hurts. I know you're scared this isn't going to work out. I get it. Okay? I'm scared, too. Everything feels hopeless. But we could still find your father. The kitsune curse can still be cured. This isn't over. We can still have a future together but only if we fight for it, and I'm always going to fight for you, Raiden. Until the end. Because I've never loved anyone like I love you."

Agonized brown eyes swim in tears as Raiden finally meets my gaze.

I'm so close to winning him over, I can feel it.

"Fight, Raiden. For us. Please."

Raiden parts his trembling lips, but no words come out. His eyes drop to the five-yen coin around my neck, and I see the moment he makes up his mind as his eyes harden and his expression turns cold. Raiden jerks his hand free. "I can't love you, Jinta. I'll never be who you want me to be. I'm yakuza. This is my life. That's never going to change."

Something inside me breaks, and I can't breathe.

Raiden murmurs, "Let's go. I'll drive you back to the hotel."

But I can't even move as he turns his back and walks away from me. It feels like I'm fifteen again, telling my parents I won't be who they want, watching my mother cry and my father rage. I'm there again as Mom tells me Katsuki's been promoted with all the pride she never showed me. I'm there, watching Takahiro cheat on me with my brother. I'm tired of never being anyone's first choice. Of being pushed away by the ones I care about and left behind. I'm so damn *tired* of never being enough.

"Forget it!" I shout. "I'll walk."

Raiden turns toward me but doesn't speak, looking miserable and resigned.

I need to walk away before I give back as good as he gave me. Before I hurt him. But I'm torn open and bleeding, my head full of rage and my heart breaking. "Go on. What are you waiting for? Run away like you always do when the going gets rough. Like your father!"

That was a low blow, but I'm too distraught to care.

Raiden flinches, hands curling at his sides. He still doesn't speak.

"I'm disappointed in you," I croak. The same words my parents have thrown in my face my whole life. I thought throwing them back at someone else would fix something inside me, but it didn't.

Wordlessly, Raiden turns away. The car door slams. The key turns in the ignition. Raiden drives away and leaves me in the pouring rain.

My chin quivers, and I break. My knees nearly give out as sobs rack my body, folding me in on myself with the force of my anguish. I can see it all so clearly now. I'm cursed, and so is Raiden. We're cursed to be trapped in the pain of our pasts, unable to move forward, haunted by ghosts that we can't escape.

I take a stumbling step, then another. There's no goal in mind, no direction. I just walk, shuddering as rain soaks me to the bone. What can I do? Where can I go? Not back to the hotel. I don't want to be alone. God. I'm so alone. There's no one I can call, nobody I can confide in to ease my pain. Ren is miles away and busy leading the pack. My brother and I hate each other.

My parents. They wanted to speak to me, didn't they? And for the first time in so long, I need them. I want to break down and let my mother hold me. Feel my father's hand on my shoulder. I want them to tell me everything will be okay. I want my parents.

My phone's in my hand and I wait, holding my breath.

"Jinta?" My mom's voice makes my eyes burn.

"H-hey, Mom," I say, a sob rising to my lips. "I'm in Osaka. Can I... can I come over?"

CHAPTER 20

Raiden

Everything hurts. My head. My heart.

What have I done?

Rain pours down around the car. It feels like I'm lost in a storm, and I'll never see the sun again. I pushed away the only good thing to ever happen to me. Who knows if he'll ever forgive me. I hope he doesn't. I'm not worthy of his forgiveness.

A pitiful sound escapes me as I slump over the wheel, needing something to hold myself up as my heart splinters in my chest. My wolf howls for our other half, for his mate, but I can't go to him. This is for the best. Jinta is better off without me and all the danger I've brought into his life.

So why does it hurt so much? It's like there are shards

of glass in my lungs, in my heart. A shuddery exhalation rattles my chest and I wipe frantically at my eyes. I can't fall apart. Not now. My father is out there, and I've got to find him and lift the curse on Jinta. After all the shit I've brought down on him, it's the very least I can do. Then he can go far away from me and this life of mine, somewhere safe.

Fuck. It hurts just thinking about it, so I shove the thoughts down and drive. The city disappears behind me as rain sluices down the windows and floods the rice paddies in the fields around me. It takes me over an hour to drive from Osaka and into the wilds of Nara Prefecture. Kodai-ji Temple is closer than ever as I park the car at the base of the hiking trail that sprawls into the woods.

But my car isn't the only one there. Three bulky vehicles are parked in the lot. The mud sucks at my feet as I go to investigate. All three cars are empty, but several sets of footprints lead away from the vehicles and into the woods. Their scents still linger in the air, and I take a breath, pulling them into my lungs.

Werewolves.

My heart sinks. *Shit*. The Horikoshi-gumi has figured out where my father is, and they're somewhere in these woods. I've got to find my father before they do, or Jinta will never be cured. Rain pelts my skin as I take off into the woods, following the tracks embedded in the mud. With the dark clouds choking out the sun, the woods only get darker as the trees press in around me.

Shapes materialize ahead of me, and I lurch to a stop and take refuge behind a tree. Men in suits prowl the woods ahead of me, ten in total. I'm completely outnumbered, but they haven't seen me yet, so I still have the advantage. I can't afford to rush in. If I get in a rough spot, I don't have anyone to back me up. I've got to stay low and quiet.

"Damn it," one of them grumbles, bald head shiny with rain. "I hate this weather."

"Quit complaining and keep your voice down," another snaps. "That bastard is somewhere in these woods. You remember what his bitch said before we tore out her throat. Spread out and search everywhere! Look for the marks on the trees."

My stomach twists. They must be referring to the woman my father ran off on our family with. They killed her. She didn't deserve that. My father dragged her into this world of his, and she paid the price. Could that have been Jinta's fate, as well? I made the right choice. Didn't I? The yakuza forge on ahead into the trees, splitting off into groups of one or two at most. I've got to get ahead of them.

Using the trees as cover, I creep around the group, keeping low and quiet on the tips of my toes. One of the yakuza, some fucker with a goatee, slinks through the woods ahead of me, grumbling when sticks tug at his clothes. I lengthen my claws and prowl toward him. My wolf hungers for blood as I bear down on him, until I'm inches behind him. I lunge, slapping a hand over his mouth, muffling his yelp against my palm.

My claws swipe across his throat, splitting the skin like parchment paper. Blood gushes down my claws, and his dying breathes gurgle against my hand. I let him drop to the floor and leave him choking on his blood as I pursue the others. One down, nine motherfuckers to go. The hunt is on. Blood fills the air, and my wolf bays for more. Black fur ripples over my arms and grows thick on my jaw.

Two others search the woods ahead of me. One looks around, water glistening in his patchy beard while his scrawny comrade with a bad buzzcut inspects a tree. "Hey, hey, I found something! These look like claw marks. We must be close to the temple!"

Patchy Beard says, "I'll howl so everyone else knows."

Shit. They can't alert the others. A growl rumbles in my chest as I sneak up on them, darting from one tree to another to stay out of sight. Neither hears me coming, not until I strike, flaying open Patchy Beard's neck. His startled gurgle alerts his friend. Scrawny spins around, and his cry of horror is cut off when I smash my fist into his face. Snaring his shirt in my fists, I slam him up against a tree.

Drink his blood. Feast on his bones! My wolf commands me.

Before Scrawny can scream for help, I fasten my fangs

into his throat and tear. Blood gushes, spilling over my tongue. There's so much that I choke on it. My clothes strain as my wolf tries to take the reins. *Shit. He's hard to control.* His fury ignites my blood and drives all reason from my head. Without my mate to soothe me, my rage takes hold.

The shift bursts from me before I can call it back. I'm still human, but barely. A snarl tears from my throat, and I charge into the woods, not caring who sees or who hears. A yakuza screams as I leap on him, sinking my claws into his chest. Blood pools around my fingers. Cries of alarm fill the woods, and footsteps thunder closer. His throat shreds to ribbons beneath my claws.

"Get this son of a bitch!" someone shouts, and a kick plows into my jaw. Pain explodes through my face as I tumble over in the grass.

"O-oh, shit! You killed Kentarou! You bastard!"

I scramble to my feet, claws dripping blood at my sides as six of them circle around me, fangs sharp and claws at the ready. One of them has already shifted to a big gray wolf, his lips curled back from his teeth. With a snarl, a big brute of a man charges me like a bull. I dodge a punch from his heavy fist, grab his outstretched arm and bite. Skin tears, blood floods my mouth, and bones crunch.

The brute screams and tries to free himself, and my fangs shred more of his arm. I use our proximity to my advantage to sink my claws into his windpipe and tear. I swing the brute around, throwing him into one of the yakuza and knocking him off his feet.

Barking, the wolf rushes me and leaps, fangs white and glistening. The wolf crashes into me, knocking me flat on my back as it lunges for my throat. I fling up my arm, snarling in pain as the wolf's jaws lock around my arm, crunching hard, fangs tearing into my skin. The yakuza cheer their shifted pack mate on. A roar of rage and pain tears from me, and I slice my claws across the wolf's eyes. The beast shrieks out in agony and stumbles off me, pawing frantically at its bloody face.

Someone rams their shoulder into me just as I find my feet, and the ground flies out beneath me. The world spins as I tumble down a steep hill. Branches smack me, rocks cut into me. When I finally roll to a stop, I'm out of breath and too dizzy to stand.

"Hold him off. The rest of you, find Noboru, now!" one of them shouts.

The wolf comes charging down the hill, rain glistening in its matted fur. It leaps for me, jaws open wide to snap around my throat. Just as its blunt fangs touch my flesh, I plunge my claws up into its exposed belly. The momentum of the wolf's jump does the rest of the job for me, ripping the wolf from stomach to groin.

It collapses on me, jaws gaping around my neck. The wet heat of its steaming innards soaks my clothes. Disgusted, I shove the wolf off me and stand. I need to follow the remaining yakuza to my father, and fast, but the terrain works against me. Mud sucks at my shoes, and my hands slip on wet rocks as I attempt to scale the hill.

A blast echoes over the trees. Was that gunfire? Someone has a gun, but it couldn't have been the yakuza, or they'd have used it. My father, maybe. *Shit. I've gotta get to him, fast!* I'm drenched in mud and blood as I heave myself over the top of the hill, clothes torn and stinking of blood and wolf guts. The yakuza left a trail of muddy footprints, so I pursue them into the woods.

Jagged claw marks are carved into the trunks of the trees. I'm close now, almost there. Panicked shouts echo through the woods before they're drowned out by another blast of gunfire. The sound is much louder this time. I crouch down and keep to the trees for cover. A cabin comes into view between the trees. One of the windows has been broken. Two dead yakuza lie in the mud near the building, blood pooling from headshots to their skulls.

"Noboru, come on out!" a man shouts. "Y-you're sur-rounded! There's nowhere for you to—" His voice is cut off by a blast of gunfire, and his remaining friend cries out in horror and anguish. Before the gunshot, I caught I glimmer of a scope in the window. He's got a hunting rifle. Approaching from the front is a bad idea. I'll have to sneak around the back and try to get the drop on him. While the shooter's attention is on the remaining guy, I give the cabin a wide berth and dart from cover to cover until I'm around the back of the house.

"N-Noboru, this is your last—" A gunshot drowns out his pained cry.

I round the corner, keeping low as I pass beneath the windows. There's a back door. The shooter fires again within the house, still occupied. Quiet as I can, I ease the door open. A man has his back to me, peering through the scope at his target. My heart hammers. I can only see the top of his silver head of hair and smell the stink of his unwashed body.

Is this him?

The rifle bucks, and there's an agonized yelp from outside. The silence makes my ears ring. Slowly, I make my way toward him. A floorboard groans under my foot. The shooter swings around, and a bright flash blinds me as he fires.

CHAPTER 21

Jinta

I never thought I'd find myself on my parents' doorstep again. It's been five years since I've come back to Osaka. Five years since I promised myself I was done giving my time and energy to people who didn't accept or support me. And now here I am, my heart in pieces in my chest as I ride the elevator up to my parents' floor. Everything hurts. Nothing makes sense anymore. I don't know what I'm doing or if anything will work out the way I want it to.

I just want someone to turn to. I can't believe I'm seriously running to my parents for support. It makes me feel pathetic, like I'm breaking every promise I made to myself to stay away. Soaking wet from the rain, I trudge through the halls to their penthouse where we all used to live as a family.

I walked these halls with my backpack heavy over my shoulders. Laughed sometimes with my brother as we raced each other to the front door. I raise my hand to knock and hesitate. There's still time to walk away and leave them hanging. I don't owe them anything. I don't need them. I... I knock and wait.

In seconds, my mother answers the door. She gasps. "Jinta! What's happened? You're soaked."

I arch one side of my mouth to reassure her, mouth trembling with the effort. "I'm fine." I couldn't be less convincing if I tried.

"What's happened?" she asks, gripping my arms.

Emotion plugs my throat. "Raiden and I had a big fight, and... I don't know if I'll ever see him again." Tears spill from my eyes in a rush.

My mother's face pinches with sympathy. "Oh. I'm so sorry, dear." She pulls me in for a hug, enveloping me in her warmth and comforting scent, and I just crumble. My mother hasn't held me in years, and it feels so good to be in her arms. Her embrace is a temple, sturdy and strong, nourishing my body and spirit. For a moment, it feels like we're a normal family. Like she loves me.

"I've missed you," I whisper, sniffling.

She sniffles, too, and squeezes me. "Me, too, dear. Come in. I'll make you some tea."

Snuffling and wiping my eyes, I step inside after her. I

take off my shoes and step into the slippers she's put out for me. My face must look terrible. I need to get myself together before my dad sees me crying. He'd always get angry if I cried.

"I need the toilet. I'll be back," I say while my mom heads into the kitchen. In the bathroom, I blow my nose and splash water on my face, trying to get rid of the ugly red splotches on my skin.

Tamano appears in the mirror behind me. "What are you doing here, Jinta?"

I squeeze the edge of the sink. "I just need support, okay?"

"I've seen your thoughts. These people treated you wretchedly. You owe them nothing."

"I *know that*," I grit out.

She arches a brow. "Do you? What are you hoping you will accomplish here?"

"I don't know."

"You do," she argues, flicking a curtain of ebony hair over her shoulder. "If you're hoping they will suddenly accept you, you're only going to be disappointed."

Her words chip away at my defenses, revealing the hope I'm guarding so close to me. The hope that this time, things will be different. They'll accept me as their son. They'll love me like they love Katsuki.

"You need nothing from them."

I swallow hard. "If Raiden has... if he's l-left me, I'm

going to be alone the rest of my life. I can't be alone." My throat aches, eyes stinging.

Tamano touches my shoulder, and I feel something. Like a cool breeze over my skin. "Better to be alone the rest of your life, than stuck with people who make you feel alone. You are a remarkable man, Jinta. How can you not see that? You worked your way into Noboru's heart and made him feel. Uncovered Namikawa's secrets. You made a life for yourself all on your own. You don't need Noboru or your family."

No. I needed Raiden. But he didn't need me. He'd made that painfully clear.

Tamano sighs. "I can see nothing I say will convince you of your worth. Very well. But do not expect something for nothing."

"Yeah. Okay," I say, but inwardly, her words make defensive anger surge through me. "Or maybe they just genuinely want to see me."

Tamano shrugs. "Perhaps. We shall see." She vanishes.

Look, historically speaking, my parents don't have a great track record. They've never gone out of their way for me, never showed me that they cared, but people can change. Taking in a fortifying breath, I pat my face dry with a towel and leave the room.

"Oh!" My father jumps as I almost walk into him.

My heart lurches. "H-hey, Dad."

He grunts, then narrows his eyes at me. "Were you crying?"

Heat races up my neck to my cheeks. "No! I'm fine."

My father shakes his head in blatant disapproval. "Get a hold of yourself. What we have to discuss is important. You can't wriggle out of your obligations to this family by being manipulative." He steps past me into the bathroom.

I'm too outraged to speak. My hands clenched, I make my way to the living room. Rain streaks down the floor-to-ceiling windows, and gray clouds obscure the normally beautiful view of Osaka and makes the apartment feel darker than usual.

"The tea will be done in a moment," Mom assures me.

"Okay. I'll be back." I want to take a look at my old room. I haven't seen my room since before I went off to college in Tokyo. Past the living room is a narrow hall that connects to the bedrooms Katsuki and I used to sleep in. My parents have a room on the other side of the penthouse. I feel like a totally different person from the teen who used to hide away in his bedroom. Teenage Jinta Onodera had drowned in loneliness and frustration, constantly overshadowed by his big brother, torn between being himself and being the perfect son his parents wanted.

I grip the knob and open the door, only to freeze in the doorway.

My bedroom has been stripped bare. There isn't a single trace of the boy I once was, like he never existed at all. There's a hollow feeling in my stomach. They must have sold all my furniture after I left to go live on campus in Tokyo. They couldn't even stand having the ghost of me in this house. The walls close in on me, and I hastily slam the door.

Curiosity, and a bit of dread, compels me toward Katsuki's room. I open the door and find Katsuki's room fully furnished. It's been updated from his teenaged bedroom, obviously, with furniture and decorations more fit for an adult. He still has all the trophies he won throughout high school on shelves. He was an excellent baseball player and helped his team win several matches.

I close the door, leaning my forehead against the smooth wood. I knew it. My parents haven't changed at all. I'm still the son they never wanted, who did nothing but disappoint them. No. Of course they sold my furniture. I'd made it clear by then I was never coming back home. Why would they keep a room for me?

"Jinta? Tea is ready!"

I swallow hard and steel my resolve before it can crumble. I need to hear them out. If they want a second chance, then they can have one. I just... I can't be alone.

In the living room, my mother sets a tray of tea and some sweets on the coffee table. My father sits in the armchair beside her, staring straight ahead. I take a seat on the sofa opposite them. "Thank you." I take my cup of green tea and one of the sweets, a steamed bun with red bean paste inside.

Mom smiles, teeth bright. "It's good to see you again."

"It's been a while." A few weeks, really. The last time I saw them was for Katsuki's birthday and that went... badly.

"Have you written any stories?" Mom asks.

I clear my throat and glance at my dad. He scowls as he swallows his tea, like it's too bitter for him.

"A few. I was working on an undercover project, but it fell through."

"Oh. Sorry to hear that."

I laugh, voice cracking. "It's fine. Everything worked out..." I still got to be with Raiden despite what I'd done. My chest tightens painfully.

Mom looks like she's going to ask more questions, but Dad sets down his tea with a hard clink against his plate. "There's something we need to discuss with you."

Nerves flutter in my stomach. "Of course."

Dad glares through his spectacles at me. "Katsuki has been fired."

Silence rings in my ears as I try to understand. Katsuki... fired? He was their heir, and last I'd heard, he'd just been promoted to manager of the Tokyo branch of their hospitality franchise. "What?"

Mom hangs her head, eyes watery. "Katsuki cheated on his fiancée. She caught him in bed with a man and sold the evidence to some gossip rag who blasted it all over the internet."

Once a cheater, always a cheater, but I keep that to

myself. He really hasn't changed. I'd say I feel bad, but he stole my ex from me and tried to flirt with Raiden. So screw him. I'm glad his fiancée got even.

Dad's nostrils flare, betraying his anger. "To save face, we fired him."

I blow out a breath. Katsuki is in hot water with my parents for the first time in his life. For once, *I* look like the golden child. "Wow. Where's Katsuki now?"

"Vacationing in the Bahamas," Mom says. "He has lost himself. Some time away will be good for him."

I bite my tongue because Katsuki was always like this. He hasn't lost his way. He was just always an asshole. "Sorry you both had to deal with that. It sounds stressful. Have you found someone to replace him?"

Dad says, "You will."

I don't know what to say as a pit opens in my stomach. I knew it. I knew this was too good to be true. Damn it, Tamano was right, and I should have listened. Disappointment wells within me, threatening to choke me, but anger swiftly replaces it.

"Dad, I've told you and Mom several times; I *have* a job. One I'm good at. One I love." How can they just refuse to accept me, time and time again, and how do I keep letting myself be disappointed by them? I'm so stupid.

Mom clears her throat. "Dear, it's time to come home. We've missed you." She smiles, but it wobbles. "Come now, we had fun, didn't we? Remember when you and

I worked the restaurant together? I taught you to cook. Wasn't that fun?"

I fight back a sigh. "It was for a while, but—"

Dad snaps, "*But* what? Enough excuses. We've sacrificed so much to raise you, invested thousands into your education, and we were ready to hand you a multi-million-dollar business on a silver platter! Do you realize how lucky you are? But you'd rather throw it all away to play with cameras and write stories!"

I flinch from his anger. "I know, and I appreciate everything you did!" When my dad scoffs, I add, "I do, Dad. Really. I loved cooking, and I wanted to be a part of the business."

Dad folds his arms. "And you chose not to because you're selfish and ungrateful."

Frustration heats my cheeks. "That's not it! Dad, come on. Don't you think it would have been so much easier to let you guys pay for my education, to graduate, and immediately have a great job waiting for me after school? I didn't sacrifice all of that just for the fun of it!"

"I'm not interested in hearing your excuses!"

"Dad—" But I give up. "Fine. You have every right to be upset. I don't blame you. I'm sure from your perspective, what I did was incredibly selfish and disrespectful, and I'm sorry you feel that way, both of you." I do mean it. I'm sorry that my actions hurt them. "But I didn't feel like staying was an option for me. It just seems, to me, that… I would have had to change who I was to make you happy."

"That's not true," Mom interjects.

"So you guys would have let me openly date a man instead of the women you wanted me to date?"

"Well..." Mom trails off.

"Of course not," Dad huffs. "You would have shamed our family. Two men together is just not traditional! You would have only done it to defy us like you always have."

Wow. I don't even have anything to say to that nonsense.

"Dear, calm down," Mom placates, touching his arm. "But your father is right, Jinta. You have a responsibility to this family after all we've done for you. Come home, son. Be a part of our family again."

And I want to say yes. I've missed my mother, and even though Dad and I have always had a rocky relationship, I've longed for him to look at me the way he looks at Katsuki—with pride and affection. This could be my chance to be the son they always wanted and earn their love.

"If I..." I swallow hard. "If I say yes, I'm not going to change who I am. I'm going to live openly. Is that something you can accept?"

Mom hesitates, frowning. "I... if that's what you want."

Dad scowls, nostrils flaring with a harsh sigh. "If we have to."

I want to be a part of their family, want to belong to someone, and be accepted.

Except what they're offering isn't acceptance, and I *do*

belong to someone, and he's never asked me to change who I am, and his love never came with conditions. Yeah, things have been tough lately for both of us. We're both as different as night and day... but somehow, he became my family, my pack, my very heart and soul.

To Raiden, I was enough just as I was, flaws and all. My own family has never loved me or accepted me the way Raiden Noboru did, even if he never said those three words. I knew it in my soul that he loved me—*still* loves me. He got scared and pushed me away, and I gave in to my insecurities and let him.

We've got to fix things between us. I'll be damned before I let him self-destruct and run off on me. I deserve better, and so does he. We both do. I deserve someone who loves me for me, and I'm done accepting anything less.

Tamano materializes behind the sofa. She arches an expectant brow and motions for me to go on. And oh, I will.

"Mom, Dad," I begin, voice shaking. "We both know I was never a part of this family."

Dad's jaw clenches. "What did you say?"

Mom looks hurt. "That isn't true."

"Yes, it is," I insist, sitting up straighter in my seat. "Family are the ones who accept you and support you in whatever makes you happy. They cheer you on and encourage you. They lift you up and celebrate your successes, and they never make you feel lesser. And you both have made me feel so small and insignificant all my life."

Mom hangs her head. "I... I didn't know that."

Dad scoffs. "Because it's not true. You're acting like a spoiled, selfish brat. We are family, and you owe us your support."

My voice shakes when I say, "No. I don't owe you anything."

Dad's lips thin. Childish fear rises in me because that's the face he always made before he struck me. But I'm not a child anymore. He doesn't control me with his anger, and Mom can't manipulate me with her guilt. "Then get out. This discussion is over."

Mom wipes her eyes. "We're disappointed in you, Jinta."

Heart racing, I rise, desperate to get out of here. Once those words would have cleaved me in two. Now, I just don't care. I've wasted so much of my life feeling like shit because I wouldn't be who they wanted. "I know," I say, and even I'm surprised when a grin springs across my face. "That's okay. I'm happy. I love my life. I don't need anything from either of you."

I turn my back on my seething parents and walk out, hopefully looking dignified. Once I'm in the hallway, my knees buckle, and the air rushes out of me like I was holding it in. *Holy shit. I did it.* I walked away from my parents' offer, and I don't even feel bad about it. I could have crumbled, could have accepted, and wasted my life chasing after their elusive affection, but I didn't. I'm officially a badass.

"Good job," Tamano says, appearing beside me. "It was smart of you to refuse."

I clutch my chest where my heart races. "Yeah, I know." I made the right choice, I'm positive.

"What now?" Tamano follows me to the elevator.

"I'll go back to the hotel and wait for Raiden." I wonder if he's found his father yet. I hope he's okay.

I ride the train back to our hotel. The sun is starting to go down, staining the sky orange. I'm sure Raiden will be hungry, so I order takeout from a restaurant near the hotel. While I wait for the food, I compose a dozen different messages to Raiden, only to erase them. What do I say?

> *I'm sorry about what I said earlier. Can we talk at the hotel? I hope you found your dad.*

I hit send before I can second-guess everything and throw my phone across the room.

My phone buzzes, and my heart does flips.

> **Raiden:** *I'm sorry, too. I'll be there soon.*

Tears sting my eyes, and I wipe them away. He wants to talk things through, and he's sorry. We can work something out. Joy makes my heart sing.

Ok!! See you soon. Love you so much.

Unable to wipe the smile off my face, I practically skip from the restaurant. Raiden wants to talk. He wants to see me. He's sorry. We can make this work. We can be together. I'm still smiling when I pass through the hotel lobby and call the elevator. My heart feels lighter than it has in hours as I seek out our room number. I swipe the card. The room is dark as the sun has already disappeared. I'm a bit disappointed that Raiden isn't back yet, but I can wait.

I pass the bathroom door and feel around for the light switch, illuminating the suite. My stomach churns with nerves. I'll need to stay busy until Raiden gets back. I wonder how soon is *soon*. I can't wait to see him.

"Do you smell that?" Tamano materializes beside me, a frown on her face.

"The food? It smells great."

"No, not that. It's something else. Metallic, almost." Tamano's lips go slack in shock. "Jinta, watch out!"

Something moves behind me, shoes rushing over carpet. I drop the takeout bag, panic gripping my heart. A clawed hand sinks into my shoulder and spins me around. A man stands behind me, a hood concealing his face, but that's all I see before searing pain slices into my belly again, and again, and again.

Blood soaks through my shirt, and the air leaves my lungs. I clutch onto my attacker's arm, the sleeve wet with blood, and grunt as he pushes the blade in deeper. *Fuck.* My insides feel like they're on *fire*.

The hood falls down, revealing Ishida's snarling face. How did he find us? "I was hoping for Noboru," he growls. "But this is even better. He'll feel all the pain I felt when my brother was killed. I'll come for him when he's drowning in grief and put him down like the dog he is!"

He rips the blade free, and blood spurts from the wound. My knees buckle, and I collapse onto the carpet. Pain eclipses everything, and the wound won't heal.

Ishida runs from the room, slamming the door behind him.

"Jinta?" Tamano's voice shakes as she appears beside me. She's translucent, fading before my eyes. "Shit. It's aconite. He's poisoned you, and the blade was silver, so you can't shift. Jinta, stay awake! Hold on until Raiden gets here!" A pained groan escapes her, back arching, and then she vanishes.

"Tama... no..." I'm all alone as my life's blood seeps from my body. I can feel the aconite coursing through my veins already, burning its way through my body. I can't shift. I can't heal. The pain is a constant, throbbing ache. It's unbearable. Too anguished to even scream, I shutter my eyes.

I'm going to die.

Panic claws at the corners of my mind as darkness comes for me.

My mate. Where is my mate? I have to see Raiden again, one more time, before—

"Raiden?" I call him across our bond, strained by distance and our fight. *"Can you hear me?"*

Please, answer me. I can't let our fight be the last moment we spent together.

I told him I was disappointed in him.

God. Why did I *say* that? I can't die. I can't. Not until I've told him how sorry I am face to face, kissed him one more time, told him I love him.

Tears trickle down my cheeks as the world around me fades away.

"I'm sorry."

CHAPTER 22

Gunfire makes my ears ring at the same time as burning pain courses through my shoulder. Snarling, I squint through the pain at the man with the rifle. He's grown out a bushy salt-and-pepper beard the same color as his long hair, but there's no mistaking those eyes, lined around the edges and cold as they are.

It's my father. Kenta Noboru.

"The next one goes through your skull," my father warns, aiming the rifle at me.

I make my claws shorten to blunt nails, holding up my hands to show him I'm not a threat. My body pushes out the bullet and begins to heal.

"Who are you?" my father asks. "You don't smell like the

pack."

I struggle to swallow or to even speak. The last time I saw this man, I was eight years old. He had his suitcases by the door, his back to me. He didn't even say goodbye as he walked out. Emotion fogs my eyes, and I clench my jaw so it doesn't shake.

"Answer me!" my father snaps, motioning with the rifle. "Who are you, and what do you want?"

I clear my throat and say, voice shaking, "I'm your son."

Noboru freezes, drawing in a sharp breath. His wide brown eyes, the same shade as mine, dart all over my face. "Well, shit." He huffs and lowers the rifle, but he keeps his finger on the trigger. "Come to kill me for leaving all those years ago?"

"Thought about it," I admit, lowering my hands. "Looks like you're still running off on people." I look outside at the corpses of yakuza strewn in the mud.

Noboru grunts, looking down at his feet. "They blamed me for the attack. I had nothing to do with it, but I was their only suspect. They'd been questioning my loyalty for months."

I scoff. "Wonder why." The man hasn't got a loyal bone in his body. If Noboru didn't betray his pack, then who fed information to the hunters that resulted in the attack?

"You look like your mother."

I clench my fists at the comment. "That's funny," I say, not feeling in any way humorous. "She said I look like you."

His gaze snaps up to mine. "You saw her?"

My fingers twitch. "Yeah."

Noboru averts his gaze, propping his rifle against the wall. He scratches the back of his neck, then asks, "So? How is she?"

"She's in the hospital. Lone Wolf Sickness." I scan his face for anything, a flicker of guilt or remorse, melancholy. Anything. But I get nothing except a surprised blink. "You really fucked her up when you left." I lean back on the wall and fold my arms over my chest, needing some kind of barrier between me and him so I don't thrash him.

Noboru huffs. "I'll probably go the same way, now that my mate is... gone."

I think I catch a hint of something in his voice, maybe sorrow, but the man before me is an empty husk. I doubt he's capable of feeling much of anything anymore. It's what he deserves. I've never believed in karma, but there's a first time for everything. "Doesn't look like it was worth it, huh?" I can't help but rub it all in his face. "Leaving me. Leaving Mom."

He glares at me through hard, narrow eyes. "No. Guess it really wasn't. But I'd still do it again. I wasn't meant to be a dad, but your mother was the breeding type. And look at how you turned out. A thug, just like your old man."

My knuckles crack across his jaw. I wasn't even aware I'd moved, not until my fist hit his face. He doesn't have time to recover before I've grabbed his dirty jacket and slammed him against the wall. "You broke my mother's heart!" I snarl, and I hit him again. His nose snaps, and blood soaks his beard. "Left us to fend for ourselves!" Noboru's head whips to the right with the force of my punch. "You ruined our fucking lives!" And just for good measure, I hit him one more time so hard my finger breaks.

Noboru slides down the wall, eyes rolling back, face covered in blood. I snarl through clenched teeth, doubled over in agony until my finger snaps back in place. My father's broken bones heal, and the cuts close, but his face is still a bloody mess. He snorts wetly and horks out a wad of blood-tinged saliva. A tooth flies out.

Wiping away blood, he says, "You throw a good punch." He rubs his bloody fist on his pants.

I want to hit him again, but I'm out of breath. Stumbling back until I'm against the wall, I sink down onto the floor. The wind howls around the cabin, and the branch of a tree scratches the roof.

"If you're not here to kill me, then what do you want? An apology for being a shitty dad?"

I pull my knee to my chest and rest my elbow over it, flexing my mended hand. "I want to know how you cured yourself of the kitsune curse."

He tilts his head, giving me a searching look. "How do you know about that?"

"After you left, Namikawa wanted us to pay off your

debt to the pack. Mom threw me at him and ran off. He made me his bitch in your absence."

Again, not even a flicker of remorse, though he does look surprised. "Your mom bailed on you? After all the times she bitched at me to give her a kid?" He scoffs.

"Because she didn't want to raise me without you," I growl at him.

He just shrugs. "And Namikawa gave you the kitsune curse?"

"He tried. Your father stopped him and died for it."

That makes him look at me, surprise in his gaze.

"In the end, my mate ended up cursed. It was the only way to save his life."

My father makes a disgusted face.

I point a finger at him and growl, "Yeah, I'm bisexual, and you lost any right to have an opinion on that when you bailed on me. So keep your mouth shut. My mate can't control the kitsune, and we need the cure now. So if you could tell me how you cured yourself, I'll be on my way."

Noboru leans his head back, gazing up at the ceiling. After a moment of thoughtful silence, he says, "I found and claimed my mate."

That makes no sense. If my mom was his mate, then why did he leave us?

As if sensing my confusion, he adds, "Not your mother. My fated mate. Yuki."

There's an ache in my chest like I've been punched. "So

my mother wasn't..."

Noboru shakes his head. "I knew Namikawa would want to pass the kitsune onto me, so I went to a mage. He believed only a fated mate's bond would be enough to cure me. I had given up on finding my fated mate in time, so I paid the mage to create a fated bond between your mother and me. Never told her, of course."

I want to punch him again. "So, you tricked her. My mother and I were just... what? Pawns to use and throw away when you got bored?" Anger makes my voice shake. My poor mother was strung along by a manipulative asshole.

"I had to," Noboru insists. "Or else I would've been bound to Namikawa and the pack for life. So I did whatever your mother wanted, even put a brat in her."

I scowl. "Thanks."

"As you know, things slowly unraveled between us. I felt trapped in a life I never wanted."

"Wonder what that feels like," I grumble, so full of bitterness it feels like I'll choke.

"I began to lose hope as our bond became more and more strained. We lived in Osaka for a few years. You were still a baby. I was the leader for the branch of the Namikawa-kai in Osaka, but Namikawa demanded I move to Tokyo so I could take on the role of his second-in-command. I met Yuki, who was the hostess at one of our clubs, and I knew right away who she was to me."

"So you cheated on my mother."

Noboru nods. "Yuki and I started seeing each other in secret. After I claimed her as mine, we made plans to leave the city together. Namikawa found out and tried to force the curse onto me, but the curse wouldn't take. The fated bond between Yuki and me was too strong to be tainted. We barely escaped Tokyo with our lives."

Outside the window, the dead yakuza have become a feast for the birds. "Shit worked out well for you, huh?"

He grimaces. "I dragged Yuki into my world and got her killed. It's a shame. People are... too complicated. All they do is hurt and get hurt by others. Used and thrown aside. So take a lesson from your old man, huh? The only one I ever taught you; you're better off alone."

Something about his words is familiar to me, like I've heard them before. My breath hitches when I realize why. All my life, I've believed some variation of everything he just said—people only hurt, I'm better off alone, and love isn't real.

And in that moment, I realize how alike my father and I really are. I criticized him for using my mother and me, but that's the exact same thing I've done for years. I've used others for sex, company, or as punching bags for the rage simmering within me. Rage at my parents. Rage at the world and my circumstances. Since I was eight, I built up walls and hid behind them, away from the world.

Jinta was right; I'm exactly like my father. He hurt the

people who loved him, pushed them away, and got them killed. I thought I was being selfless with Jinta by putting up a wall between us, giving him the opportunity to have a safe life without me. But I know now that it was nothing but a cowardly tactic to protect myself from being hurt when he ultimately realized I can't give him what he needs.

Why would Jinta ever decide that? He's made it so clear from the beginning that what he feels for me isn't going away, and because I was too damn cowardly to trust him, I could have ruined the best thing to ever happen to me.

I'm on my feet in seconds, fueled by a determination that makes my heart gallop. "Keep your advice," I snap. "I don't want it. Look at you!" I motion around this piece of shit cabin as empty, cold, and miserable as the life he's led. I see myself in him, alone, bitter, and closed off from the world. God. I could end up just like my father. The very idea fucking terrifies me. I don't want to be that person. This cycle of pain and trauma will keep on turning unless I shatter the damn wheel myself.

He sneers. "You think you're so much better than me? I see those tattoos. You're a thug, boy. Like father like son."

"No," I snarl. "I will never be like you. These tattoos are my past, but they're not my future. I'm going to make a life for myself. A good life. A normal life. I won't be a fucking failure like you. I won't end up alone. I have someone who loves me, really loves me, and I will not hurt him like you hurt my mother. I'll be happy. I'll be so happy, just to fucking throw it in your face!" I'm panting by the time I finish talking, shaking violently as years of pent-up anger surge from me. I almost feel... lighter? Like this great weight's been lifted off of my back. It feels like freedom.

I'm done letting the pain of the past define me. I'm going to live in the present with my mate—after I've got down on my knees and begged for his forgiveness, that is. I turn my back on the man who's haunted my life since I was eight and walk out of that wretched cabin.

The sun's going down when Osaka comes into view, glittering like diamonds off the windows. My heart beats faster, and my wolf howls for our mate. *Fuck*. My poor sunshine. I could hit myself for being such a coward. I've got to fix things between us. Our bond is strained, but it's still wrapped around my heart.

I'm done denying how I feel for him, and I'm done running from us. I want a future with Jinta by my side. I want to be free of the yakuza, to be the man he deserves—so I'm going to damn well do it. Fear starts to rise in me, a roaring tide of what-ifs, but I focus on our bond and breathe through it.

Love is scary. Scarier than a bullet fired from a dark alley or the flash of fangs as a wolf lunges at you. But Jinta is worth it, all of it. I just wish I'd realized this sooner.

My phone buzzes from the dashboard, propped up so I can follow the GPS. It's a text from Jinta. My heart gallops. Is it possible he wants to talk about our fight? Looking both ways, I pull over into the grass and grab my phone. Please, give me a second chance, please...

> **Jinta:** *I'm sorry about what I said earlier. Can we talk at the hotel? I hope you found your dad.*

He's sorry. He wants to talk. Thank god. I didn't ruin things between us after all. How did I hit the jackpot with such a sweet mate? I don't deserve him. My fingers fly over the keyboard as I type.

> *I'm sorry, too. I'll be there soon.*

> **Jinta:** *Ok!! See you soon. Love you so much.*

He loves me. Jinta loves *me*. Despite all my flaws, all my insecurities and my baggage, this man has decided I'm his person. For the first time, those words don't fill me with dread, but with such relief it makes my eyes burn.

I love him, too. I love Jinta Onodera.

He's *my* person. The man who's made me believe in love when all my life, I thought love wasn't real. But it is real. I love Jinta, he loves me, and we're going to be together. I slump over the wheel and break down, laughing in sheer relief until my eyes are damp.

My phone rings, jolting me from my happy meltdown.

Fuck. It's Ren. In all the chaos and heartbreak of this morning, I forgot to check in with her. Guess I'm a shitty friend, as well as a shitty boyfriend. I swipe to answer, keeping my eyes on the road and hands on the wheel.

"Everything okay?" I ask.

She's panting and takes a few seconds to answer me. "No. Remember my stalker? It was Ishida. He broke into my home last night. He and some friends of his made me come with them. I only just managed to get away."

My blood begins to boil. "Did he hurt you?"

"Don't worry about me! Listen, Ishida took some of my blood. I'm worried he took it to Charlie so he could figure out your location. This was hours ago! That's long enough for him to trace your location, jump on a flight to Osaka, and plan an ambush!"

A pit opens up in my stomach, sucking in all the remnants of my joy like a blackhole. Ishida is here in Osaka, and he knows where we are. Foot throttling the gas, I hurtle up the freeway. Charlie's magic is precise, so the tracing spell would lead Ishida right to our hotel. *Fuck!*

"I've gotta go, Ren! Call Jinta, tell him to stay the fuck away from the hotel!"

Fear wraps around my lungs and squeezes, choking me. *Jinta. No. Fuck. No.*

Ishida hates me for what happened to his brother. If he

finds Jinta in the hotel, it won't matter if it's not me in his place. He'll kill Jinta to hurt me the way he was hurt. Jinta could die, and I'm not there to protect him!

Please be okay. Please. I can't. Nothing can happen to Jinta. My love. My mate. My destiny.

I drive fast, and for the first time, I pray to every god I know to protect my mate or let me take his place in death.

Chapter 23

Jinta doesn't answer any of my calls. Or maybe he can't. My heart won't settle, beating out of my chest for my mate. I drive fast, dangerously so, but my preternatural reflexes help me weave in and out of traffic. Ignoring the angry honks of the other drivers, I don't let up until I've crossed into the city.

Jinta's bond flares in my chest. I'm finally close enough to feel him. Pain stabs into my chest, so sudden and fierce I almost lose control of the vehicle. My lungs tighten, and breathing around the pain is impossible. Something's wrong. Jinta is hurt. *Damn it! I'm too late!*

"Raiden? Can you hear me?"

Jinta's voice echoes through our bond, his voice weakened and full of pain.

"I'm sorry..."

"Jinta?" I call back to him through our bond. *"Hang on, okay? I'm almost there!"*

But he doesn't reply. The thread around my pinky finger begins to unravel. Despair grips my heart. I'm losing him. My mate is dying. I slam on the gas and race to the hotel.

The moment the hotel comes into view, I brake and scramble from my car, not even bothering to close the door. My feet pound the pavement. I can't lose him. I can't. I haven't told him I love him. Haven't said how damn sorry I am for being so stupid and scared. There's so much we still have to do together.

I crash through the doors and run, the lobby blurring around me. The elevator takes years to come, stopping on what feels like every damn floor. My wolf snarls beneath my skin, ready to tear the building down until I find Jinta. I give up waiting and run to the nearest staircase, jumping the stairs two at a time. My lungs are on fire, legs screaming when I arrive at our floor. I swipe the card at our door and stumble into the room.

Immediately, blood hits my nose, so thick and pungent it makes me choke.

"Jinta?"

Nobody answers my hoarse cry. I hurtle around the corner and the carpet squelches beneath my shoes. Jinta lies on his side, skin as pale as snow. His shirt is soaked in blood below his chest, drenching the carpet. My entire world stops turning, and my hopes for a future shatter like glass.

My knees hit the floor. A scream lodges in my throat and gets trapped inside. The anguish, fear, and despair is simply too big for any human sounds to express. I crawl to him. His blood soaks into my knees and stains my hands. I lift him off the floor and haul him to my chest. "I'm sorry," I say. "I'm so sorry. Open your eyes. Please. Please don't leave. I'll be better for you, I promise. I'll be the man you deserve."

He's not healing. Why isn't he healing? *Fuck*. I've got to get him out of here, get him help now, or I'll lose him. What do I do? *Fuck!* What can I do? The breath escapes me in ragged pants. My ears ring. I can't breathe. Call Ren. My fingers smear blood on the screen as I call, putting her on speaker phone. I lay Jinta down and grip my hair, tugging. Need to stop the bleeding.

My legs nearly give out as I sprint to the bathroom. I find a first aid kit and rush back to Jinta.

"Raiden? Hello? Hello?"

"Ren!" I yank up Jinta's shirt and flinch. Blood weeps over Jinta's pale skin, and there's so much of it, I can't tell where the wounds are. The stink of silver and aconite makes my throat prickle. "Fuck. Ren. Jinta's hurt. He's really hurt. He's not healing. I... I think he's been poisoned, or—"

"Take a deep breath. If he's been poisoned, he needs a doctor who can treat it, and fast. Hang on." Frantic typing comes from her side of the phone.

I wind bandages tight over Jinta's middle. "Hurry, Ren!" The blood soaks through before I can bandage him.

"Okay, okay! I'm checking our contacts. And... all right! There's a doctor in Osaka." She rattles off the address while I wind an entire roll of bandages around Jinta's stomach. Blood seeps through. I gather him into my arms. This isn't over. I've got to keep my head. Jinta can still be saved. He's going to be okay, and when he recovers, I'm going to kiss him and tell him how much I love him.

We're going to be together, and we're going to be happy for the rest of our lives.

Hoisting Jinta into my arms, I run from the room and take the stairs back down. My heart thunders in my ears, eclipsing every other sound. Heads turn as I hurtle through the lobby. People scream in shock and fright, hurrying out of my path. Back at the car, I carefully set Jinta into the front seat and buckle him in.

Once I'm behind the wheel, I tap in the doctor's address. Blood smears my screen. The tires squeal as I spin the wheel violently and take off down the street. "Jinta, you're going to be okay. I promise. I'm going to get you help, and if you ever do this to me again, I'll—"

A sob chokes me, but I swallow it down. I can't fall apart, not until he's safe. The city lights blur outside the windows. Every time I stop for the light, I check on him. Jinta's head flops to the side, eyes closed, and blood-stained lips parted.

Once we're at the doctor's, I carry Jinta from the car toward the clinic. She meets me at the door, and she and her team take him from me and strap him into a stretcher. They roll him away, and the fate of the man I love is out of my hands. My knees give out, and I collapse into a chair. His blood is drying on my hands, shaking violently in my lap. My head falls back, bumping into the wall.

The nurse asks me questions about Jinta to relay to the doctor. She asks me who he is to me. "My mate," I croak. Hot tears sting my eyes, and I make my teeth ache trying to hold them back. "He's my mate."

I can't give up, not yet. I won't despair, not while there's the slightest chance Jinta can be saved. My mate is a fighter, and he needs me to be strong.

I hang my head between my knees and start to wait.

"...boru? Noboru?"

My eyes fly open. The doctor stands before me in her scrubs. Did I fall asleep? No. I'm exhausted, every bone in my body aching. I must have just zoned out. My throat is bone dry, and my heart is stuck somewhere up there and beating fast.

I scramble to stand. "How is he?" My voice shakes.

The doctor touches my arm. "Please sit down." Her eyes are pinched with sympathy above her surgeon's mask.

She sits beside me when I sink into the chair, knees shaking too badly to support me. "We cleansed the toxin from his body." She speaks softly, like I'm a small child. "Stitched his wounds. However, the poison, his deep wounds, and the silver in his bloodstream had already taken a toll on his body."

I don't understand what she's saying. Did she heal him or not? I try to ask, but the words are caught.

"I'm very sorry but your mate has passed away," she says.

I can't speak. Her words don't make sense. Jinta's not dead. He can't be. We were supposed to talk. I was going to apologize to him, tell him I love him, finally claim him as mine so we could begin our lives together.

"No." It's all I can say, shaking my head. "No, that's not true. That's bullshit." Before she can speak, I'm on my feet. "Where's his room? I'm leaving and taking him with me. We'll go to another doctor who can actually do their job!"

How dare she lie to me? Jinta's not dead. She's full of shit.

"Noboru!" She rushes after me.

I follow the scent of cherry blossoms and blood through the halls. "Jinta?" He doesn't answer. "Jinta!" His scent disappears behind a door. This doctor is a moron. She doesn't know what she's talking about. Jinta isn't dead. He's not.

I throw open the door. "Jin—"

A pungent scent chokes out the sweet aroma of cherry blossoms. One I've smelled many times before. My throat prickles, but I swallow down my nausea. Jinta lies in bed, a white cloth placed over his eyes. My feet won't move. The room is silent. There's no heartbeat. I try to speak, but I have no words. My eyes sting and burn as a violent shudder racks my body.

No. No, he isn't—he can't be—

I make myself move toward his bed. "Jinta. We're leaving. I'm getting you out of here."

When I reach toward the cloth covering his face, my fingers won't move. Come on. I have to move. Get him out of here. Get him help. Sucking in air, I grip the cloth and pull it from his face.

The light has left his eyes. They aren't a sweet chocolate-brown anymore. They're black. Empty. I choke on air. The cloth ripples to the floor as I turn away, covering my eyes as my entire world shatters around me. My pinky finger feels cold as the single thread connecting me to Jinta unravels and crumbles to ash.

I know what it means. But it can't be. It isn't true.

This wasn't supposed to happen. We were supposed to have more time.

My cheeks are wet.

Everything hurts, every breath like glass in my lungs, every pulse of my heart is a stabbing pain.

I stumble to his bedside and fall to my knees. My chest heaves around a great wrenching sob as those empty eyes stare through me. Fingers trembling, I reach out and touch his cheek. The warmth is fading fast from his skin. He was always so warm, like sunshine in my arms.

"I'm so sorry," I croak. I run my fingers through his soft hair. "I'm sorry, okay? I didn't mean it. Any of it. I swear."

I sniff hard and lean in, pressing my lips to his forehead. "I'm here. I'm here. I came back. We can go wherever you want. Japan. America. I don't care. I'll leave the yakuza. Open up a restaurant. We can cook together every day. I'll make you so happy. I promise."

My tears dampen Jinta's pale cheeks, and I wipe them away. I kiss him everywhere, his cheeks, the tip of his sweet nose, and cover his mouth with mine. His lips are cold and unresponsive.

A shudder racks me. I'll never feel him kiss me back. Never hear him say my name. He'll never smile like a ray of sunlight and laugh.

I frame his face in my quaking hands, but I can't see him through my tears. Stroking my thumbs over his cheeks, I kiss him again and again, nuzzling my forehead against his.

"I love you," I whisper, three words I've never said to anyone in my life, three words I'll never say to anyone but him. "I love you so much. You're my destiny. My good fortune. My mate. You're everything to me."

I should have told him. *God*, why didn't I tell him?

My wolf howls a song of anguish as I clamber into bed and pull Jinta into my arms.

I rock him back and forth, burying my face in his neck, and weep for the only man I've ever loved.

CHAPTER 24

Raiden

Nothing hurts when I wake up. Not at first.

Dawn light streams in through the blinds. The world is quiet and still. Jinta lies in my arms, his cheek to my chest, like he's sleeping. It starts in my bones, an ache that goes soul-deep. My lungs tighten, and my chest feels heavy when I look into his lifeless eyes.

What am I going to do without him? There's no point in trying to live when a part of me has been torn from my chest. This whole world can burn down for all I care. All I want is to join him in death. Kissing his forehead, I squeeze my eyes shut as a spasm of pain racks me.

I can't feel Jinta anymore. The bond between us is gone. My wolf has fallen silent, and his presence is barely there. I feel closer to a human than ever before, and I can't imagine I'll be able to shift again. I don't know what happens when a wolf loses his mate, but I'll find out soon enough.

Tears burn my eyes, and I cover Jinta's cold skin with kisses, then bury my nose in his hair. His cherry blossom scent has faded, or maybe I just can't smell him anymore with my wolf so weak. They'll come for Jinta soon to prepare him for burial. I hold him tighter. They'll have to pry him from my cold, dead arms. Or cremate me with him. I'll never get to have him in my arms again, feel him against me. This is all so wrong. We weren't supposed to say goodbye.

A chill creeps over my skin, raising the hair on my arms. A breeze tickles the nape of my neck, but the windows were closed, weren't they?

"I am sorry for your loss." It's a woman's voice. She stands at the foot of the bed, clothed in a red kimono. She's pale and black-haired and has a narrow, foxlike face. She can only be Tamano-no-Mae. I'm not sure why I can see her, but I don't really care.

"Piss off." I focus on brushing Jinta's hair off his forehead. I can't imagine a world where Jinta doesn't exist.

"There's no time to grieve."

I glare at her. "Fuck you. You did nothing to save him!"

"Because there was nothing I could do," she snaps.

"If you hadn't possessed him, none of this shit would have happened!" The hunters wouldn't have targeted us. Ishida wouldn't have gotten pissed and betrayed our group. Or maybe not. Maybe all of this was preordained, but I just need someone, anyone, to lash out at. "Do us both a favor and fuck off! Go burn the world down like you said you would. I don't care."

"Are you done?" She folds her arms and glares at me. "Time is running out! Now, do you want to save your mate or not?"

I can save Jinta? Did I mishear? How is it possible he can be saved when he's lying cold in my arms? No. I can't afford to hope. If I'm let down, I'll never recover.

"If you're playing a trick, kitsune, I swear I'll—"

"You can't feel Jinta, but I can, and furthermore, I can see him! That's why I'm able to communicate with you, because of his bond to you."

My heart skips a beat. "R-Really? Where is he?"

"He's a spirit. You can't see or touch him. But he can see you. He's been sitting beside you all night, sniveling like a pup."

Sorrow chokes me. "Where?"

She waves a hand, motioning to my left. There's no one there. I have no idea if she's telling the truth.

"He—" She sighs like she's embarrassed. "He wants me to pass on a message to you before he leaves."

"Leaves?" Fear grips my heart. "What do you mean?"

"Spirits can only linger so long after death. Once he has gone to Yomi and eaten from the banquet hall, he will be a part of the world of the dead forever and able to wander as a spirit."

"No. He can't. Jinta, don't go. Please, don't go." I wish I could see him. "Is he okay? Is he in pain?" Please let him be at peace...

Tamano is quiet a moment, then she says, "He says he is fine. But he's scared. He doesn't have much time left."

Tears nip my eyes. "Don't be scared. I'll be right here," I whisper to the space beside my left shoulder, wishing I could see him.

Tamano clears her throat and grimaces. "He... he wants to tell you that he's sorry."

Swallowing around the lump in my throat, I say, "Me, too, Sunshine. I'm so sorry.

"He says you're not a disappointment. You're the love of his life. He loves you, and he always will."

I press my lips hard together as they tremble, a tear spilling down my cheek. This pain is like nothing I have ever felt. As I brush a kiss over his forehead, it feels like I'll break apart. "I love you, too. I'm sorry. I'm so sorry." Wiping my eyes, I look at Tamano. "What else? Tell me what else he said!"

Tamano hangs her head. "He's vanished. I can no longer see him. He has passed into the afterlife."

A broken croak escapes me, and I clutch Jinta's body.

"But there is a way we can save him."

My broken heart races in my chest. "Don't lie to me."

"It's not a lie," she insists. "The longer Jinta remains as a spirit, the weaker his connection to the world of the living becomes. You may not feel his bond from your side, but he still feels yours. However, it is decaying. If you want to save him, we must enter Yomi and find him."

Yomi-no-Kuni. The land of the dead. I have no idea what risks there are to entering such a realm, but I don't care. "I'll do it," I say without hesitation. There's nothing I won't do if it means bringing Jinta back to me.

She smiles at my enthusiasm. "You remind me of my Konoe. We were as close as you and Jinta. We must act swiftly. Bring his body."

"Where are we going?" I have no idea where the entrance to this spirit world might be.

"To Yomotsu Hirasaka, the boundary between our world and the land of the dead. There is said to be an entrance in Shimane Prefecture. But to open the way, you will need the help of someone who can communicate with the dead."

"A necromancer. I can have Ren look for one while we drive there." But first, I have to get Jinta out of the hospital without drawing any attention to myself. An idea comes to me. I gently lay Jinta down, then kiss his cold hand. "I'll be back soon." I don't care if he can't hear me now. His spirit is still out there, and I won't rest until I've brought him home to me.

I've got to clear the building. If I can find a fire alarm,

that would give me the perfect distraction. I search the halls until I finally spot one. Looking both ways, I wait for a nurse to round the corner, clipboard in her hand. I break the plastic seal and pull. The alarm blares through the hallway as I jog back to Jinta's room. On my way back, I grab a wheelchair and roll it toward his room.

Once inside, I carefully lift Jinta from the bed and position him in the wheelchair. I wince when his head flops, his chin touching his chest. I yank the sheet off his bed and drape it over his lap. People rush past our room, calling out to evacuate the building. I take in a breath to calm myself, hoping nobody tries to stop us. Then, I roll Jinta along the hallway, keeping a distance from staff, though they all seem preoccupied.

I don't let myself breathe until we've made it outside, and then I rush toward the car. I get Jinta into the passenger seat, then climb in beside him and start up the car. We leave the clinic behind, and at the next light, I quickly tap in our route. Shimane Prefecture is four hours away by car in the Chugoku region of Honshu.

Hang on, Jinta.

I'm bringing you home. I promise.

"I've reached out to a necromancer in the region," Ren says

through my phone. "She'll meet you at Iya Shrine for the ritual."

I blow out a relieved breath, adjusting my route in the GPS. "Thanks." It's really happening. Soon, I'll be reunited with Jinta.

"Of course. Are you okay?" she asks softly.

I don't know how I can answer that question when my mate is dead in the seat beside me, his hand ice-cold in mine. A part of me has died with him and won't ever be whole until we're together again. "I'll feel better when I see him again."

"Promise you'll come back in one piece. Oh! And take pictures."

I scoff. "Not happening."

"And hurry back." Her voice takes on an urgent note. "There's something else," Ren adds, and there's an intensity to her voice that surprises me.

"What?"

"Don't freak out, but… one of Takada's own men came to us."

I grip the wheel tight. "Did you kill him?"

"No."

"Why not?" I growl, hoping she has a damn good reason.

"Because it was Hirano Kasamatsu. Saito Takada's second. He had good information on Takada. Information we can use to bring him down for good. I'll tell you more when you're home."

I wish I cared, but until I get Jinta back, nothing else matters. "Stay safe. Keep everyone on their toes. I'll be back tonight or early tomorrow. With Jinta."

Or I won't come back at all.

I park the car at the entrance to Iya Shrine. The woods around me are quiet and serene, my footsteps crunching over pebbles as I open Jinta's door. "Come on, Sunshine." I carefully lift him into my arms, adjusting him so his head rests on my shoulder. I kiss his cold forehead. "I'm almost there. Wait for me."

With my mate in my arms, I set off through the woods. When I pass beneath a wooden gate, I'm heading in the right direction. As my foot touches the ground beyond the gate, a strange sensation prickles up my spine, and my stomach swoops, like I've missed a step on the stairs. Magic hangs like a mist in the air, invisible to the eye, but undeniable. The air grows colder, the woods darker as the tree branches obscure the sunlight.

The Iya Shrine is dedicated to the goddess Izanami, creator of the world. A woman stands before the shrine, head bowed and hands clasped. She turns toward me, face covered by a surgeon's mask. Her hair is stained gray, her eyes lined. "Let us begin," she says and motions toward the shrine. "Place him upon the altar."

Right to business. Good. Heart thumping, I lower Jinta onto the altar.

"Hold his hand tightly. Do not let go, or you will be lost."

I lace my fingers with Jinta's and squeeze, closing my eyes tightly.

The necromancer begins to chant in low, guttural tones as the wind kicks up, growing cold. A flash of light makes me wince even through my closed eyes. A portal yawns wide beyond the altar. Mist pours from it along with a salty aroma, like we're near the ocean. The light gets brighter, threatening to blind me.

I clutch Jinta's hand and refuse to let go, even as the portal swallows us whole.

CHAPTER 25

Jinta

The banquet is in full swing around me as spirits dine with Izanami herself.

A sea breeze curls into the temple, and from my seat by the window, I have views of the endless horizon and the waves as they crash against the rocky face of the cliff far below. It's beautiful here, but the urge to weep has left a lump in my throat for hours now that comes and goes.

The goddess herself welcomed me to the land of Yomi. It had been, well, flustering. I bowed so low I hurt my back, face hot. She'd invited me to dine but warned me that once I ate in her temple, I would never be able to return to the world of the living. I would pass on to whatever realm awaits me after this one. Paradise, maybe? Or I could refuse the food and linger on as a spirit.

I don't know what would be worse; passing on and never seeing Raiden again, or being able to see him but unable to touch him and speak with him. It tormented me to see him cry over my lifeless body; to hear him finally tell me he loves me without being able to say it back and hold him in my arms.

Lips quivering, I touch the severed thread around my finger. It's been slowly unraveling into nothing but strings. I'm losing my connection to him by the minute. This wasn't supposed to happen. That stupid, *stupid* fight should never have been our last conversation. It isn't fair.

Alone by the window, I watch as the spirits rise from the banquet table, and the goddess leads them to a door at the end of the temple. As she slides the doors open, the twittering of birds echo from beyond, and golden rays of sun shine upon the tatami mats. The spirits are always overjoyed at whatever lies beyond the door and pass through without hesitation, some even crying out the names of what I assume are loved ones.

So, the afterlife does exist. Or at least, the Shinto interpretation of the afterlife. I wonder if different religions have something similar to Yomi. I've successfully unraveled one of life's biggest questions. Too bad I'm too bitter and heartbroken to care. Maybe if Raiden and I got to grow old and gray together, I would be happier to be here.

Izanami approaches me and offers a smile. Black hair

frames her round, pale face, and the hems of her white robes trail over the tatami. "Waiting for someone?" she asks.

"Yes. I don't want to go without him." No matter how long it takes, I'll wait for Raiden to join me.

"Your loyalty and devotion are beautiful. You're welcome to wait for him beyond the door, as well."

"Will I... will I know when he's here if I go through?" My eyes sting.

"Of course."

At a loss, I turn away and gaze out over the ocean to hide the tears in my eyes. The ground beneath me rumbles, and the temple begins to shake. The spirits cry out in alarm, and plates of food spill onto the floor. The thread around my finger begins to levitate, pulling taut toward the front doors.

My heart soars as a familiar presence glows warm in my chest, the dormant bond bursting to life like flowers in spring. I'm on my feet, staring spellbound at the doors as the red string of fate around my finger glows.

The doors burst open, and Raiden fills the doorway. His eyes are wide and wild, chest rising and falling fast. Joy surges through me, lifting my heart and bringing tears to my eyes. He's here. Somehow, Raiden is here, and as our eyes meet, his yuzu scent sweet in the air, I run to him.

Raiden meets me halfway, arms flying around my shoulders. He pulls me in close, wrapping me in the warmth and strength of his arms. A shudder racks his body, the salty scent of his tears stings my nose. "Jinta," he whispers my name like a prayer again and again.

My own tears course down my face, and I throw my arms around him, clutching him to me. "I never thought I'd see you again," I confess, finally allowing myself to admit a truth too terrible to face alone.

"I know," he whispers, framing my face in his big hands. Tears cling to his eyelashes, and his face is wet. I've never seen him so vulnerable.

A sob escapes me. "You're not a disappointment. You're not. I don't know why I said that. I'm so sorry."

Raiden wipes away my tears with the gentle caress of his thumbs over my cheeks. "I was a coward, and I was being selfish. You're right. I was acting just like my father. I'm sorry I pushed you away. I'm sorry I hurt you. I'm done letting the bullshit from my past come between us. I swear to you, Jinta, I'm going to spend every day of my life being the man you deserve. I love you, my sunshine, my mate, my love."

I can't stop the flow of my tears. I was so afraid I'd never hear him say those words to my face... that I'd never be able to say them back. "I love you, too."

Raiden pulls me in close, capturing my lips with his. I curl my trembling fingers in his hair and lose myself in his warmth and scent. "I love you," Raiden whispers as he kisses each of my eyelids. "Love you." He touches his lips to each of my cheeks. "Love you." He caresses my forehead with his lips, then swoops back down to claim my mouth again.

The thread around my finger vibrates, making me look down. The thread reaches toward Raiden and wraps around his finger, connecting us, making our souls one. Raiden holds my hand tight as he kisses each of my fingers, including my pinky, right over the red thread.

"How can you be here?" I ask, voice shaking. "You aren't... dead too, are you?" The thought is too terrible to dwell on.

Raiden doesn't answer right away, raining kisses over my neck and up to my jaw. "No, but we don't have a lot of time. I've got a portal waiting for us."

"Well, I was hoping for a horse-drawn carriage, but I suppose a portal will do."

He chuckles low in his throat and leans his forehead to mine. "I'll remember that for our bonding ceremony." Clearing his throat, Raiden averts his gaze, then takes in a deep breath. When his eyes find mine again, they're bright with determination. "Jinta, the only way you can leave with me is if I claim you as my mate. You're a spirit now, but I'm mortal, and that connection will make it possible for you to return. This wasn't how I wanted to do things, but—"

I cradle his face. "I don't care. I never thought I'd see you again. Claim me."

Raiden's throat bobs when he swallows, eyes flooding with emotion. Cupping my cheek, he leans in for a kiss so sweet and reverent, my own eyes sting with tears. I'm breathless when Raiden pulls away, but he doesn't stop. He brushes his lips over my jaw to my chin. Closing my eyes, I tip my head back, savoring the caress of his soft, warm lips as they flutter over my pulse point and lower to the spot between my neck and shoulder.

Raiden takes my hand and squeezes. "Love you now and forever," he whispers, and he bites down, fangs sharp.

I gasp in pain, but the pain is washed away as pleasure and warmth rush through me from head to toe. The thread tingles around my finger and his, fluttering until it forms an infinity symbol between us. I'm not knowledgeable enough in the paranormal world to quite understand what's happening, but I do know one thing.

I'm his, and he's mine. Now, forever, and on into eternity. That's all that matters to me.

Raiden lifts his face from my neck. The wound heals into a scar in the perfect shape of his fangs, marking me as his. His lips tremble when he gazes into my eyes. "There's no one else I want but you," he whispers.

"I know. I feel the same." Closing my eyes, I lean in for a kiss so sweet, it feels like my heart has grown wings.

"Cheers!" a chorus of voices erupts.

And that's when I remember we have an entire audience watching us. Raiden glares at them, growling low. I chuckle and pull him back down for a kiss. "You can't kill them, they're already dead."

"Too bad," he mutters. "That spirit was checking out your ass."

"Was not."

Someone clears their throat. Izanami has come up beside us. "Congratulations," she says.

Raiden bows low. "Goddess. Thank you for looking after my mate."

"It's been my pleasure. But you shouldn't linger. The portal is getting smaller. Ah! There's a face I haven't seen in some time." She spins toward Tamano, who has just walked in.

The kitsune smirks at us. "Done embarrassing yourselves?"

I'm surprised by how happy I am to see her. "Nice to see you, too."

"Will you be passing through?" Izanami asks after she and Tamano have bowed in greeting.

Tamano doesn't answer right away, gazing at the doors to the realm beyond with longing plain in her eyes. "I..."

The doors open. "Tamano?" a voice cries, and then a man rushes through the doors. He's garbed in regal robes.

Tamano gasps. "Konoe! My beloved!" Her voice shakes with emotion.

They run to each other, and Konoe holds her tight for a long moment. I turn away to give them some privacy. I suppose Tamano will want to go with him, but she can't. I sigh. "It's too bad she can't stay." She's still bound to me thanks to the curse.

The edge of Raiden's mouth twitches for some reason. "She could."

"How?"

Joy like nothing I've seen before lights up his face. "You're cured, Jinta."

I blink at him, honestly dazzled. "What?"

Barking a laugh, he gently shakes my shoulders. "You're cured! My father told me that only a fated mate's bonding bite could break the curse. It's how he was able to escape Namikawa."

Is that true? There is a part of me that feels lighter than I have in a while. "Are you sure?"

"He's right, Jinta." Tamano walks over, hand in hand with Konoe. "The curse lifted the moment he claimed you."

I laugh, hardly able to believe it. "This is perfect! So, you're free, too."

"I am, at last. This is Konoe."

He bows. "It's a pleasure. Thank you for reuniting me with Tamano. We can finally be together again."

Tamano frowns. "My love, I'm going to stay with them a little while longer."

"You don't have to!" I insist. She was just reunited with her lover. She shouldn't have to leave him again.

"Of course I don't have to." She huffs. "As if you could make me do something I don't wish to do. I want to stay until I am sure you are both safe. You two are awfully sweet together, and very entertaining to be around. As soon as the Takada-kai and the Blades are defeated, I will return, Konoe. I promise."

He smiles, though it's bittersweet. "Come back to me soon." He pulls her close for a kiss.

Raiden wraps an arm around my shoulders. "Let's get back to the portal. Last thing I want is to be stuck in here watching them make out for the rest of my eternal life."

Laughing, I take his hand, and together, we walk back toward the light of the portal, toward our future together.

The sudden kick of my heart jerks me awake. I open my eyes to blue skies above me. My lungs burn with the need to breathe and expand rapidly as I suck in a greedy gulp of sweet air. Warmth spreads throughout my body as my blood starts pumping. I'm... I'm *alive.*

"Jinta? You okay?" Raiden asks, but I don't answer right away, sitting up and taking in grateful breaths. As a spirit, I didn't need to breathe, and I had no heartbeat. I was alive in a sense, but not. Closing my eyes, I savor the earth beneath my hands, sun-warmed soil and soft grass.

"I'm fine," I assure Raiden. "Just... taking it all in."

Raiden sits beside me and takes my hand, threading his fingers through mine. The bond between us sings with pulses of relief and joy and love. Are those his feelings or mine? Maybe both? Emotion chokes me, and I fall into his arms and hold him tight.

"I'm alive," I whisper, needing to affirm this to myself. I'm really here. I'm with the man I love. We can still create a future together.

Gentle lips brush over my forehead. "Yeah, Sunshine. It worked. Not even death can keep you from me."

My body shudders, and I feel like I'll burst with the cascade of joyous emotion flowing through me. "You've set the bar so high, baby. I mean, you literally followed me into the afterlife to get me back. How am I ever going to top that?" A laugh escapes me as I sniffle, rubbing my cheek against his chest.

Raiden cups my chin and lifts my face. "Cook meals with me every day. Fall asleep next to me every night. Wake up with me every morning. That'll be good enough."

My face hurts from how hard I'm smiling. "Sounds like a proposal to me. Do werewolves get married?"

Raiden shrugs. "Not really. Mating bites are the equivalent of marriage to us. Marriage, it's just paperwork and symbolism to us. But mating bites bind us together for life, body and soul. When you die, I will, too. We'll be together for life."

A delighted shiver runs through me. I can't imagine anything better.

"That made you happy."

I flush. "How can you tell?"

Raiden rubs his chest. "I bit you, bonded you to me. I can feel everything you feel."

"Really? Everything?"

"Yeah. Your happiness. Sadness. Pleasure." He nips my ear. "It'll all be doubled for me. I'll never have to ask *what's wrong*. I'll know and be able to look after you."

I frown. "But I can't feel that from you."

"Because our bond is incomplete. You still need to bite me."

"Oh!" I like that idea. Very much. I'd like to bite him as soon as possible. "I want to claim you, too. But not here. Somewhere private and more romantic."

Lust darkens Raiden's eyes. "That can be arranged."

"I'd still like a ceremony after we're bonded, though."

Raiden chuckles and kisses my forehead. "Sure thing." With his hands in mine, Raiden helps me stand. "We better get back to Tokyo as soon as possible."

Oh. I guess that means I won't be able to claim him yet. The thought of returning to all our problems kills the fluttery feelings inside me. We still have to face Takada and the hunters. We'll need a plan. I wait for Raiden by the gate while he pays the necromancer for her services, and then he joins me as we walk back to the car together.

"Where to?" I ask.

"The airport. We can't afford to waste any time." He meets my gaze and smiles knowingly. "But don't worry, you'll have plenty of time to claim me for yourself." He waggles a brow, and my blood heats with anticipation.

"Really? How?"

"A private jet?" I squawk, jaw falling open as Raiden walks me down the tarmac toward the jet awaiting us.

"I'm sick and tired of being crammed into overpacked planes. This way, we'll have the whole plane to ourselves, and I can feel you up without getting kicked off the flight." He slips his hand down my back and gives my ass a pat.

Now, I'm actually excited about the trip back rather than dreading it. At least we'll have time to ourselves up in the clouds before we have to face all our problems back in Tokyo. The interior of the jet is beautiful and spacious, with sleek leather furniture, a wall-mounted television, a dining area, and a queen-sized bed covered with silky sheets.

We take our seats while the jet ascends into the clouds. A cheerful attendant offers us food and drink, though Raiden declines. Being dead really works up an appetite, so I order some food and sit on the sofa with Raiden. He drapes an arm over my shoulders and watches some movie while I eat and enjoy his presence.

"Wow. This is amazing," I say, sighing like a sap as I nuzzle into his side.

He rests his cheek against my hair. We've left our worries and cares far below us. It feels like we're in our own little world, far away from anyone who can hurt us. Raiden nuzzles his nose against my ear. "Hey, Jinta."

"Hmm?" I take his hand and squeeze.

Raiden's breath warms my ear when he whispers, "I'm ready. I want you to claim me."

My heart swoops as I look at him, his whiskey-brown eyes a deep, molten hue. "I'd love that," I rasp, voice gravelly with want.

The warmth of Raiden's hand glides up my thigh. "I mean, in every way."

The breath gets stuck in my throat. Does he mean...

Raiden drags his lips down my jaw and stops inches from my mouth. "I want you inside me while you claim me as yours."

I swallow as I start to harden, my heart racing fast. "Are you sure?" My eyes close as he caresses his mouth against mine in a barely-there kiss.

"Never been so sure." His breath scorches my lips, his scent deepening with the same desire coursing through me. "I want that with you."

I'm so hard, I can barely think, but I know he's been

hurt before. "O-okay. But if we try it and you don't like it, or if it brings up anything painful for you, you need to let me know. I won't be upset. Okay?"

Raiden blinks fast when he meets my gaze. "Y-yeah. I know."

"Are you okay?" I run my fingers over his cheek.

"Yeah. Yeah, just... nobody I've been with has ever put me first. You know?"

Leaning in, I deepen our kiss, nipping his lower lip. "You'll always come first, and you're going to be my last. There's never going to be anyone else for me but you. But I've never topped before."

"Really?"

"It sounded overwhelming." I'd worried I wouldn't be able to make the other person feel good, so I'd preferred to bottom.

Raiden frowns. "We don't have to if—"

"I do," I insist. "But just... tell me if you don't like something I'm doing, let me know what you want, what you like. Okay?"

Raiden's lips tremble against mine. "Got it." Then, I'm hoisted off my feet and thrown over his shoulder. My squawk of surprise turns to laughter.

"Shouldn't I be the one doing this?" I ask, squirming over his shoulder. "You know, since I'm going to ravish you."

Raiden snorts. "Yeah, I'd like to see you try to carry me."

Okay, he has a point.

Raiden grabs his bag off the floor and shoulders open the bedroom door.

"Do not throw me!" I yelp, but of course he does. I howl laughter as I crash into the soft sheets. Raiden's grinning wide and bright as he tosses a bottle of lube onto the bed beside me, then peels off his shirt and reveals all his beautiful tattoos. I'm going to kiss every single one of them. Kicking off his shoes, Raiden steps onto the bed and crawls over my body.

I need him. Now.

Taking his face in my hands, I haul him down to me, moaning as our lips collide in an explosion of passion and want. Raiden kisses me with such intensity it makes my mouth tingle, sucking on my lip, nipping, then swiping his tongue over my swollen lips. I let him in, bucking my hips up against him as our tongues tangle. Kissing him always feels so good, and having him so close makes my head spin from longing.

This man just went to the afterlife and back for me so we could be together. I have got to show him how much it means to me that we can be together. Hooking my legs around his waist, I arch against him, and Raiden lets himself be rolled onto his back. We're panting as I break the kiss. A hurricane of emotion whirls through me at the sight of this powerful, beautiful man on his back beneath me, trusting me with his pleasure and to give him what he needs. Awe and love take me by storm.

"What?" Raiden's throat jumps when he swallows.

"I love you," I tell him, and it doesn't feel like enough. What I feel for him is so much more than those three words can ever hope to express. So I'm going to show him how I feel by worshipping this gorgeous man from head to toe.

Raiden smiles, soft and beautiful. "I know."

My throat aches, my eyes stinging with sudden feeling. Leaning down, I capture his lips with mine, dipping my tongue inside to deepen our kiss, tongues gliding together. I let my hands wander down his powerful body, squeezing his thick pecs and rolling his nipples between my fingers until they harden.

When he moans against my mouth, I break our kiss and chart a course down his body with my lips. The spot between his neck and shoulder radiates a scent so sweet and tempting it makes my fangs sharpen. I want to bite him here and now, make him mine forever, but not yet. I kiss that sweetly scented spot, heart racing when he arches beneath me. His hard cock ruts against mine, making my stomach muscles clench with need, my hips flexing for more pressure.

I drag my tongue over warm, tattooed skin and flick his hard nipple, then worry it with my teeth until he groans beneath me and grabs at the sheets. "Fuck." He's panting. "Feels good. That's good, Sunshine."

My stomach swoops from knowing I've pleased him,

kissing and licking my way down his taut abs. His cock strains the front of his jeans, and he growls when I palm him through the material. "Get these off me," Raiden pants. "Wanna feel your hand around my cock."

His wish is my command. I'm grateful he's communicating so I know exactly what he wants. I've never topped before, but so far, I'm loving every second of it. I yank his pants and boxers down, peeling them over his knees, and he kicks them the rest of the way off. My mouth waters as his thick cock curls against his abdomen, the head already shiny with precum.

I open the lube and coat my fingers, waiting a moment to let the slick warm, then take him in hand. He feels so good in my hand, so hot and hard. Raiden arches beneath me, lips parting around a groan as I start to stroke.

"Fuck, Jinta. That's good. Just like that." Raiden bucks his hips, fucking into my fist. Pulling off, I kiss my way down his hard length. When I suck on each of his balls, Raiden grabs my hair, pulling. "Y-you doing what I think you're doing?"

Grinning, I blow a puff of air against his hole. "Mayyybe..."

A quiet curse escapes him. "Damn tease. Gonna make me beg?"

I kiss his ass cheek, then introduce my teeth. "If you wouldn't mind."

"Fuck." I can almost hear his molars grinding together.

I start off slow, teasing him with my hot breath against his sensitive skin, giving him the faintest kiss of my tongue. Raiden squirms above me, breath getting shorter as the seconds drag into nearly a minute.

"Damn it, Jinta!" Raiden suddenly says. "Do it. Eat my hole. Make me nice and sloppy for your cock."

My dick jerks at his filthy words. "With pleasure."

I dive in, circling his puckered skin with the tip of my tongue. Raiden's body jerks, fingers tugging on my hair. A slew of curses tumble from his lips as I slip my tongue inside him. It's an entirely new experience for me. I know what I like, I just hope he likes it, too. Sliding my hand up, I tug on his cock while I work my tongue in and out.

Breathy sounds escape Raiden, hips rolling to take my tongue deeper while he bunches the sheets in his fists. I've never heard such soft, sweet sounds from him. Knowing this strong, powerful man is letting me take control gives me a high I've never felt before.

"J-Jinta. Shit..." Raiden tangles his fingers in my hair. "More. Don't stop."

I alternate between fucking him with my tongue and toying with his rim, flicking, licking and sucking until he's drenched with my spit. My other hand cups his balls, squeezing gently and making him pant and curse. They're nice and heavy already. I want so badly to let my fingers go lower, but I need to make sure he's okay with that first. "Want my fingers inside you?"

Raiden tenses beneath me, swiping his tongue over his lips. "Y-yeah, but... just go slow."

Leaning down, I kiss him. "Of course."

I'm determined to make this good for him. Applying more lube to my fingers, I go lower until my finger caresses his puckered entrance. Raiden's breath hitches, and he clenches against my finger. "Go on. Wanna feel you inside me."

"Okay. Breathe. Relax for me, baby."

My heart racing, I let the tip of my finger sink inside him. I bask in how perfect he feels, his walls so soft around my finger. "You feel so good. Fuck, baby."

Raiden gazes up at me, eyes dark as he groans quietly. "Can't wait to see how you react while you're fucking my hole."

I might just blow the second I'm inside him. If he's this hot, this soft around my finger... fuck, he'll feel so good squeezing my cock. "More?" I crook my finger inside him, and his back arches off the mattress.

"Yeah. Yeah, give me more."

I slide my finger deeper into his body, biting my lip as I start to push in and out. Raiden's chest hitches, hips jerking with every curl of my finger inside him. "Want another?" I ask, and when he nods, I press another slick finger against his hole. "Relax for me." Raiden breathes for me, and his body loosens up enough so that my finger slips easily inside.

Working my finger in and out, I lean down and suck on the head of his cock, lapping up the stream of precum dribbling down his length.

"Fuuuck," Raiden says, legs thrashing on the sheets as I stretch him wider. Slowly, I work him open on my fingers, pumping them in and out, curling them against his velvety walls. With his permission I add a third, and his face pinches with discomfort, but he says, "Don't stop. Keep going." To distract him from the discomfort, I take his cock in hand and stroke while I fuck him with my fingers, and slowly, his body relaxes beneath me.

When I find his prostate and start to rub, he squirms. "F-feels like I have to take a leak."

I chuckle. "That will fade, I promise."

As I massage his prostate and alternate between stroking and sucking his cock, Raiden's breathing quickens, gasps spilling from his lips as his toes flex, and he grabs at the sheets. My own cock pulses and throbs with longing.

"Close," Raiden croaks. "I'm close. Fuck. Feels so good."

"Yeah?" I pant, stretching him on my fingers. "Want me inside you?"

He nods frantically. "Yeah. Want your cock. Fuck me, Jinta. Claim me. Now."

The sound I make is downright feral. "Lift your hips." When he obeys, I push a pillow beneath his ass. His legs are already up over my shoulders as I shuffle closer on my knees. His hole is exposed to me, leaking lube and twitching in anticipation.

I slick up my cock until it's slippery with lube, then add an extra dollop to his hole, pushing it in with my fingers. It's probably excessive, but I need to make sure this is as smooth as possible. "Ready?"

He groans impatiently, nodding.

I don't need telling twice. Holding my breath, I sink slowly into the perfect heat of his body. He bears down on me, and even after all that prep, there's some resistance at first. I keep my eyes on his dark, lidded gaze, watching for any signs of discomfort. When I breach him, Raiden's lips part, and he grabs my elbows hard. I fist the sheets, urging myself to take things slow as his body welcomes me in.

"You... you feel so amazing," I whisper. Even though it's just the head of my cock inside, it feels incredible. "Are you okay?" I brush my knuckles over his cheek, and he nuzzles into the touch.

"Y-yeah. Fuck. You feel huge."

I chuckle. "That's good?"

He gives his hips an experimental rock, and we both moan as I slide in deeper. The glide into his body is effortless and so slick. "So good." He runs his hands up my arms and twines them around my shoulders. "More."

Biting my lip hard, I make myself stop. My balls are aching, and he feels so good around my cock. "N-need to go slow, or I'll..."

He nods frantically. "Okay. Okay, just... fuck. I need—"

"I know," I grit out, panting. "I'll fuck you, baby. Give you what you need. Just... just let me—" I bottom out inside him. The noises we make are both feral as my hips smack his ass. Raiden pants hard beneath me, his walls clenching around me. I clamp my lower lip between my teeth, *begging* myself not to cum, not yet. I slow my breathing and wait for my body to settle, stroking his cock to keep him satisfied.

Slowly, I start to move inside the hot grip of his body in short, gentle motions. Raiden's cries get louder, making my cock throb inside him. When he starts to move his hips, meeting me thrust for thrust, I have to snarl out, "C-can't hold back if you do that, baby."

Mischief curls his mouth. "Don't hold back. Fuck me hard. Wanna see you let go for me."

Oh, fuck. My self-control snaps, and I let loose, crying out as I slam inside. I pull out almost all the way, leaving only the tip inside, then fill him up again and again. With every slap of his hips, pleasure sparks up and down my cock.

"Fuck, yes!" Raiden shouts beneath me, tearing at the sheets. The mattress creaks beneath us, dipping beneath our weight. He claws at my hair and tugs me down. Our mouths crash together, and I claim his mouth while I claim his body, sharing desperate moans.

Nothing has ever felt as good as he does. I feel like a god

when I'm inside him, untouchable and safe as his arms wrap around me. A snarl escapes me as his claws bite into my shoulders, the pain only fueling my pleasure. I feel feral, unhinged, as we fuck like animals. I never want to leave his body. He's mine. My mate. My love. Mine to cherish and fuck and care for.

Something swells at the base of my cock, and I realize what it is. I'm going to knot him. I've never done this before, but I should have thought about it. I'm a shifter now, and I'm toping. My instinct screams at me to fill him with my cum and knot him to me. But will he let me? "Baby, fuck, I'm going to knot! Can I?" I have seconds. In my panic, I try to pull out, but Raiden locks his legs around my hips and clenches his ass hard around my swelling cock.

"Don't you dare stop," Raiden growls. "Knot my ass, then put your teeth in me and make me yours."

I spit out a curse as I let go, fucking him into the mattress. The harsh slap of my hips meeting his ass fills the room, the bed quaking beneath us from my frenzied movements. If he wasn't moaning beneath me, I'd worry I was hurting him. My orgasm barrels down my spine. Tightening my balls. Making my cock buck inside him. I'm so close. Need to cum. Need to claim him as mine and mine alone.

When my knot locks us together, Raiden cries out beneath me. My entire body tenses up, his name escaping me in a howl as I start to cum inside him in spurts that feel like they'll never end. When Raiden's head falls back and he bares his neck to me, I don't think.

My fangs pierce his skin, his blood citrusy sweet on my tongue, and it's like a dam breaks inside me. All of Raiden's passion, his love, and his pleasure rushes through me, prolonging the intensity of my orgasm and taking me to new heights. I fuck him through my orgasm until his ass spasms around me and his cum splashes against my stomach. My mind goes blank, vision whiting out as the ecstasy of his own release surges through me, and I cum again with him.

The aftershocks feel like they last hours after I've collapsed into his arms. We hold each other close as the sweat cools on our bodies, shivering and gasping between slow, tender kisses. His bliss flows through me in a feedback loop of contentment and tender feeling that passes from him to me and right back to him.

Tears sting my eyes, and a sob shakes my body. I never knew it was possible to connect so deeply with someone. We're connected now in body and soul. Raiden soothes me with gentle strokes up and down my back.

"Y-you feel that, too, don't you?" He must, but I want to hear it.

Raiden presses a lingering kiss to my cheek. "Yeah. I do. It's amazing." His own voice is thick, his eyes bright with emotion when I look down at him. He swallows hard. "I... I never knew it would be like this. How good it would feel.

It's... *right*. You, me, us. I'm sorry I made you wait. Sorry I was so scared and—"

Lying down, I kiss away the tears that fall. "Don't. Baby, don't. I'm here, we both are, and nothing's coming between us. Not ever."

Wiping his eyes, Raiden's face relaxes in a wobbly smile. "Damn right. From now on, it's going to be you and me, and fuck everything else."

His determination rushes through our bond. We're going to take on the world, and this time, we'll win.

I claim his mouth with mine and kiss the man I love until we're both breathless.

Nothing is parting me from my mate.

Not even death itself.

CHAPTER 26

I could watch Jinta fuck me for hours.

As much as I love having him beneath me, there's something so hot about how feral he looks as he's pounding into me. And the way he makes me feel? It's unlike anything else. Sex has never been so intense before, especially now that we're bonded.

Every time he bucks up into my body, his own pleasure surges through me, enhancing my own as I ride his cock hard and fast. Jinta digs his hands into my ass hard enough to bruise, head thrown back in ecstasy as he pounds my ass with the speed and force of a damn jackhammer. I never knew my mate could move like this. I've been seriously sleeping on his talent.

"Fuuuck, Jinta!" His name is a snarl from my lips as his cock nails my prostate again and again. Precum weeps down my cock, puddling on the tight muscles of Jinta's stomach. I thought I'd feel vulnerable bottoming. Instead, I feel like a damn king as Jinta pants through clenched teeth.

"So close. Gonna cum. Hurry."

I slam my hips down, burying him completely inside me, and clench my ass around him. "Hurry, what?"

"W-want you to finish first."

A grin lifts my lips. "Oh, yeah? We'll see about that." Now I'm determined to make *him* blow before I do. Problem is, my orgasm is tingling in my balls, ready to erupt. I pinch just below the head of my dick—hard enough I grit my teeth. Then, I double down, fucking myself on Jinta's cock for all I'm worth, making sure to clench around him.

"Not fair," Jinta moans, slapping my ass.

"Want me to stop?" I smirk at him.

"No! No, don't stop." He looks so beautiful with his sweat-slick hair stuck to his forehead, pale cheeks flushed, eyes black with lust. My cock throbs despite my own efforts.

"Shit, Sunshine. Gonna cum just watching you. You look so hot fucking my ass."

Jinta shushes me, clenching his jaw tight. "Stop. Gonna... gonna cum if you say stuff like that."

Fuck, it's so hot seeing him try to fight off his release.

I roll my hips, bouncing on him at a pace that has my eyes rolling back. "Love the way you feel inside me. So close. Haven't even stroked myself, but you're gonna make me cum all over you completely untouched. You want that? Want me to cum on your cock?"

"Raiden," Jinta whines my name, brows pinched, his hips slamming against my ass. His knot begins to swell, stretching me so perfectly.

"Cum for me, Sunshine. Fill me up. Want your knot in my tight ass as you breed my hole."

Jinta cums like a damn geyser inside me, screaming hoarsely as he fucks me through his orgasm. Just the sight of him as he loses himself in pleasure tips me over the edge, and I cum so hard it feels like my soul leaves my body. I crash down into his arms, and we recuperate together, clutching each other close. I roll us onto our sides, wincing as his knot tugs at me and kiss his sweaty forehead. I've never felt so close to another person except when I'm with him, basking in the afterglow of the pleasure we shared.

"I wish we could stay up here forever," Jinta whispers, breath warm against my chest.

"Me, too," I confess. I lift my head and peer out the window. "We should be landing soon." Jinta groans. I know how he's feeling. Literally. His fear floods our bond. "Hey." I rub his arms, making him look up at me. "We're going to be okay. We've got the kitsune under control this time. You won't be a threat to the pack. You can use that giant form of yours to help us this time."

He nods, though that uncertain furrow to his brow remains. I try and smooth it out with my thumb.

"What are we going to do? We need a plan."

I shrug. "Drive into his territory, tear up his clubs and provoke him into attacking us, kill them all, then go home."

Jinta scoffs, fondness brightening his sweet face. "Brilliant. Except for the fact that they outnumber us."

I grin and pat his hip.

"What?"

"You and the kitsune are the ace up our sleeve that we need to win. Well, along with a little something else." Excitement bubbles up in me. "Ren told me one of Takada's own guys, Hirano Kasamatsu, has dirt on him. Ren thinks it's enough to bring him down."

Jinta's mouth pops open in surprise. "Really? What is it?"

I kiss his cheek. "Guess we'll find out once we're home."

That we will, and maybe it's all the amazing sex or having my mate back, but I'm feeling optimistic about the future.

Before we land in Tokyo, I've already arranged a meeting

with my pack. Apparently, Ren had also reached out to the bosses of different wards and invited them to the meeting. Whatever dirt Hirano has on Takada must be huge if all of Tokyo's yakuza bosses are getting involved. A mixture of nerves and excitement tingles in my stomach when Ren picks us up from the airport and drives us into the city.

Since Namikawa's traditional home in the suburbs is so big, that's where we're meeting. The sun is setting by the time we arrive at Namikawa's home. I take Jinta's hand and don't let go until we're outside the door where the bosses have gathered. I take in a breath and give Jinta's hand a squeeze. "Let's do this."

"Yup," Jinta says, offering a smile that soothes some of my nerves.

Whatever happens in this room, I have a feeling it will be the end for Saito Takada.

I slide open the doors.

The most powerful and influential bosses of Tokyo have gathered around Namikawa's big table. The sliding doors are open to let the evening breeze curl in, jingling the wind chime hanging from the eaves of the house. All rise and bow, and Ren and I return the gesture before I take my seat at the table.

"Thank you all for coming," I say. Jinta touches my leg beneath the table, his hand warm and comforting. "Ren has called you all here because Saito Takada, in Hirano's words, has betrayed us all." I turn my gaze to Hirano. "Tell everyone here what you told Ren."

Hirano nods and says, "I have proof that Takada has been cooperating with the Blades of the Onryō to destroy yakuza clans in Tokyo."

My heart lurches, outrage heating my blood. The bosses around us express their shock and anger.

Hirano reaches into his briefcase. He pulls out a tiny USB and a laptop. Once the laptop is on, he sticks in the USB and says, "I suspected something was wrong. So I hid a camera on his person. Please watch and listen closely." He turns up the volume on his laptop as a video starts to play.

In the video, the camera points right at Akira, who has a cup of tea in front of him. Takada's voice says, "Thank you for meeting with me."

Akira sips his tea. "Just spit it out."

A low growl comes from Takada. "Sounds like you really put those Horikoshi-gumi fools in their place. For the intel I provided on the group's location, you owe me one."

The ward bosses begin to whisper among themselves, and tension stiffens my spine.

Through the screen, Akira scoffs. "Oh. Is that so?"

"The Atsushi-kai. I want them gone. They'll be holding a meeting in one of their pachinko parlors. They'll be vulnerable." Takada pushes a briefcase across the table. "I will make it worth your while."

Akira opens the case and counts out bundles of cash,

setting them on the table. The conversation goes on, with Akira agreeing to strike the Atsushi-kai. A shiver goes through me. I remember that day. I'd shown up to aid them in the attack, and the hunters overwhelmed us. I had no idea that brutal attack was Takada's doing. So, this is how Takada was able to get Akira to cooperate with him, through bribery. One by one, the bosses start to mutter among themselves, the scent of their fury palpable.

I ask, my voice thick with anger, "Why would he do this?"

Hirano says, "To expand his own territory. Many bosses were killed during these attacks, leaving a vacuum he wishes to fill, thereby growing his power throughout Tokyo and beyond. This is not the righteous path of a yakuza, but of a coward and a traitor! He must be stopped."

The bosses voice their heated agreement.

Once the room has quieted, I say. "Thank you, Hirano. Takada will answer for what he's done." And I know just where to start. "Please excuse me." Pulling out my phone, I dial his number and walk out into the hall.

"Noboru," he purrs into my ear, making me shiver in revulsion. "It's been some time since I heard from you. Is the kitsune dealt with?"

Growling lowly, I say, "Jinta is dead."

Takada is silent.

"I had no choice but to put him down. My wolf is going crazy. I'm losing my damn mind."

Takada's swallow is audible through the speaker. "What do you want, Noboru?"

"I... accept your offer. I can't face the hunters on my own, not with my wolf ready to rampage out of control. Come and claim me. My wolf needs you, Takada. We'll destroy the hunters together. Namikawa's house. Meet me."

I can hear the lust dripping from Takada's voice when he murmurs, "I'm on my way."

He hangs up, and I snort. I've always been his greatest weakness.

And now... we wait.

An hour later, tires crunch outside the house. The front door in the hall opens. "Noboru?" Takada's voice calls, breathless and eager.

I sweep my gaze around the bosses. They're ready. I call out, "In here!"

Footsteps pound the hardwood as Takada marches through the house. The sliding door flies open, and Takada stumbles to a halt. The frenzied lust darkening his eyes shifts to panic as his gaze darts from the gathered bosses to me and then to Hirano, who stares him down.

"What's the meaning of this?" Takada asks, a tremor

barely audible in his voice. His eyes bulge when they land on Jinta. "I... I thought..."

I motion to a chair. "Have a seat, Takada." Oh, it feels so good to see him squirm.

Takada's throat bobs, sweat breaking out on his forehead as his scent betrays his panic. He takes a seat. "To what do I owe the honor?" he asks, attempting a smile at the bosses glaring at him.

I motion toward the laptop where the screen shows Akira sitting across from Takada. Hirano plays the video, and Takada's face goes pale. "It's... it's a trick," he stammers, eyes wide and panicked. "Someone's framed me."

"Really? You've got a body double out there with the exact same voice?" I point out.

Takada swallows hard, eyes close to bulging. "I... I can explain—"

"You have no honor!" one of the bosses says with a snarl. "Traitor!"

Takada seems to shrink into his seat as the accusations pile up. There's no coming back from this. Takada has been disgraced in front of the most powerful men in Tokyo. The most honorable thing to do would be to take his own life as repentance, but Takada has no honor.

I hold up a hand, silencing everyone. "Leave him to me."

One by one, the bosses leave the room until only myself, Jinta, Ren, and Hirano remain.

Nostrils flaring, Takada glares at me. "You little shit. I

was ready to give you everything!"

Jinta clears his throat, catching Takada's heated attention. "He already has everything." And he tugs down his collar and flashes his mating mark.

Takada's claws scrape over the table. "You filthy little human. You dare taint what belongs to me! I'll kill you!" He leaps from his seat.

I shove back my chair, claws out, and fangs sharp. "No," I snarl, putting myself between Jinta and my old enemy. "You won't lay a finger on him."

With a furious roar, Takada charges me. We clash, claws flying, fangs gnashing at whatever we can reach. Razor claws rip across my chest, tearing my shirt and shredding my skin. Takada rams me into the wall, pounding his fists into my stomach. I slash both claws over his ears, making him double over with a scream, then slam my foot into his stomach. Takada crashes down, and I tackle him. Red-faced with rage, Takada grabs my throat in his clawed hand. His claws puncture my skin, drawing blood, but before he can shred my windpipe, I lunge forward.

Takada screams beneath me when I puncture his left eye with my claws until it pops in the socket. His scream is cut off when I punch him, knuckles cracking across his nose. Heart pounding, I hit him again, for the boy whose fragile innocence he stole. I hit him again, for making me believe that he cared for me. I hit him again and again, for every single time he put his hands on me. For hurting me. For breaking me down to nothing. For violating my body. For making me think every single fucked-up thing he did to me was *love*.

I descend into a red haze of fury and pain and hatred, hatred for myself, hatred for this monster.

Fuck him for touching me. Fuck him for hurting me.

"Raiden. Raiden, stop."

Somewhere in this fog of fury and pain, a cherry blossom tree blooms, filling the air with the scent of spring, of renewal, and hope.

"It's over. He can't hurt you anymore. He's gone, Raiden. He's gone."

I draw the scent of my mate into my lungs, let it heal me from the inside and out. I open my eyes, dragging in air through clenched teeth. Blood soaks my fist and my clothes and left spatters on my face. Takada's face is a mass of swollen, bloody flesh. Completely unrecognizable.

Swallowing hard, I stumble off Takada's body and catch myself against the wall. My fist throbs, and it's because the bones have broken, leaving my fingers crooked and bent at agonizing angles. With loud pops, the joints fit back into place on their own, bones tingling as they heal. I stare down at the corpse of the monster who groomed me and raped me, and I let his death sink in. Takada will never haunt me again. He'll never threaten the ones I love.

My lips tremble, eyes stinging as a sudden wave of emotion crashes over me. Jinta's there in seconds, arms around me, and I clutch him to me.

Takada is gone. He's gone forever.

I take in a few calming breaths, then rub Jinta's back. "I'm okay," I say hoarsely. Jinta kisses my cheek, then steps out of my arms. I clear my throat, cheeks warm when I look at Hirano and Ren, who have been speaking quietly among themselves and very obviously trying hard to give me space.

"Takada's gone," I say, catching their attention. "But the Blades of the Onryō still need to be dealt with."

"How? We need a plan," Ren says.

I smooth back my hair and straighten my tie. "The hunters want me, and they want the kitsune. They've been patient enough. It's time we give them exactly what they want."

CHAPTER 27

Jinta

My stomach is twisting itself into a pretzel by the time Raiden and I arrive at Akira's home in the suburbs. Raiden called the hunter ahead of time, demanding we meet and strike a deal. No one else came with us, except Ren, who squeezes the wheel tight and stinks of nerves. Hirano stayed in the city to spread the word of Takada's death and assume the mantel of the pack's new leader. Raiden was insistent we handle this alone and not involve anyone else in the pack.

Ren stops the car outside Akira's home. It's a gated property, and the home is huge with three levels and a vast sprawling garden. Ren glares at us. "If either of you die, I'll pay that necromancer to resurrect you so I can kick you both in the balls."

I snort. "Point taken."

"Are you sure you won't need backup?"

Raiden nods stiffly. "If anything happens to me, someone has to lead the gang."

My heart sinks. Raiden isn't going to get hurt. Not if I can help it.

Ren shakes her head, lips trembling. "You asshole."

"We'll be fine, Ren," Raiden assures her and steps out.

Tamano materializes in the seat beside me. "It's almost over," she says as we follow Raiden.

"Yeah, I hope so."

She scoffs. "Have some faith in me, won't you? Have I let you down so far?"

"Well, there was the time—" I chuckle when she growls. "Truthfully, there isn't any other kitsune I'd rather have been stuck with."

Her cheeks flush. "I suppose you aren't that bad... for a human."

"Come on, you love me, and you're going to miss all the shenanigans of this world."

"I certainly will not!" Tamano huffs, then she vanishes into pearly white smoke.

Before we enter the gates, Raiden suddenly grips my shoulders and steers me up against the tall wall that encircles the property. His mouth finds mine, stealing my breath with a hungry, urgent kiss. "Anyone touches you, and I'll tear them all to pieces," he growls against my mouth.

I sink my teeth into my bottom lip so I don't moan. "I should *not* find the idea of you committing violence sexy."

A smirk brightens Raiden's face. "That's because you're a freak."

I grip his shirt to pull him closer. "True, but I'm your freak."

A pleased rumble escapes Raiden as he kisses me again with such heat and passion, my toes curl. "Damn right." He drags his fingers through my hair and curls them possessively at the nape of my neck. "Let's do this."

Raiden yanks on my hair and marches me toward the gates with sudden roughness.

"Ow! Not so hard," I say through our bond.

"Thought you liked it rough?" his teasing voice replies. *"Sorry, Sunshine. Gotta look convincing."*

The guard behind the gate sneers at us.

"Open up," Raiden snaps. "We're here to see Akira."

"Cause any trouble, wolf, and we'll mount your furs on our wall." The guard buzzes us in. Through the windows above, Akira's guards patrol the home, and another stands watch at the door. The guard at the door directs us to the office on the third and final floor.

My heart pounds faster with every step we take toward Akira's office, and before I'm ready, we're through the door. Akira beams like a child on Christmas as we enter.

Fear flips my stomach over. All I can hope is that my ability to control the kitsune will be enough to get us out of this.

"Sit," Raiden grunts, pushing me toward a chair.

I fake a glare at him, then drop into a seat. Raiden stands behind the chair and stares down Akira.

"The Wolf of Asakusa and a kitsune," Akira says, rubbing his hands together. "I couldn't imagine a more perfect gift. Although, I'm a bit confused. Last time we met, you were ready to kill us all before we touched the kitsune, Wolf. What's changed?"

Raiden says, voice thick with feigned anger, "I thought I could control the kitsune, that it could be a weapon to unleash on my enemies, but it's impossible to control. It's become a threat to myself and to my pack. Nothing but a burden."

Even though I know he doesn't mean it, I still wince hearing those words from the man I love.

"How disappointing," Akira says, smile only growing. "But why bring it to me? What, you think I want your deadly, uncontrollable beast? Because, of course, I do." He laughs low in his throat. "But forgive me for not entirely trusting in your questionable intentions."

Raiden clears his throat. "I've brought you the kitsune as a peace offering. Take it, do whatever you want with it, but leave me and my pack alone."

Akira's beady eyes sparkle with mirth. "My, my. You must be truly desperate to even think I'd accept such an offer."

Of course, Raiden and I aren't stupid. I know for sure that Akira will take the kitsune spirit and use it for himself, then turn on Raiden and slaughter the entire pack in seconds. The kitsune will make him a killing machine capable of wiping out every werewolf and witch in Japan, and who knows if he'll stop at paranormal creatures?

But if Akira thinks Raiden is desperate and stupid, it works in our favor.

Raiden growls, "Will you take it or not?"

Akira rolls out his neck, considering our offer. "Bring it outside."

My heart lurches in anticipation. "R-Raiden," I say, voice shaking as he yanks me from my seat. "Please don't do this. I'm sorry!"

Raiden squeezes my arms tight, the gesture comforting as he forces me to follow Akira out into the courtyard. Akira's hunters gather around to watch, jeering with excitement as they cage us in. Akira forces his way to the front of the crowd and motions to the center of the Zen garden. "Place him there."

Jaw tight, Raiden marches me to the garden and forces me onto my knees. As he leans down, he whispers in my ear, "Don't be afraid. I won't let any of these fuckers touch you."

Tears sting my eyes. "I know," I whisper back.

Raiden steps back toward the hunters, breathing hard as

his gaze remains locked with mine.

"Priestess, if you will," Akira calls.

The priestess he'd hired to do my exorcism makes her way toward us. She begins the ritual, spreading a circle of salt around me. Fear makes cold sweat break out over my body. *"Ready, Tamano?"* I ask.

She materializes beside me, hands clenched at her sides. "Yes. All we need to do is wait."

The priestess chants a liturgy as she waves her staff over my head. The kitsune writhes beneath my skin, snarling in discomfort, but still under my control. Harsh pants escape me as the kitsune rises to the surface. Fur sprouts on my arms, and my fangs lengthen.

My instincts scream at me to fight, to shift, *now*! But I can't. I have to let this happen. Still, I put up a show, thrashing and acting like I'm *trying* to fight and failing.

Akira throws back his head and howls laughter. "Poor little fox. How cute that you think you're strong enough to fight back. You weren't even strong enough to control the kitsune, but I will be!"

Raiden whirls on him, snarling, "That wasn't part of our deal!" There's no surprise in his scent. We expected this, and Akira has no clue. Raiden makes like he's going to storm over to Akira, only to be grabbed by two thuggish hunters who pin him to the ground.

The kitsune roars with fury in my soul, demanding we protect our mate, but I can't. Not yet.

Akira smirks at me. "As if a weakling like you could ever be good enough to control such a powerful creature. Now, look at you. You weren't enough for your pack, and they've tossed you aside."

Those words light a spark in me that surges into a roaring flame. All my life, I've heard variations of those words. I'm not good enough. Strong enough. Obedient enough. I'm a disappointment. *A burden.*

My parents thought they could give me shit. So did my brother. My ex-boyfriend. Takada. Now, it's Akira, standing over me, looking down on me, thinking I'm so weak, so *stupid,* that I'd just let him win.

Well, I'm not going to take it.

The kitsune surges up my throat, choking me as the spirit billows from my mouth in black smoke. The smoke takes the shape of a fox, curling protectively in on itself. Retching, I catch myself on my elbows, coughing hard as I struggle for air.

Akira is wide-eyed with awe. "Priestess, hand it over."

I squint up at the priestess through watery eyes. She looks uncertain.

"Now!" Akira snarls, reaching for the short sword at his hip.

"Y-yes..." The priestess summons the kitsune spirit through the salt barrier.

The moment the spirit is in reach, Akira cups the little fox spirit in his hands. "Huh," he says, a note of surprise in his voice as he watches the smoke churn in his hands. "that was... easier than I thought it would be."

Too easy, in fact. Before, to transfer the curse, it required a sacrifice. But the kitsune's feral rage has been tamed, free to do whatever it wishes and no longer bound to the whims of whoever hosts the spirit. As Akira is about to find out.

"At last," he says breathlessly, eyes gleaming with excitement. "The kitsune is mine to control!" The black smoke crawls up his arm. Akira's chest rises and falls faster and faster, eyes bulging with anticipation. The smoke flies toward him and plunges down his throat, crawls in through his eyes, and ripples violently under his skin. Akira's eyes run black, and his throat bulges as the smoke forces its way into his body. The hunter doubles over, coughing and gasping for air.

"I... I can feel it!" He cries, spreading his arms wide. "This power, it's incredible!"

"Now, Tamano!" I shout.

Akira screams and grabs at his chest. His limbs jerk and flail, eyes rolling back as he howls in anguish before his body explodes, blowing apart in chunks of flesh and shards of bone. Blood sprays all over the hunters nearest him, who shout in horror and disgust, then in terror.

The spirit of the kitsune towers over the hunters, an enormous fox shrouded in black smoke. Red eyes blaze, and long, sharp fangs gleam as the kitsune snarls. "I have been held captive for long enough! Never again!"

Tamano lunges, snapping up dozens of hunters in her huge jaws and crunching down. Blood spatters the earth in a shower of crimson rain. I can't look, covering my eyes as the screams of the hunters, the grotesque crunch of bone, and wet squelch of blood assault my ears.

"Jinta, I'm here!" Raiden cries, and his arms are around me as he holds me close.

I hide my face in his chest, shaking violently at what we've unleashed, until the world falls silent. The kitsune makes a loud swallowing sound, and my stomach lurches. When I dare to open my eyes, the kitsune looms over us. She lowers her body to the earth and bows her head.

"I thank you for setting me free. I go now to my beloved. Perhaps one day, we will meet again."

Raiden stands and bows. "Thank you for your help, Tamano."

My knees shake, but I rise and bow, too. "Thank you. Say hello to Konoe for us."

The kitsune bares her bloody fangs in a hideous leer. Howls of laughter escape her long snout, and then she bunches her muscles and soars high into the star-strewn sky, nine tails rippling after her. The clouds swirl overhead, opening into a portal that glows with light. "Konoe, here I am!" she calls, voice full of joy. Her tails are the last to vanish into the portal before it closes. The winds disperse, clearing the clouds from the sky, and the world falls silent.

My shaky knees give out, and I slump into the grass. I can't believe it. It's over. The hunters are all dead. Not a single piece of them remains. Takada is no more, and with Hirano as their leader, the long rivalry between the packs will one day turn to peace.

"We did it," Raiden says, sitting in the grass beside me.

"Yeah…"

He scoffs. "You don't sound so convinced."

I don't know how to feel. How can it be over after all this time? "I don't know," I say, shrugging. "I guess I'm just waiting for something else to happen."

"Like what?"

"Anything. An earthquake or a tsunami. More hunters. Another big yakuza rivalry. Godzilla."

Raiden slaps a hand over my mouth. "Shut up, you'll jinx us!" And then he bursts into hysterical laughter and tackles me into the grass. As his warmth envelops me, his laughter sweet in the night air, I hold on to him tight.

My mate's lips find me in a kiss so full of joy and relief that it chases away all my worries and doubts.

It's over. Raiden and I can finally be free.

Raiden breaks our kiss, eyes bright, teeth bared in a grin. "Get up. Come on. There's something I want to show you."

"Baby, my nerves are shot. Please, no surprises."

"Come on! You always love my surprises."

That is true. For our first date, he brought me to his favorite garden in the city, then took me home and pounded my brains out.

If anyone is good at surprising me, it's my guy.

"Jinta? Hey, wake up. We're here."

I jolt awake with an aborted snore, not realizing I'd fallen asleep. We've parked along a side street in Shinjuku. The streets are mostly empty except for a few drunks stumbling home under the light of dawn that streaks the horizon. Raiden opens the door for me, mouth twitching at the corner like he's fighting back amusement. "Close your eyes."

I give him a suspicious look but obey. "Kinky."

He chuckles and tugs on my hand. "Good boy."

My eyes still closed, I let my mate lead me a few steps from the car until we stop. "Keep 'em closed," Raiden orders, and tugs his hand free. There's a rattling sound, like keys, then the unmistakable click of a lock. He takes my hand and leads me onward. A door closes, and the noise of the outside world is muffled. There's a smell like plaster in the air. I'm not a kitsune anymore, and while that's a relief, I enjoyed having more enhanced senses.

"Open them!" Raiden's voice is so full of excitement that my heart skips.

I open them and find a big empty room with strings of lights hanging from the ceiling. In the center of the room is a blanket with boxes of food and a bottle of sake. I'm still not sure what I'm looking at, but it's a sweet gesture. "When did you find time to do this?" He never ceases to amaze me.

Raiden circles behind me and wraps his arms around my shoulders, fingers lacing against my chest right over my heart. "I had some of my men put the dinner together. I bought this place a few months ago. Couldn't figure out what to do with it, though. Until now. It's ours if you like it."

"A big empty room?"

Raiden sighs at my teasing. "No! It's a restaurant, Sunshine. Our restaurant."

My heart swoops. I spin around to face him, searching his face for any sign he's teasing me. "A restaurant. Just like your grandad."

Raiden nods. "Yeah. I've got to make a choice before tomorrow." Wetting his lips, he paces away from me. "I'm thinking cozy. Like my grandfather's place. Somewhere families can come for a meal. I still have my grandfather's recipes for ramen and curry and rice bowls. If you want anything else included on the menu, let me know." He motions toward the big windows up front. "We can have some tables there. Some plants. Put some artwork on the walls. Make it our own." His voice comes to life with excitement.

Tender emotion wells in my throat as he paints a picture for me. I see him at work in the kitchen, chopping scallions with practiced ease. At the door, I bow and welcome guests to their tables. There's no yakuza, except a few associates from the pack who stop in for meals and to say hi to Raiden. Ren visits and oohs and aahs over the place. Pictures on the walls tell a story of us, me and him, and the life we've built together. A life full of happiness, good food, and love.

My eyes are wet when I put my arms around my mate and hold him tight. "I love it," I whisper hoarsely into his neck, rubbing my hands up and down his strong back.

Raiden sighs in relief and holds me tight, nuzzling his forehead against mine. "Then it's ours."

I laugh softly, blinking back tears. "Are you sure? You won't miss the excitement of yakuza life?"

He shakes his head and brushes his lips over my forehead, thumbs caressing my cheeks. "I'll hand over the pack to Ren's care soon and leave the Namikawa-kai behind me for good. I never had a choice in joining the yakuza, Jinta, but I have one now, and I choose you. I choose us. Now and forever."

I push myself onto my toes and kiss him again and again, tangling my fingers into his soft hair. "I love you."

Raiden shivers against me, then kisses my lips, my cheeks, and my forehead. "You, too."

I've never felt more loved, more cherished, than I do when I'm with him. "Let's eat, and we can talk more about the restaurant."

Raiden squeezes my hand. "Sounds good."

Together, we sit on the blanket beneath the strings of gently glowing lights. We eat and drink sake and talk long into the night. For the first time since we met, Raiden opens up about the future he sees for us without fear or doubt, and I allow myself to dream of the life we'll have.

I can't wait to see what we'll create together, and with Raiden by my side, I know I'm in for an adventure.

Chapter 28

Raiden

"**T**he Namikawa-kai Ascension Ceremony will now begin!"

Ren holds my gaze as she drinks from her cup until it is empty. She then folds it in special paper and tucks it into her robe. Lifting my own cup to my lips, I drink until there are no drops left.

Bowing low before me, Ren says loud and clear, "Please accept my pledge!"

When her eyes find mine, I dip my head as pride for my friend warms me from head to toe. "I accept."

Ren Makoto is now the leader of the Namikawa-kai, the first woman to ever hold such a title in this organization.

And I... I'm free. As we clap rhythmically together

as a pack, I remember the day when I first joined the Namikawa-kai. It felt like the end of the life I'd once known, a life of poverty and hunger and despair, but it also felt like leaving one cage and entering another. All my life, I believed I would live and die a yakuza. The tattoos will never fade. My criminal past will always be a part of me, but it doesn't have to define me.

Jinta and our little restaurant... that will be my future.

After the ceremony has concluded, we continue the celebrations at my home in the suburbs. There's food and drink, and many of us shift to wolves and run in the woods, hunting anything that moves. I sit out on the porch and enjoy the quiet of the night. Ren comes out to sit beside me, face upturned to the moon.

"Congrats, boss," I tell her.

Ren smirks. "I like that title."

"It suits you more than me." I take a sip of sake. "So, what's next on the agenda?"

"Recruiting more women for a start," Ren says without hesitation. "There's far too much testosterone in this pack. But before that, Hirano wants to meet and talk about a lasting peace between our packs."

"You think he means it?"

She nods confidently. "I do. He's a good man. Far better than Takada."

"It's not hard to be a better man than that slimeball."

She laughs. "No, guess it isn't, but I trust Hirano. We

couldn't have exposed Takada without his help. And what about you two? Got any plans?"

I rest my elbow over my knee. "Jinta likes the restaurant, so I bought the place. He's got all sorts of ideas about furnishings and menu items."

"That's nice." Ren smiles. "He'll be busy with his job and the restaurant."

"He's quitting."

I chuckle when her eyebrows rise. "Really?"

"Yeah. Says that part of his life is over. He wants us to work together." Just telling her floods my heart with happiness. I can't imagine anything better than working with the man I love.

"You're so gross." Ren makes a gagging noise. "Too sappy. Too much love. Going to be sick!"

Laughing, I shove her shoulder. "Shut up." It's true. I've gotten so damn soft, but I don't care. This is the happiest I've ever been in my life. With Jinta at my side, I'm going to create the life I only ever let myself dream of. A normal life filled with the love I thought I'd never find.

"Hey." Ren punches my shoulder, eyes sparkling with happiness. "I'm proud of you."

A sappy grin bursts across my face. "Me, too."

She rolls her eyes. "Ass."

My laughter echoes into the night.

"Come on! Let's shift and show these puppies what real wolves look like!"

Taking to my feet, I bound after my friend and into the woods.

By the time I return home, my muscles are pleasantly sore, and my throat aches from howling my head off. The house is quiet, and I turn off the lights as I pass through the rooms until I'm upstairs. Jinta lies in bed, reading some romance manga called *The Dragon's Betrothed*. He's been pestering me to read it, but I don't need romance manga, not when I'm living one.

Dropping into bed beside him, I curl myself against his chest and kiss along his collarbone. Jinta sighs happily and runs his hand through my hair to cup my nape. "Have a good run?"

Parting my lips, I suck a kiss into the scar of his mating bite. "Yeah."

Moaning softly, Jinta angles his neck to give me better access to his skin. "And... the ceremony? How'd that go?"

I kiss my way up his neck until I'm a breath away from his soft pink lips. "It's over. I'm a free man." Emotion gets stuck in my throat. Somehow, saying it aloud makes it more real.

Jinta winds his arms around my shoulders and holds me close. "I'm so glad."

"Me, too."

"You really won't miss it? Or get bored with a normal life?"

I know what he really means. Will I get bored with *him*. "Not a chance, Sunshine." As I claim his lips, Jinta melts against me. "You're..." I scowl, struggling to find the right words. "You're everything to me."

Jinta's eyes are soft and warm as he holds my gaze. "So are you."

We kiss and kiss until my eyes grow heavy, and I'm nearly asleep as my head hits his chest, his heartbeat lulling me deeper.

When I open my eyes, the room is dark. All the sake has gathered in my bladder, so I untangle myself from Jinta's warmth and go to the bathroom down the hall. My head throbs, and my mouth feels like I stuffed it full of cotton. I really overdid it with the drinking.

The stairs creak as I head downstairs to the kitchen. I pour myself a tall glass of water and down it in a few gulps.

My wolf stirs within and whispers, *Danger*.

I freeze, straining my ears for the slightest sound as the hairs on my neck stand on end. Something's wrong. Drawing in a breath, I parse through the scents in the room. My heart lurches as I catch an odor that shouldn't be here. Another wolf. Right behind me.

Growling, I spin around, claws out, only to freeze as something sharp digs into my neck.

"Forgot about me, didn't you?" Ishida whispers, eyes glowing in the dark, claws sharp at my throat.

"Not at all," I admit, fury rising within me. This son of a bitch killed Jinta. "I've been waiting for you. Knew you'd show your face eventually, so I could rearrange it for what you did to my mate."

Ishida's lips curl in a silent snarl. "Your human pet got what was coming to him!"

A furious growl rises from my throat, but it cuts off as Ishida squeezes my neck.

"You think you can just settle down, live the easy life? After getting my brother killed? No, no, no. I'm going to kill you, Noboru, and then I'll kill that bitch Makoto. You took a human for a mate. Now you're letting a woman lead? You should have died! Not my brother. I'll take over. The pack will revere me for killing the Wolf of Asakusa."

I snort. "Are you stupid? I sent out letters to every yakuza organization in the city, letting them know you'd been exiled. You're done for, Ishida. You'll never work as a yakuza again. Find another occupation. Like, I don't know, a garbageman."

Ishida's eyes widen, crazed with fury. "You... you've ru-ined everything!" In the shadows behind him, Jinta prowls closer and closer, armed with the short sword he keeps under our bed. Now that he can't shift, I've been teaching him how to use it. Just in case.

I stare Ishida down and growl, "So go and kill me, but if you do, you better be ready to run because the Namikawa-kai will hunt you for the rest of your life. Makoto will see to that."

Ishida's hand shakes against my throat, then his eyes narrow in determination. His claws dig in, drawing blood to the surface, but before they can penetrate my flesh completely, Ishida grunts and stumbles into me. Grimacing, I side-step him, and Ishida crashes over the counter, the hilt of a blade protruding from his back right where his heart is.

Before my eyes, Jinta rips the blade out and stabs him again and again. "Fuck you, you piece of shit!" he shouts, eyes wild as he brings the blade down more times than I can count.

"Hey, easy, Sunshine." I grab his arm. "You're getting blood all over my kitchen."

God damn. My mate is a fucking savage.

I'm about to tell him how hot that was, but Jinta's eyes are wide. Stumbling back, he drops the sword. His hands shake as they drip with blood. *Shit.* Jinta's so soft and sweet, he's gotta be in a state of shock.

"Hey. It's okay. Ishida was scum, he deserved it!" I grip Jinta's heaving shoulders. "Sunshine, look at me. The first kill is always the hardest. I know mine really fucked me up for a while, but—"

Whatever I was going to say is cut off when Jinta lunges in and kisses me hard, pushing my lips back against my teeth. His scent darkens with arousal, and I quickly realize he wasn't breathless from shock.

I groan against his mouth, head spinning as Jinta's tongue plunders my mouth and slides against mine. I keep forgetting that for as soft and sweet as Jinta is, he's got a dark side, too. And apparently, killing for me really gets him going.

"Wanted to do that for so long," Jinta pants between ravenous kisses, moaning when I grab his ass and squeeze. "That son of a bitch nearly took me from you. He deserved it."

I bite down on his bottom lip. "You liked that? Revenge? Killing for me?"

"Yes," he whimpers as I nip and suck on his earlobe.

"Good," I growl, and I grip the back of his thighs and lift him into my arms. "Like killing for you, too. I'd burn the whole fucking world down for you."

"I know!" Jinta grabs my face in his hands, kissing me until my lips are sore and tingling. "Do anything for you, baby. Anything."

The moment we're upstairs, my back is to the mattress and Jinta's above me. I tear at his clothes until I've stripped him naked. When Jinta grinds his hard cock against mine,

I see stars. I yank open my robe, exposing my cock, and Jinta already has lube in his hand. He slicks me up, then preps himself, blanching his lip with his teeth as he fingers himself open.

Panting, Jinta straddles my waist and bears down until I'm notched against his hole.

Gripping his hips tight, I say, "Next time you ever doubt how fucking strong you are, just remember that you had the Wolf of Asakusa on his back beneath you. Remember how you took what was yours."

"Mine," Jinta says, lowering his hips.

"Yours," I snarl out the word as my cock slips inside him.

We both moan as Jinta drops his hips, taking me in until I'm balls deep, and starts to ride me so hard the bed shakes beneath us. Hauling him down, I devour his lips, losing myself in the incredible heat of his body and his urgent kisses.

All right, so maybe our lives will never be normal. *We'll* never be normal. We can't be, not after everything we've been through.

As Jinta chants my name as he cums, and I hold him in the exquisite aftermath of our passion, I don't care what's normal and what isn't.

We're going to take this life and make it our own, and I can't wait to see what adventures we create together.

Jinta

"Will it hurt?"

Ren grins at the nervousness surely written all over my face. "A little bit."

The tattoo artist, Ren's girlfriend, Misaki, turns on her needle. "Don't be scared," she says, lips dancing with mischief. "Just think about how much he'll like the design when it's done."

The design Misaki made for me based on the vague description I gave her really is beautiful, and I can't wait to show it to Raiden when it's done. Misaki brings the needle close to my exposed chest, and I squeak. Ren laughs, earning her a glare. "Hey, I brought you along for emotional support, not to mock me," I remind her.

"Sorry, sorry! You're just so innocent. It's cute."

I snort and take her hand, holding tight. She wouldn't say that if she knew I'd let Raiden eat my ass until I'd cried last night. Just remembering makes me blush.

"Ready?" Misaki asks.

I nod, but I end up closing my eyes tight and squeezing Ren's hand so hard she yelps. When the needle touches my skin, I gasp in pain. It feels like the sharp sting of a bee, but as the minutes pass, the adrenaline kicks in, and the pain starts to become more tolerable.

"I can't believe it's been five years since your ceremony," Ren says, distracting me from the needle buzzing over my skin.

The memories of our wedding still make my heart flutter. Even though werewolves don't get married, Raiden didn't hesitate to help me plan the ceremony.

We'd picked a beautiful temple and said our vows before a roomful of employees from the restaurant, coworkers and sources I was friendly with from my days as a reporter, and dozens of yakuza from both the Takada-kai and the Namikawa-kai. After, we'd picked up our certificate of partnership, gone out to an amazing dinner, and fucked our brains out during the flight to our honeymoon in Thailand.

It was amazing. Well, aside from a bit of drama, but let's face it, it wouldn't be us without a little excitement now and then.

"I know," I say, all breathless and dreamy. "It still feels like yesterday. How are things with the yakuza?"

Ren shrugs. "Can't complain. Sometimes, I miss running the Blue Lotus. We should go for drinks sometime.

You can meet the new bartender."

Ren keeps us up to date on everything that goes on in the Namikawa-kai. Thanks to her and Hirano's mutual efforts, there's been lasting peace between both yakuza groups. So far, hunters have left Tokyo alone. It's hard to say if that's because of the combined forces of Ren's and Hirano's packs or because of a rumor that Raiden Noboru singlehandedly slaughtered every single member of the Blades of the Onryō. Either way, I'm glad none of us have to deal with them anymore.

"How's the restaurant?"

A full-on grin spreads over my face. "It's great. We've been working on this exclusive curry recipe that goes on the menu this weekend!"

Nothing makes me happier than cooking with Raiden and running the business together.

"I can't wait to try it!" Misaki chimes in, moving the needle over my skin. "The okonomiyaki you make is some of the best I've ever had, by the way."

My cheeks flush with pride. "I'm glad to hear it."

For the next hour, we gush over food. Finally, Misaki sets down the needle, cleans the area she tattooed, and covers the tattoo with plastic wrap. "And, done. How's it look?"

Jumping up, I go and look in the mirror for a better view. "Whoa..." It's perfect. Somehow, Misaki made it look even better than the sketch she'd done for me. It's a simple design, nowhere near as elaborate as Raiden's beautiful tattoos, but I think he'll really appreciate the symbolism. Since it's our fifth anniversary, we both decided to surprise each other with tattoos symbolic of our relationship. I wonder what design Raiden will get.

After Misaki has given me instructions on how to care for my tattoo as it heals, Ren gives her a kiss, and we leave the parlor together. The sun shines bright in an ocean of blue sky, and the air is hot with the arrival of summer. Ren checks the time. "I need to get back to headquarters, but I'll bring Misaki over to the restaurant for dinner."

"Sounds good," I say, giving her a wave. "See you later!"

Her guard holds the car door open for her, and Ren steps into the big black vehicle before it speeds away into the sea of rushing cars.

After a quick train ride from the parlor, I arrive at Hideyoshi's Izakaya. The sight of our restaurant always fills me with pride. I walk beneath the banners waving in the doorway, and the smell of home-cooked ramen broth, grilled meats, and spicy curry sauce makes my mouth water.

The tables are packed with people, several of whom I recognize. There's the salarymen on their lunch break who wave at me. Foreigners having a liquid lunch at the bar as they pore over maps. The mother who lives down the street has brought her baby and small son in for a meal. Of course, there are some members of the Namikawa-kai stuffing their faces with bowls of ramen. They dip their heads at me as I pass.

The sight of so many familiar faces fills me with joy. Through food, we've fostered a community of friendly faces, regulars who always come back for more and never leave unsatisfied. Raiden and I have created something beautiful, something all our own.

Of course, just because I'm retired from reporting doesn't mean I've given up photography. I've filled the walls with photographs of iconic attractions throughout Tokyo, of Raiden hard at work in the kitchen, and the food we've created. The restaurant's namesake has a few photos, too, older photos of him with a much smaller, younger Raiden in the kitchen together.

Even though my relationship with Hideyoshi became complicated at the end, I'll always be grateful to him for raising the man I love and providing him with the father figure he never had. He deserves to be honored for that much.

"Hi, everyone!" I chirp as I sweep into the kitchen. Steam billows from dozens of smoking pots and pans. The chefs greet me enthusiastically. "Keep up the good work! Where's Raiden?"

"In the office," one of our chefs says, stirring a big vat of curry sauce.

I can't wait to show him my tattoo. Biting my lip, I make my way into the little office. We've made it into a cozy den with a sofa big enough for both of us to sleep on at the end of a long, hard day when neither of us felt like going back to the penthouse. Behind the big desk, Raiden scowls as he types away into the computer, a stack of paperwork beside him.

I kick the door shut and grin at him. "Hey."

He grunts, clacking away on the keyboard.

"*Hey, Jinta. What's up? I missed you*. Aww, thanks, baby. I missed you, too."

Amusement hooks the corner of his cheek before he taps a key and says, "And, done. Thank fuck." He groans and leans back into the chair, then gives his lap a pat. Those dark, lidded eyes tempt me closer until I'm straddling him in the chair. Cupping his face in my hands, I lean down and brush my lips over his. Raiden sighs against my mouth and sweeps my lips with his tongue, deepening our kiss when I let him in.

"Hard day?" I ask, nuzzling the tip of my nose against his.

Raiden rolls out his neck, muscles popping, and sweeps his hands down my back to give my ass a squeeze. "Much better now." Parting my collar, he brushes his mouth over the mating bite on my neck. "Even the hardest day is better than my yakuza days."

I'm pleased to hear it. I kiss his forehead. "Happy Anniversary, baby."

A low, pleased rumble escapes him as he claims my mouth. "Happy Anniversary."

I'm practically vibrating with excitement. "Can I show you my present yet?"

His eyes light up. "Go on."

Grinning, I unbutton my shirt. Raiden parts the fabric, and his breath catches. Gently, he runs his fingers over the plastic wrap protecting my tattoo. My heart soars as a soft smile touches his eyes, filling them with warmth.

On my left pec is a black wolf just like his, a little yellow yuzu clutched in his jaws.

Raiden gazes up at me like I hung the moon. "It's beautiful." His happiness and affection flow through our bond. "What's with the fruit?"

"I never told you? It's a yuzu. It's what you smell like to me."

He snorts. "I smell like a sour citrus?"

I laugh. "Well, now that you mention it..."

Chuckling, he slaps my butt.

"Don't worry, you're sour, but you can be sweet, too. Come on. Show me yours."

Unbuttoning the first few buttons of his shirt, Raiden pulls it open. After he became the boss, he had a tattoo right in the center of his chest of the Namikawa-kai's crest. Now, it's been covered up. In its place is the sun, shining through the branches of a cherry blossom tree. It's so vivid, as if I'm gazing through the window of his heart and out into the open sky.

Emotion tightens my windpipe. "Wow, baby. It's beautiful."

Raiden guides my hand to the tattoo. His heart beats beneath my palm. "I'm not always proud of my past, but I'll never regret my time with the yakuza."

"Yeah?"

Leaning in, he brushes his forehead against mine. "It put me on the path that led me to you. To this life we've made together." He kisses the wedding ring on my finger. "It was worth it, all of it."

Tears prick my eyes as I kiss him, sighing when he caresses my cheek. "Shut up, you're going to make me cry."

"You're pretty when you cry." He kisses me once more, so gentle and tender it feels like I'll melt.

"Nobody's ever made me feel as cherished as you do," I whisper. I haven't seen my family in five years, and I'm happier than I ever thought I'd be without them. I don't need a thing from them, not when I have so many people in my life who love me just as I am. Raiden is my family, and so is Ren and every friend I've made since I left Osaka all those years ago and fell into his arms in a packed bar.

"And nobody else ever will. You're mine, and I'm yours." Raiden pulls me close to kiss the crook of my neck. "Love you, Jinta." No matter how many times he says those precious words, words I once thought I'd never hear, it's as heart-stopping as the first time.

"I love you, too." And I mean every single word.

For a moment, we're quiet, basking in each other's presence. "Is it busy out there?"

"Yup." Pride lights up my voice.

He frowns. "Guess there isn't time to give you your other present, then." He squeezes my ass, making my breath hitch with longing.

I nip his soft lower lip. "I always have time for presents from you."

Raiden growls, "Then lock the door."

Jittery, I jump up and fly across the room to do as he says. When I turn around, Raiden snaps his laptop shut, sets it aside, then pushes all the paperwork off his desk. With a roll of his shoulders, he sweeps the shirt from his body, baring his beautiful tattoos that are a roadmap of the path that brought us together.

Smirking, he gives the desk a pat. "Now, come over here and take what's yours, Sunshine."

THE END

Thank you for reading Raiden and Jinta's story! I sincerely hoped you enjoyed their adventures as much as I did writing them.

If you're not ready to say goodbye just yet, don't worry, you're invited to Raiden and Jinta's wedding! Catch this sweet and spicy bonus epilogue when you sign up for my newsletter at www.CJRavenna.com.

Until next time!

xoxo

CJ

About CJ

CJ Ravenna loves to tell stories where the ordinary meets the extraordinary. Her books often feature an explosion or two, possessive and protective werewolves who adore their mates, steamy and swoony romance, and of course a happy ending. Connect with me on:

My website: cjravenna.com

My Facebook group: Ravenna's Ravens

Instagram: @cjravenna

TikTok: @cjravenna

Goodreads: goodreads.com/cjravenna

Bookbub: bookbub.com/authors/cj-ravenna

Get bonus shorts, sneak peeks of upcoming books, and more on my Patreon: https://www.patreon.com/CJRavenna

The Lycanthrope Protection Agency Series

To Hunt A Moonborn Beast (Gabe & Max)

Child Of The Moon (Gabe & Max)

The Moon Aways Rises (Gabe & Max)

The Moon Over The Oak (Zach & Ryan)

Redemption Under The Moon (Ben & Isaac)

Fire and Moonlight (Eddie & Vico)

A Paranormal Yakuza Duet

Secrets & Sake (A Paranormal Yakuza Duet Book 1)

Curses & Kitsune (A Paranormal Yakuza Duet Book 2)